ONE SPECIAL MOMENT

Colby reached out and placed her hand on Sterling's arm. She felt his tensed muscles relax with her touch. Their eyes met as he returned his hand to her waist. And then to her complete surprise he lowered his mouth to hers. Oblivious to the cameras flashing around them, he kissed her. The kiss was soft, warm and tender. And although it only lasted mere seconds, the feel of his lips on hers, as always, totally consumed Colby.

"As I said, gentlemen," Sterling stated in a husky voice as his eyes continued to gaze into Colby's, "my reasons for rushing into marriage with Miss Wingate are purely selfish ones. Goodnight." Then he tenderly gripped Colby's elbow and led her into the restaurant.

Colby tried to dismiss the brief kiss they had shared. She knew it was all a part of the playacting they had agreed to do, but as usual, it had a whirlwind effect on her. Sterling looked into Colby's eyes and he thought he saw something flicker in their dark depths. A silent question formed in his mind . . . When the time came, how on earth was he going to let her go?

Other Books by Brenda Jackson

TONIGHT AND FOREVER (Justin Madaris' story)

IN A VALENTINE KISS ANTHOLOGY—
"Cupid's Bow"

WHISPERED PROMISES (Dex Madaris' story)

ETERNALLY YOURS (Clayton Madaris' story)

ONE SPECIAL MOMENT

ONE SPECIAL MOMENT

Brenda Jackson

Pinnacle Books
Kensington Publishing Corp.
http://www.arabesquebooks.com

ACKNOWLEDGMENTS

I would like to acknowledge my family, my friends, and my faithful readers, who continue to believe in me and who give me their undying support. Thanks for all those special moments.

Very special acknowledgments to my sisters, Robin E. Ware, Cynthia H. Powell, and Lisa L. Hawk. Thanks for making being the oldest so rewarding, as well as challenging.

To Brenda Arnette Simmons for her helpful feedback on the finished product. You are a jewel.

And most importantly, to my Heavenly Father who makes all things possible.

If you can find a truly good wife,
she is worth more than precious gems!
Her husband can trust her,
and she will richly satisfy his needs.

Proverbs 31:10–11
(Taken from *The Living Bible*)

Chapter 1

This would be the biggest gamble of her life.

That was Colby Wingate's very thought as she glanced up at the tall, impressive structure that housed the law firm of Stewart, Heard, and Mathers. Summoning up much needed courage, she entered the building determined to go through with her plan. She couldn't get cold feet now. The future of her brother's company depended on her.

The main lobby of the huge building contained a spectacular eighty-foot atrium populated with numerous flowers and plants, and a huge breathtaking tinkling waterfall. She couldn't help admiring a painting on a wall that showed a stunning scene of turquoise waters and snow-capped mountains.

She stepped into the elevator, the doors slid shut, and it carried her to the twenty-ninth floor. The door of the elevator opened, and a smiling secretary seated in the spacious and elaborately decorated foyer eyed her curiously when she gave her name.

"Mr. Stewart's on the phone right now, Ms. Wingate. Please have a seat. He'll be with you shortly."

Colby nodded and sat in the leather chair offered. To pass the time, she picked up the latest issue of *People Magazine* from a nearby table. There on its cover, bigger than life, was the one man who could save Wingate Cosmetics, movie actor Sterling Hamilton.

She studied his features and decided that although Denzel Washington was her favorite actor, Sterling Hamilton was definitely a good-looking man. His eyes, the color of rich, dark chocolate and fringed by thick ebony lashes, appeared to be staring right at her. His face, sable in color, contained full sensual lips and a blunt jaw. His slightly arched nose appeared to have been broken at one time. That wouldn't have surprised her. According to her sister-in-law, Cynthia, who was probably one of Sterling Hamilton's biggest fans, he performed most of his own stunts. Instead of blemishing his features, the slight indention in his nose somehow enhanced his looks. Centuries of African heritage were etched in his features, and his prominent cheekbones hinted at the possibility of Indian ancestry as well.

As she cataloged his explosively attractive looks, she knew that here was a man who had a masculine force about him. He had a quality of male assurance not many women could easily ignore, or forget. There was no doubt about it, the man definitely had appeal. And she hoped he would agree to use that appeal and endorse Wingate Cosmetics' newest masculine cologne called Awesome. His endorsement would guarantee the cologne's success and the survival of the company.

Colby was grateful Mr. Hamilton's attorney, Edward Stewart, had agreed to meet with her, and she had been delighted at the expedience with which he had done so. She understood Sterling Hamilton was out of the country filming a movie and was not due back in the States for another month or so. Edward Stewart handled all of his business affairs while he was away.

"Ms. Wingate, Mr. Stewart will see you now." The secretary's words snapped Colby out of her thoughts. She stood, refusing to think anything but positive thoughts.

The door to the office opened. Taking a deep breath to settle the feeling of butterflies in her stomach, she walked inside the spacious room. The first thing she noticed was that Mr. Stewart hadn't completely opened the window blinds in his office to allow the California sun to shine through.

Colby looked up into the face of the older gentlemen who stood when she entered the plush office. He was a little on the heavy side, slightly bald, and had a square wall of a forehead with heavy brows for a base. His face, although firmly set in deep thought, was friendly.

"Please have a seat, Ms. Wingate, and thank you for coming," he stated, coming forward to shake her hand.

"Thank you for agreeing to see me, Mr. Stewart," she said, smiling and taking the chair he offered.

He nodded. "How was your flight to L.A.?"

"Fine."

"And your hotel accommodations?"

"They're excellent. I didn't expect you to take care of my flight nor my lodging."

He gave a warm chuckle. "Of course we took care of them. We sent for you to come to California, didn't we?"

Colby drew in a deep breath of excitement. "Yes."

"Well then," he said, placing a folder in front of her. "The proposal is ready. I'll cover all the specifics with you in detail before you leave my office."

Colby's head came up. "It's ready? But I haven't given you all the information you'll need to make a sound decision."

Edward Stewart smiled, waving off her words with his hand. "There's really no need. Sterling was quite taken with the history and background investigation that was done."

Colby was surprised. "You did an investigation?"

"Of course. Under the circumstances, such measures had to be taken. This is very important to Sterling."

Colby was stunned. It was a known fact that on numerous occasions Sterling Hamilton had refused to endorse or have his name linked to any products. She'd been prepared to vigorously plead her case. Why was this endorsement very important to him? Why did he suddenly have a change of heart about doing them?

She was assaulted with a satisfying sense of relief. Whatever his reasons, she was grateful for them and glad Wingate Cosmetics would ultimately benefit.

"After our meeting, I'll give you a copy of the proposal. I suggest you look it over carefully. Although, I'm sure you'll find everything satisfactory and in order. When Sterling decides to do something, he doesn't do it half measure. And I do hope you understand that due to the nature of this matter, you're not to disclose this business arrangement between you and Sterling with anyone. That stipulation is included in the proposal and will be outlined in the final contract."

"But what about my brother? I'm sure you'll want to meet with him."

A confused frown covered the older man's face. "I don't understand. Why would we?"

Before Colby could answer the door behind her opened.

"Sterling? This is a pleasant surprise," Edward Stewart said, smiling at the man. "I didn't know you were back."

Colby glanced over her shoulder to look at the bearded man who entered the room. She took a deep breath as her eyes collided with Sterling Hamilton's. Even with the window blinds slightly closed, his very presence in the room radiated light . . . and something else she couldn't help but notice, sensuous heat. The very idea that she could think such a thing surprised and fascinated her.

He was distinctively dressed in a pair of charcoal gray

triple-pleated slacks, a colorful printed shirt, and a double-breasted navy blue blazer. Tall and masculine, his clothes fit his body well.

Their eyes held. Apprehension touched Colby's body. An emotion she couldn't put a name to flooded through her with a force that left her speechless. For the first time in her life, a man had evoked an immediate and tangible response from her. She was vaguely aware of Edward Stewart making introductions and found herself getting to her feet on wobbly knees.

"Colby Wingate, how are you?" Sterling Hamilton's deep masculine voice seemed to radiate through the room.

Colby suddenly found her soft fragile hand encompassed in the strong firmness of his. His eyes held her spellbound and seemed to probe deeply into hers. She didn't miss the look of pure masculine appreciation in them. For an intensifying moment, her heart thumped against her rib cage.

She took a deep breath. Nothing could have prepared her for this meeting. Because of her sister-in-law, Cynthia, she had seen many of his movies, but seeing him in the flesh was very unnerving. The man was bigger than life and just as sexy. She found her voice and replied shakily. "I'm fine, Mr. Hamilton, thank you."

"Please call me Sterling."

Edward Stewart took a quick glance at the both of them. He cleared his throat. "I . . . er . . . think it would be a good idea if I left the two of you alone awhile to discuss the finer details of the contract. I'm sure Sterling will be able to answer any questions you might have, Ms. Wingate. I'll return later and make any modifications to the final contract the two of you deem necessary." Then he left the room.

An irresistibly devastating smile tugged at the corners of Sterling's mouth. "Please have a seat, Ms. Wingate."

"Thanks, and please call me Colby."

"All right, Colby." He took a quick glance around the room. "Edward isn't one for a lot of light," he said, opening the window blinds some more.

Colby sat down, staring at him. If she thought he was one fine brother in the dimly lit room, in the bright sunlight he was undeniably awesome. Never had a man radiated so much sensuality. It wasn't just in his looks, but was in his walk, his stance, his stare, and even his smell. The fresh, clean scent of him flowed through the room.

Sterling Hamilton turned from opening the blinds and stared at Colby in a way that went deeper than just casual observation. He leaned against the desk, enjoying the way the sunlight slanted through the windows and highlighted her nut-brown coloring. The stunning two-piece navy suit she wore gave her a look of sheer sophistication. Her thick mass of brownish-black hair flowed past her shoulders. Its glossy strands cascaded around her face like silk, softly framing her delicate features of almond-shaped dark eyes, high cheekbones, a straight nose, and succulent red lips that belonged in a Fashion Fair lipstick ad.

He couldn't help but notice her perfume was totally alluring. It was a fragrance he wasn't familiar with but one he definitely enjoyed inhaling. His nose had picked up the luscious scent of her the moment he'd walked into the room.

Sensing her nervousness from his open scrutiny, Sterling took the seat across from her. He couldn't remember the last time a woman had completely captured his full attention. He found it incredible that any woman could do that. He was accustomed to beautiful women, but the one sitting across from him not only had captured his attention, she was holding it tight.

"Mr. Stewart indicated you would cover the specifics of the contract," Colby said nervously, breaking the silence that had enveloped them. She felt under a microscope with his sharp, blatant appraisal of her.

Sterling nodded, not relinquishing his assessing stare.

"I can't believe how swiftly things are moving along," Colby rushed on conversationally. "I'd just contacted Mr. Stewart a few weeks ago. I'm glad you decided to do it."

"Really?" Sterling replied, watching her with curious intensity. "It's been on my mind for quite a while. I decided the time was right."

Colby liked the sound of his voice. It was deep and husky. "I'm glad you think so. I believe everything will work out fine for us."

Sterling stroked his bearded chin, regarding her carefully. A hint of a smooth smile touched his lips when he responded. "I'm sure they will. I don't foresee any problems, Colby. Do you?"

"None whatsoever. In fact, a name has already been chosen."

Sterling's face registered his surprise. There was a sudden degree of coolness in his voice when he replied. "There was no need for you to do that, Colby. I already have a name picked out."

Now it was Colby who showed surprise. The heavy lashes shadowing her cheeks flew up. "You do?" At his nod she shrugged. "Well, I guess it's negotiable."

Sterling's dark eyebrow raised questioningly, and the line of his mouth tightened. "There's nothing to negotiate."

Colby was stunned by his words and his curt tone of voice. "I think J. C. may have something to say about that."

Sterling stared at her through dark, brooding eyes. "J.C.?"

"Yes, James Cameron Wingate. My brother."

"Your brother?" Sterling stood and stared at her, blinking. Confusion lined his features, and his mouth took on an unpleasant twist. "What does your brother have to do with any of this? This is strictly a business venture between the two of us."

Colby shook her head and gazed up at the man towering over her. "No, it's not," she replied angrily, getting to her feet so she could face him squarely. She knew he wielded a lot of power in Hollywood, but he was wrong if he thought for one minute he was going to run roughshod over her or Wingate Cosmetics. *Of all the nerve! Just who does he think he is?*

"I'm sorry if you were given the impression I'm alone in this, Sterling, but James has a lot to say about what happens. After all, it will be his creation, not yours."

Fury shone in Sterling's eyes and his face was set in a stormy expression. "His creation! How do you figure that? I don't know what kind of sick game you're playing but—"

"How are things going?"

Sterling and Colby turned their furious glares from each other to Edward Stewart as he reentered the room. His smile faded when he saw their angry looks. "Have we encountered some sort of problem?"

"That's not the tip of it," Sterling replied heatedly, placing both hands on his hips. "She's trying to drag her brother into this! The contract is suppose to be between the two of us. No one else! I thought you made sure she understood that, Edward."

Colby's anger was boiling and topped the scale with Sterling's stone-faced expression. "How can I not drag James into this? After all, he owns the company."

"What company?" both men asked simultaneously, completely baffled.

Now it was Colby's time to be confused. "Wingate Cosmetics."

The two men looked at each other uneasily. And Colby didn't miss the questioning gaze that passed between them. Then Edward Stewart spoke softly. "Ms. Wingate, just why are you here?"

Colby's eyes narrowed. "You should know that, Mr. Stewart, since you're the one who sent for me. Your office called me a few days ago and said you were ready to discuss the proposal with me."

"And just what proposal do you think you're here to discuss?" Sterling asked in a somewhat menacing voice. A flicker of a frown appeared on his face. His expression was still dark and angry.

Colby's eyes flashed irritation. "The one I sent to you in care of Mr. Stewart asking for your endorsement of Wingate Cosmetics' new cologne for men which, has already been named *Awesome.*"

Edward Stewart cleared his throat. "Then you're not here because of the ad?"

Colby stared at both men blankly. "What ad?"

Sterling answered. "The one that ran anonymously in various newspapers in selected cities around the country."

She eyed him with a bemused expression. "I have no idea what you're talking about."

Sterling weighed her answer with a critical squint. "Evidently you don't," he said with agitated calmness. "It appears that a mistake has been made, a very big mistake. Somehow your name got mixed up with the numerous women who answered the ad."

He released a disgusted whoosh of air, shaking his head in total disbelief, wondering how such a thing could happen. "Of all the women who responded to the ad, you were the one who impressed me the most. But the funny thing about it is that you really hadn't responded at all. Yet, *you* were the one I chose."

Colby lifted an arched brow. "I was the one you chose? What on earth for?"

Neither man answered.

Colby looked from one to the other, flashing them a

dark look. "Have the two of you suddenly gone deaf? I asked what was I chosen for?"

A few moments later Sterling Hamilton broke the uncomfortable silence when he answered her question in a clear distinct voice. His eyes, indecipherable as water, met Colby's directly.

"You were chosen to have my baby."

Chapter 2

Colby was stunned into silence by Sterling Hamilton's statement. When she gazed into his face, he returned her stare with bland indifference. Mr. Stewart, however, seemed to have gone a little pale.

"Now wait just a minute," Colby said, raising her chin and keeping her expression stern. "I asked a simple question. The very least you gentlemen can do is not play games with me and give me a straight answer."

She watched as Sterling sat down on the edge of the desk facing her. Her eyes involuntarily shifted from his face to where his slacks stretched tight across his thighs. She was so caught up in her close study of him that she was startled when he spoke.

"We did give you a straight answer. You were chosen to have my baby. That's the reason you're here and not for some cologne endorsement I most certainly won't be giving."

A wave of anger surged through Colby. She glared at him. "You can't be serious about a baby!"

Sterling met her glare. "I *am* serious."

Colby stiffened. If she didn't know better, she would think her reaction to this entire escapade amused him. "Then I suggest you do what most people do—fall in love, get married, and make one!"

She could tell her suggestion hit a sore spot with him. She watched as his eyes radiated bits of stone.

"I plan on getting married and making one, but I have no intentions of falling in love," he snapped. "Of that you can be sure."

Colby shook her head and walked over to the window. It afforded her a breathtaking view of the city below. She turned back around and glanced at Edward Stewart. "Is what he wants to do legal?"

Edward Stewart cleared his throat before answering. "Yes, it's legal as long as the two parties involved agree."

Colby was aghast. "What woman in her right mind would go along with such a thing?"

"Evidently quite a few, Ms. Wingate," Edward Stewart continued. "We received over a hundred responses."

Colby still was not convinced. "Did you tell them exactly what they would be doing?"

"We told them enough without exposing Sterling's identity. However, it wouldn't have mattered if we'd wanted them to have a baby by Godzilla, the thought of a million dollars would make most people do anything."

"A million dollars!"

"Yes, with an extra half million dollar as a bonus in the end."

Colby stared at the two men. This couldn't actually be happening. She'd come all the way from Virginia to discuss a cologne endorsement, and they were only interested in paying someone to have a baby.

"This will be strictly a business deal between me and the woman," Sterling spoke. "No love, no romance, and no till death do us part. When the child is six weeks old, we will end the marriage in a no-contest divorce with me getting full custody of the child.''

"And the child's mother?"

Sterling continued to meet her glare. "She can go on her merry little way. I'm sure my one and a half million dollars will make it a lot easier and sweeter for her to do so.''

Colby was appalled by his callous statement. Surely no man could be so heartless about the notion of separating a child from its mother. "Well, I wish you much success in your repulsive endeavor, Mr. Hamilton. Now if you gentlemen will excuse me, I've wasted enough of your time already.''

Giving both men one last glare, she turned around and without so much as a glance back, she walked out of the office.

A few hours later, Colby was relaxing in a pool of bubbles in the huge bathtub in her suite at the Beverly Hills Hotel. She had been more than surprised when she'd arrived the day before to discover reservations had been made for her here. The beautiful hotel was a California landmark known to be frequented by numerous movie stars. She had noted quite a few when she had checked in. In fact, she had been speechless when Nicholas Cage had gotten on the elevator with her that very morning.

She'd let out a low whistle when she had entered her suite. It was exquisite. The room had been done in soft colors of peach and cream. The carpet felt like mink and the furnishings made hers back home seem obsolete with the Victorian velvet covered sofa and chairs, marble-top tables and a four-poster king-size bed. Never had she stayed in a place so elegant. The sight of it had almost taken her breath away. However, it was the over-sized bathroom that definitely made a statement. The tub was shaped in the style of a huge clam with fixtures in the shape of seashells. And it was big enough to fit at least four people comfortably.

"Ahhh," she moaned as she lay against the back of the tub. What a way to relieve the tension and unpleasantries of her earlier meeting with Sterling Hamilton. In the morning she would catch a plane and return to Richmond, disappointed that she had been unsuccessful in accomplishing her goal. At least she hadn't jumped the gun and told her brother about what she'd plan to do. He thought she was in California visiting a girlfriend from college. She hadn't told him the truth because she wanted to surprise him with the news once Sterling's endorsement agreement was a done deal.

For the past year and a half, Wingate Cosmetics had shown incredible profits. However, those profits were nothing in comparison to the likes of Flori Roberts and Fashion Fair. Both of those well-known cosmetic companies had something Wingate Cosmetics didn't have, celebrity endorsements.

And she had been determined to change that.

It was the least she could do for the brother who'd single-handledly taken on the responsiblility of raising her after their parents' death in a plane crash. She had been ten at the time and James had been twenty. Because of her, he had turned his back on a full scholarship to Harvard and dropped out of college to become her parent, brother, friend, and protector. A year or so later, he was able to enroll in night classes at a local college and complete his studies, obtaining a bachelor's degree in chemistry. He then continued and a few years later got his M.B.A.

She smiled. If all they had needed for the Awesome ad was a handsome face, then James would have been perfect. Her brother was a very good-looking man who stood well over six feet. A lot of women had tried capturing his attention and his heart, but none had succeeded until the beautiful and perky Cynthia Johnson entered the picture. James had been smitten instantly. However, it was only after Colby had graduated from high school and left home to attend Hampton University, that James and Cynthia got married. She adored her sister-in-law and knew she was the best thing to ever happen to James.

Closing her eyes, Colby inhaled the scent of the bubbles. Nearly eight years ago for her eighteenth birthday James had created a special cologne just for her and named it *Colby*. It had a subtle, incredible scent of a variety of flowers and had been made from natural ingredients known only to James. His refusal to expose the ingredients had led to him losing his job as a chemist with one of the largest pharmaceutical firms in the country. James had tried explaining to his superiors that the fragrance had been created for her as a gift and was not to be marketed and worn by other women.

Later, he had started his own cosmetic company, sinking every penny that he owned into it. Then as a gift for her twenty-first birthday, he had developed the fragrance *Colby* in both bath oil and bubble bath just for her. Every time she wore the cologne, bathed in the bubble bath, or used the bath oil she thought of how blessed she was to have a brother like James.

"I think it's about time you got out of this tub. Your toes are beginning to shrivel."

Colby's eyes flew open. She blinked, unable to believe who she saw. Standing next to the tub at a towering height and a stance that was forbearing was Sterling Hamilton. A shriek escaped her lips. Covering her chest with her hands, she sank deeper in the bubbles. "What are you doing in here? You have no right to be in here!"

A smile tilted the corners of his lips. "The reason I'm here is for us to talk, and since I'm footing the bill for you to stay in this place, that gives me the right. Now, I'm going to leave you to get out of the tub. If you take too long, I may be tempted to come back and hurry you along."

Colby's eyes narrowed. "Why do we need to talk?" she asked angrily. "As far as I'm concerned, we have nothing to discuss."

Sterling's smile turned into an insipid grin. "Oh, I think we do, Colby. There's definitely unfinished business between us."

Colby watched as he turned and with the cool, collected swagger he was famous for and that was known to drive female moviegoers out of their minds, he boldly strutted out of the room.

Chapter 3

Colby's jaw dropped. *Just who does he think he is?* she asked herself as she quickly got out of the tub. Hurriedly she began toweling herself off with one of the huge, thick velour towels.

Slipping into her robe, she swiftly walked over to the closet looking for something to put on. She finally settled on a light blue skirt set.

She could care less that he was footing the bill for her to stay in this place. No one asked him to. It was their screwup not hers. She shook her head when she thought about the fact that Sterling Hamilton, of all people, was actually sitting in the other room waiting for her to appear.

Colby's eyes brimmed with amusement in knowing that Cynthia would give anything to be in her shoes right now. Correction, she thought looking down. Cynthia would give anything to be in her bare feet. Her sister-in-law would die at the thought of coming within ten feet of Sterling Hamilton. She saw all of his movies, some more than twice, and purchased any magazine if his face appeared on the cover.

In fact, Colby thought, as she rubbed some Colby Bath Oil onto her skin before slipping into her outfit, it had been Cynthia's constant chattering about Sterling Hamilton's sex appeal that had given her the notion to approach him with the idea of an endorsement.

A few minutes later, Colby entered the sitting room of the suite where Sterling sat lazily reclining on the sofa scanning a magazine.

Sterling looked up. His gaze swept over Colby's appearance. Somehow she seemed to have gotten prettier since their meeting earlier that day. He noted she was no more than five feet four inches tall and had what he considered one helluva voluptuous figure. It was an enticing contrast to the figures of the women he usually dated. Most of them thought too much meat on their bones was a crime. They were totally obsessed with their thinner, willowy frames.

He thought there was something blatantly sexy about Colby Wingate's small waist, curvy childbearing hips, and her nicely rounded behind. And with her full breasts and shapely legs, all her feminine attributes were enough to make any man take a second look.

So he obliged himself and took a second look before getting to his feet.

"You made excellent time, Colby. But I only asked you to get out of the tub. You didn't have to get dressed on my account."

Colby glared at him. For some reason he appeared even taller than he had in Edward Stewart's office. She suddenly felt rather small in the room with his six feet three inches of towering height. If he thought he would use his height to intimidate her, then he had another thought coming. James was just as tall, so tall men didn't bother her one bit. But, she thought as she continued to glare at him, although his height didn't bother her, his penetrating stare did. She had been fully aware of his close scrutiny of her when she had entered the room. She had seen his gaze make a slow journey down the full length of her body and had wondered just what he thought he was looking at. She knew most men preferred pencil thin, size-five women. Pencil thin she was not, but she felt completely comfortable and satisfied with her size-ten figure.

Placing her hands on her hips, she asked. "What do you want, Mr. Hamilton?"

Sterling's gaze again roamed over her figure before he brought his eyes back to hers, with mesmerizing intensity. His perusal caused an unexpected quickening of Colby's pulse and made her feel momentarily light-headed. She struggled to control her body's reaction to him.

"I asked what you wanted, Mr. Hamilton." She repeated nervously and with a little less force.

Sterling walked over to her slowly, with the ease of a predator stalking his prey. His dark eyes were sharpened and held Colby transfixed in place. She couldn't have moved if she wanted to.

He reached out and tipped her chin so he could see even deeper into her eyes. "I'm glad you asked because I have every intention of telling you exactly what I want, Colby Wingate. I want *you* to have my baby."

"No," Colby murmured in a choked whisper. Her head began spinning at his words. And to make matters worse, her body began aching in a very private place. What was wrong with her? She took a step back and out of his grasp. Finding her voice, she replied. "We've gone over this before and my answer is still the same. We can't always get what we want."

Sterling chuckled. "But I usually do."

She tilted her chin. "Usually isn't the same as always."

"That's true. Then maybe I should rephrase my statement so there won't be any misunderstanding. I *always* get what I want. Eventually."

Colby swallowed again. "Not this time."

Sterling's gaze penetrated hers. He noticed the color of

her eyes had darkened even more. There were traces of fire in them as her gaze challenged his. He gave her just as good a glare as she was giving him, and wondered when the last time was that a woman, any woman, had gotten under his skin like she was doing.

He moved in closer and lowered his face over hers until their lips were less than mere inches apart. His hand cupped the center of her back. "On the contrary, Colby. Especially this time," he whispered hoarsely. "I'll get everything I want . . . and more."

Colby saw his intent and quickly twisted away from him. She walked swiftly to the door and opened it. "Please leave."

"I will if you really want me to, but if you really love your brother and care about what happens to him and his company, you'll let me stay."

Colby drew in a deep breath. Her throat became congested with fear and uncertainty. "What do you mean by that?"

"If you'll allow me a few minutes of your time, I will tell you," he said, returning to the sofa to sit down.

Colby eyed him narrowly. If there was something concerning James and Wingate Cosmetics, she wanted to hear it. "All right," she said closing the door. "You got five minutes. No more and possibly less." She took a chair opposite the sofa. "I'm listening."

A soft chuckle escaped Sterling's throat. Although he didn't want to, he actually liked her. She was an amusing change from most of the women he came in contact with. He couldn't remember the last time a woman had acted as if he'd crawled out from under a rock.

"We could have shared the sofa. I don't bite."

"Your bite is the least of my worries, and you're down to four minutes, Mr. Hamilton. My patience is wearing thin."

Sterling laughed. "So is mine. And I prefer you call me Sterling, or anything else you may find endearing."

Colby gave him a withering glance. "There's nothing about you I find endearing." She knew to him this was just a game. A game she wasn't interested in playing. Women threw themselves at him constantly, and she had no intentions of being one of them. He was way out of her league.

Sterling reached for a briefcase on a nearby table that Colby noticed for the first time. He leaned back against the sofa and proceeded to review a stack of papers he took out of it. He didn't bother to look up as he began speaking.

"After you left Edward's office I made a few calls and found out some rather interesting information regarding your brother's company."

Colby cocked an arched eyebrow. "Such as?" she asked blithely.

He looked up and wished he hadn't. Heat surged through his body just from looking at her. He quickly looked back down at the papers he held in his hand. What was wrong with him? You would think Colby Wingate was the first woman he'd been around in a long time, but that wasn't the case. He'd just flown in from Paris, where he'd been surrounded by numerous beautiful women on the set of his latest movie. What was there about her that drew his gaze to her tempting mouth time and time again? He shook his head and took an exasperated breath.

"I'm waiting for an answer, Mr. Hamilton."

He looked up again and met her gaze, grateful he was a little better in control. "Such as the fact that Wingate Cosmetics is about to be faced with a hostile takeover attempt by Morton Industries."

Colby sat up straight and stared at him with open-mouthed shock. "What? Are you sure?" she asked in a whisper.

"I'm positive. A very good friend of mine named Jacob

Madaris, is a top-notch player on the New York Stock Exchange. He handles most of my investments and is known to have inside information about a lot of things."

Shakily, Colby reached out to steady herself by grasping the arms of the huge chair she was sitting in. "But why? How?"

Sterling watched her reaction to the information. "Correct me if I'm wrong but according to my sources, Morton Industries released your brother from their employment several years ago when he failed to divulge the ingredients of a certain perfume he had created. I gather they liked the fragrance and wanted him to sign over the rights to them."

Colby sighed. "Yes," she replied softly. "He created it as a present for my eighteenth birthday and named it after me. It's called *Colby*. I'm the only woman who wears it."

He nodded and inhaled the tantalizing aroma of her. It was a subtle but extremely potent scent. There was something about it that was totally alluring. He was familiar with various feminine fragrances, but somehow the one Colby wore seemed unique and exclusively hers. He couldn't imagine the scent on any other woman.

"What your brother may not have known is that he did exactly what they expected him to do by going into business for himself. They sat back and waited patiently for him to make it into a lucrative company. Now they're ready to take things over."

Colby gasped. "You can't mean that."

"Yes, I do. I doubt your brother is aware of it, but Morton's about ready to file with the SEC. It's only a matter of time before their intentions are made public. Then it will be virtually impossible for him to do anything about it. If they're successful, they will gain complete control of Wingate Cosmetics. If the perfume *Colby* is registered with the company, regardless of the fact it is not being publicly marketed for sale, it will become the property of Morton

Industries. And I have a feeling nothing will please them more than to put it on the market. Also, this new creation of your brother's, the one you called Awesome, will fall into their hands."

"I can't let that happen."

Sterling met her gaze. "You can't stop them."

Colby stood quickly to face him. "But you don't understand. I have to do something. Everything James's ever owned is tied to that company, his life savings, his heart and his soul. He's worked so hard to make it a success. He and his wife are expecting their first child and the pregnancy is a risky one. It's not fair that Morton Industries can just come in and reap the benefits of his hard work."

Sterling witnessed her outburst. The anger she was feeling was openly expressed in her features.

"It's not fair," she said. "It's just not fair, and I won't let them do it."

"And just how do you plan to stop them?"

Colby slumped back down in her seat knowing she didn't have a clue. "I don't know, but I'm going to call James immediately. He'll think of something."

"It's too late. The wheels are already in motion. There's nothing he can do."

Colby frowned. "How can you say that? It's his company."

"Not for long. Anytime a company goes public with stock options something like this can happen. Especially if the company is doing well financially. And according to this," Sterling said, spreading out a financial report on the table in front of them, "Wingate Cosmetics is doing rather well. Your brother should be proud of what he's accomplished."

Colby appreciated his compliment of her brother's hard work. "It wasn't easy for him. He works hard and long hours," she said softly, thinking back to how his marriage had nearly suffered because of it.

Then she looked at Sterling for a long, taut moment before speaking again. "I would like to know how you got this?" she asked, indicating the financial statement spread out on the table.

"The financial position of any company is a matter of public record."

"Are you saying James should have anticipated this take-over attempt by Morton Industries?"

"No," he said calmly. "It appears Morton Industries' planned acquisition of Wingate Cosmetics was a calculated move on their part. I believe their reasons for wanting it are both business and personal. Your brother didn't leave on the best of terms. He was their top chemist and had created quite a number of successful products for them. Homer Morton took it as an act of betrayal when he left to form his own company."

Colby lifted a brow as she sat curled up in the chair. "And just how do you know all of that?"

A tiny corner of his mouth lifted in a smile. "I have ways of finding out anything I want to know."

She stood and began pacing the room. After a while, she turned toward Sterling. "And you're absolutely sure about all of this?"

Sterling eased out of his seat and came to stand before her. "It's all there in the report. I suggest you read it for yourself. So far, Morton Industries has acquired the minimum amount of outstanding stock they need before filing with the SEC. Since it appears they'll be doing a filing relatively soon, I can only assume their plan is to start going after a vast quantity of shares of Wingate's stock available on the open market. All Morton needs is enough stock to give them control of your brother's company."

Colby turned and walked to the window. She stood there stunned for several minutes and felt moisture gathering in her eyes. This couldn't be happening, she thought. She closed her eyes briefly, hoping that when she reopened them, the events of today would have been a dream. She wanted to open her eyes and find herself back in Virginia, in her classroom taking care of her rowdy third-grade bunch. But when she reopened her eyes, that was not the case.

Sterling sat down and watched Colby. He knew she was upset. The anger and hurt had been obvious in her expression before she had walked over to the window. And he was perceptive enough to know she was crying. For some reason that bothered him, and he was surprised by the protective feelings she'd awakened in him. They were feelings he wasn't used to. He wanted to go to her and comfort her.

In one swift movement he stood and walked over to where she was standing. Turning her to face him, he gathered her into his arms, enfolding her in the firmness of his form to absorb her trembling body.

"Your brother means a lot to you, doesn't he?" he asked her softly.

She nodded, then tearfully, she told him why James meant so much to her and the sacrifices he had made throughout his life for her.

"Shhh, Colby," Sterling whispered in her ear. "Maybe there is a way you can help your brother."

Colby's body was stiff and unyielding for a moment, before she drew in a deep, unsteady breath. She raised tear-stained eyes to him. "How?" she asked brokenly.

"Come sit down with me and we'll talk about it."

Colby allowed him to lead her to the sofa and sit her down close to him.

"If you'll agree to have my baby, I'll provide your brother with whatever financial backing he needs to keep his company. And I'll do whatever endorsements are needed to ensure the success of his newest creation."

Colby stiffened and pulled herself out of the comfort of his arms. She glanced up at him. "You just don't get it, do you? There's no way I could carry a baby inside of me for nine months and then turn it over to you, relinquishing my ties to it. I'm an elementary school teacher, Sterling. That means I love kids. I couldn't just give away my child."

Sterling's features hardened. "Not even to help your brother?"

Colby swallowed. "James wouldn't want me to give away my child to help him."

"No, I'm sure he wouldn't," Sterling said, his voice was like a soft caress as he continued. "A few minutes ago, you mentioned all the sacrifices he's made over the years for you, Colby. What real sacrifices have you made for him?"

Colby rose from the sofa to face him, her expression pleading for understanding. "But you're asking me to give up a baby, something that will be a part of me, my own flesh and blood."

Sterling stood. "Yes. That's exactly what I'm asking you."

"But a baby needs its mother."

His jaw hardened. "You can't convince me of that. I didn't need mine."

Colby lifted a brow. From his remark she could only assume his mother was not around while he was growing up, and for whatever reason, it had left him bitter. "You may not have had a mother around, Sterling, but you can't convince me you didn't need one."

She watched him move to the window and gaze out. After a few brief minutes he slowly turned back to her, giving her a long, hard look. "It's important you understand that if you decide to go along with me on this, once I get custody of my child, you'll never be a part of its life again. I will be its only parent."

"But you constantly travel all over the world. You'll never get an award for being a stay-at-home family man. What kind of life can you offer a child? When will you have the time to spend with it?"

"My child will be the most important thing in my life,

and it's the quality of time and not the quantity of time that makes a difference. I will be both father and mother to my child."

Colby swallowed. What could she say? He was convinced a mother's love wasn't necessary. "What if the woman decides after the baby is born that she wants to keep it?"

"I'll have the contract to back me up," Sterling answered. "I've taken extra precautions to make sure it's not contestable."

Colby then asked the question that had nagged her since leaving Edward Stewart's office. Sterling Hamilton was known to be a man whose name was constantly linked to some of the most beautiful women in the world. He was the man both *People* and *Entertainment* magazines referred to as one of the country's most eligible bachelors, as well as an extraordinarily gifted actor. The media thoroughly enjoyed keeping the public informed of his bad boy life-style. It was often rumored nothing in a skirt was safe from him, especially if that skirt-wearing female caught his eyes. From everything she'd read about him, he preferred a certain type of woman; tall women with long legs and pencil thin bodies. She had none of those faculties.

"Why me, Sterling? Why was I the one chosen?"

He stared at her a few minutes before speaking. "I found the information on you very interesting. Foremost were the facts that according to the medical information I obtained, I don't have to worry about you giving me any-thing other than a baby; and you don't have any gynecologi-cal problems, so there shouldn't be any difficulty with you getting pregnant."

"And what about you?" Colby snapped, angry that he had invaded her privacy by obtaining information about her. "Maybe you should be concerned about just what *you* might give me. You're the one with the widely acclaimed global sex life. And what if there's a problem with you?"

Colby asked, lifting her chin belligerently. "What makes you so sure you can get someone pregnant?"

An amused look glinted in Sterling's eyes. "The tabloids like to sell those sleazy papers, and the media likes to keep America's ears buzzing. You're too intelligent for me to stand here and deny every intimate detail you've heard about me, so I won't. But I will say most of what you've read is not true. Although I do date a number of women, I don't believe in taking unnecessary risks. I love life too much not to be selective and cautious. It's plain suicidal these days not to. And at the risk of sounding boastful, getting you pregnant won't be a problem. However, to arrest your concerns, according to a recent physical I had, my sperm count is more than adequate to accomplish what I need to do."

Colby blushed furiously. Then she asked her next question. "What about you and Diamond Swain? At one time the two of you acted like you were joined at the hips. Why can't she give birth to your child?"

He was silent for so long that for a while Colby didn't think he would answer her question. When he finally did, his tone was serious, and the look in his eyes held no signs of humor. "Diamond Swain is very special to me but not in the way the media has claimed. She and I are very good friends and that's all you need to know."

"That's not all I need to know. If you plan on sleeping with the both of us then—"

"I wouldn't do that, and I refuse to discuss Diamond any further."

Colby's anger increased. She wondered just what his relationship was with the woman who was the leading lady in most of his movies. According to Cynthia, at one time rumors had circulated that the two of them were even married.

She looked at him and his gaze held hers. His expression was unreadable. She knew he was waiting for her to make some kind of flippant comment about what he'd just said. But she had no intentions of making his day. Her eyes narrowed at him but she said nothing.

"What's the matter, Colby? Suddenly at a loss for words?"

When she didn't reply, he shrugged indifferently. "Now where were we? Ah, yes, I was explaining how you were chosen. Another thing that impressed me about you was that you're an extroadinarily bright young woman. You graduated from high school at the age of sixteen."

"There was nothing bright about that," she said quietly. "James was taking classes at night at the college and didn't want to leave me home alone so he took me with him. I discovered I could get credit for a lot of my required high school classes if I took similar classes at the Continuing Education Center located on campus, so I did. In the end, I had taken enough hours to waive my senior year of high school. I was able to graduate a year early."

Sterling nodded as he listened carefully to her explanation. "You also completed four years of college in three years and still managed to graduate valedictorian of your class. You also got your master's degree in half the usual time."

Colby shrugged. "So what of it? I merely took classes year round and studied hard."

Sterling again nodded. Unlike a lot of women he knew, she wasn't one who liked to toot her own horn. "Lastly, according to my information, you're not seriously involved with anyone and haven't been for some time. All those things are important to me."

His gaze suddenly became serious. "If you decide to go along with what I proposed to do, no one is to know of our agreement. The only person who'll know our marriage isn't one made in heaven is Edward. You're to tell no one, not even your brother. We'll do everything within our power to convince everyone we're in love. Because of who

I am, our relationship will become news. The media is always fishing for a story. It's very important that we put on a good show.''

"Why? From what I've read, you've never cared one way or the other what the media has thought. Why are you doing so now? Besides, even if I went along with what you're suggesting, James would never believe it. He knows me too well and knows I'm not serious about anyone; especially not serious enough to rush into marriage.''

"The reason I'll be courting the media is because I don't want my child growing up with the circumstances surrounding his birth an issue. Neither do I want there to be any speculation about why you and I got married. As far as your brother is concerned, it'll be up to you to convince him our marriage is a match made in heaven,'' Sterling said calmly.

Colby got out of her seat and began pacing again. Moments later she turned to Sterling. "I can't do it.''

He came from the window to stand before her. "Yes, you can. You love your brother too much to let him lose everything he's worked hard for. You will make the ultimate sacrifice to help him.''

"James would turn the company over to Morton Industries on a silver platter before he'd let me do what you're suggesting.''

"Are you willing to let him do that? I really don't think you are.''

Colby's head began spinning. Things were moving too fast. "I need time to think.''

Sterling shrugged. "I wish I could tell you to take all the time you need, but I can't. I want your decision as soon as possible, preferably in the morning over breakfast. If you decide to go along with this, you should make plans to stay in California a few more days so Edward can modify the contract.''

He pointed to the papers he had left on the sofa. "I'm

leaving those for you to take a look at. Maybe then you'll understand the seriousness of the possibility of your brother losing his company.''

He eyed Colby closely, seeing her look of anger and frustration. ''Giving up your child won't be the end of the world. No doubt you'll remarry one day and have other children.''

Colby didn't make a reply to his statement. What was the need? He actually believed what he was saying. How could anyone think one child could possibly replace another?

She took a deep breath. ''I'll give you my decision in the morning. How can I reach you?''

''Didn't you know?'' he asked as his mouth curved in a lazy grin. ''I'm in the adjoining suite.'' He walked over to the connecting door. ''Although I have a home in Malibu, I prefer staying at this hotel whenever I'm in town and have important business to take care of.''

His smile widened. ''And you are important business. I'll see you in the morning, Colby.''

She watched as the door closed behind him. Then she walked to the door and locked it. Feeling monumentally drained, Colby went over to the sofa, curled up in the corner and began reading the documents Sterling had left. A few hours later, she was still sitting curled on the sofa. The impact of everything was seeping through her mind and her heart.

Then she went into the bedroom and began getting ready for bed. She drifted off to sleep still uncertain as to what she would do.

Chapter 4

Colby dragged herself out of bed the next morning after having endured a sleepless night. The report Sterling had left clearly indicated Morton Industries was strategically planning a hostile takeover attempt of Wingate Cosmetics. And with Cynthia's at-risk pregnancy, a potential loss of the company was the last thing that her brother needed to deal with.

She felt the need for a hot shower to relax her. After checking to make sure the lock on the connecting door was still securely in place, she went into the bathroom.

During her shower she decided to go downstairs to the dining room for something to eat. Sterling had indicated he wanted the two of them to get together for breakfast, but he was the last person she wanted to see. Hopefully, he was still in his room sleeping.

Moving quickly, she got dressed in record time. Grabbing her purse, she was about to leave the room when there was a knock at her door.

"Please don't let it be him," she said under her breath. She slowly walked to the door. "Yes?"

"Ms. Wingate, it's Edward Stewart."

A quick glance through the peep-hole confirmed Mr. Stewart's identity. She was relieved it wasn't Sterling, but curious as to why his attorney would be paying her a visit before eight in the morning. She opened the door with a quizzical expression on her face.

"Mr. Stewart, this is a surprise. I hadn't expected to—"

"Ever see me again," he interrupted. He managed a smile as he looked at her. "I can understand your surprise but it's no greater than my own."

Colby raised a brow, but before she could respond, Edward Stewart continued. "Sterling had an unexpected appointment this morning. He called and asked me to be your escort to breakfast."

Colby couldn't help but grin at something so absurd. "My escort?"

Edward Stewart nodded and grinned back. "Yes, and it appears I'm just in time. You were about to leave."

She shook her head. "I don't need an escort, and I don't know why Mr. Hamilton would think I would."

"Neither do I, but let's just humor him shall we?"

Colby frowned. "I'm in no mood to humor Sterling Hamilton. The man is despicable."

Edward Stewart's laughter was not what Colby had expected. She allowed time for his amusement to subside before asking. "Did I say something funny?"

A rueful smile touched his lips. "I apologize for my outburst, Ms. Wingate, but you're so unlike the women who're usually around Sterling. I find your candidness refreshing. I don't know too many women who think Sterling Hamilton is despicable. Most of them think he's the best thing since the banana split."

Colby raised her eyes toward the ceiling. She knew that, unfortunately, Cynthia was one of those women. "Then that explains why Sterling and I can't get along."

At Edward Stewart's confused expression she added. "I'm allergic to bananas."

Colby shook her head when the man burst out laughing again. To her way of thinking, it didn't take much to amuse him.

"My dear you *must* join me for breakfast. If you don't do it to humor Sterling then do it to humor me. I'd love your company."

Colby hesitated for a second then said, "In that case, it will be my pleasure."

Moments later they entered the hotel's elegant dining room and were given a table near a window with a scenic view of Sunset Boulevard. After Colby accepted the menu from the waiter, she looked out the window and was amazed at the number of Mercedes and Jaguars that went by.

"Coffee, Ms. Wingate?" Edward Stewart asked.

Colby turned to him. "Yes."

After the waiter poured their coffee and left to give them time to look over the menu, Edward Stewart shook his head, chuckling. "After you left my office yesterday, it took me a good twenty minutes to calm Sterling down."

"He was that mad, huh?" she asked, smiling, getting a little satisfaction in knowing she'd been the cause of Sterling Hamilton's anger.

"No, he wasn't mad. He just couldn't contain himself for laughing so hard," Edward replied, chuckling as he informed her.

"Laughing?" Colby looked up sharply from pouring cream into her coffee. It had not been her intention to be funny yesterday. "And just what did he find so amusing?"

"The fact that you walked out on him," Edward answered. "No woman has ever done that before."

Colby rolled her eyes. "Then it's about time someone did. He has a lot of nerve in what he wants me to do."

"He's determined to go through with it."

Colby shook her head. "I know, and that's the sad part."

The look Edward Stewart gave Colby hinted that he agreed with her. And for some reason she got the feeling he was trying hard not to expose his own thoughts on the matter. "Sterling has his reasons for taking the approach he's taking," he finally said.

Colby snorted. "I can believe that. The man is a cold, calculating, arrogant, egotistical, conceited person who will stop at nothing to get what he wants. Any decent man wouldn't use what's happening to my brother's company as a bargaining tool to force me into doing something I'm totally against."

Edward Stewart slowly expelled his breath, frowning thoughtfully. "I know Sterling didn't make a good impression on you, but believe it or not, he's none of the things you just described him to be. In all actuality, Sterling is the most decent man I know."

"Then you must not know too many people."

Edward Stewart chuckled. "On the contrary, I know a great number of people and like I said, Sterling's the most decent person I know. He's a warm-hearted individual and a loving man who would make a wonderful father. His own father, Chandler Hamilton, was that kind of man." He smiled. "The media was in awe over the relationship between Tiger Woods and his father, but even their close relationship can't hold a light to the one Sterling and Chandler had."

"Had?"

"Yes. Chandler passed away unexpectedly last year. He died in his sleep from a heart attack."

"Did you know him personally?"

"Oh, yes. My friendship with him went all the way back to when the two of us were kids growing up in a small lumberjack town in the mountains of North Carolina."

Colby hesitated a moment before asking. "Did you know Sterling's mother as well?"

Edward Stewart set down his coffee cup. A long, weary sigh escaped him. "Yes."

Colby decided to press for answers to questions that bothered her. She was sure Mr. Stewart wouldn't hesitate to let her know when she was inquiring about something that wasn't her business. "I understand she wasn't around while he was growing up."

Edward Stewart lifted a brow. "Sterling told you that?"

"No, but it wouldn't take a rocket scientist to figure it out. I get this feeling that as far as he's concerned, the whole idea of motherhood sucks."

Again Colby got the distinct impression Edward Stewart was desperately struggling not to say something. At that moment, the waiter came to take their order. After the waiter left, she decided to pick up where they'd left off. There were things she needed to know about Sterling's childhood; things she needed to understand.

"Mr. Stewart?"

"Yes?"

"I know as Sterling's attorney you're very loyal to him, and I can appreciate that. But I want you to try and understand my predicament. I have some important decisions to make. They are decisions that will not only effect my life and Sterling's, but decisions that could very well effect the life of a child."

She breathed in slowly in an attempt to steady her voice, which had gotten rather shaky. "Sterling expects me to give him my decision today. Even now, I'm still totally against what he wants me to do. But I'm also torn by the thought that my brother might lose his company without Sterling's help. But when you think about it, me being the one chosen for what Sterling wants to do doesn't make any sense."

After taking a sip of coffee, she continued. "Sterling claims he did a thorough investigation of me. In that case, I would have been the last person he would have chosen.

I love kids. I was named Teacher of the Year in my home-town last year, and I'm on various committees that benefit children. Someone who loves kids as much as I do wouldn't easily give one up. He should have sought out a woman who doesn't like kids or who's indifferent to them."

She took another quick sip of her coffee "If a builder wanted to tear down an old building, he wouldn't employ the services of a person who's a member of the historical perservation society to do it, would he?"

Edward Stewart looked long and hard at Colby before finally answering. "No, he wouldn't."

He sat back in his chair. To his way of thinking, she was absolutely right. He had wondered about that very same thing himself. He'd seen the intense look on Sterling's face while he had first viewed the video tape on Colby that had been part of the investigator's completed report. The one scene that had captured Sterling's attention more so than any of the others had been the one showing Colby's interactions with her class on the playground. The smile that had been on her face indicated she was enjoying the children's little games as much as they were. From playing hopscotch with the little girls to kick ball with the little boys, it was apparent she was having a great time.

Inwardly, Edward believed Sterling wasn't just seeking a woman to bear his child, he was subconsciously looking for a woman who was the epitome of a perfect mother. Something his own mother was not.

He heaved a sigh. Sometimes attorneys had gut feelings about things. And he felt this was one of those times. Colby Wingate had summed it up perfectly. Her being chosen didn't make sense. It was a very irrational act on Sterling's part. And he'd never known Sterling to act irrationally. Which meant he'd been so taken with Ms. Wingate that he'd thrown sensibility right out the window.

Edward Stewart's gaze suddenly grew luminous with admiration as he watched Colby begin eating. He had a strong feeling she could very well be the one person to erase the terrible pain and hurt Sterling had suffered over the years because of his mother. It had been so easy for Angeline to just walk away and leave her husband and six-week-old baby in search of a life that was better than the one Chandler could afford to give her. Not only had she not looked back, but she had wanted them completely erased from her past forever. But what she hadn't counted on was five-year-old Sterling recognizing her from a photo Chandler had kept sitting on the dresser in his bedroom. She'd been on television with her new husband, Alan Chenault, a highly respected, wealthy businessman from Florida. The couple, to the television viewers, had been extremely happy because they'd just had a baby boy. "My very first child," Angeline had smilingly told the reporter.

It was apparent her husband did not know about her first husband and the child she'd left behind, and she was determined to keep it that way. But the icing wasn't put on the cake until the following year when Sterling had come face to face with her for the very first time. He had gone to Charlotte, North Carolina, with a youth group, not knowing that his mother, her husband, and their one-year-old child were there. He had recognized her immediately in the lobby of a hotel, and with the innocence of a child, he had walked up to her and asked when she was coming back to him and his daddy.

Unfortunately, Edward thought, he had been one of the group leaders and hadn't realized what was happening until it was too late. He didn't know such cold-hearted selfishness could exist in any person. In front of all of Sterling's friends, his mother had denied even knowing him, and had gone so far as to summon hotel security claiming Sterling was harassing her and her family.

That night Sterling had cried himself to sleep. But upon waking the next morning his small face had been expressionless, and in a solemn little voice he'd said. "Mr.

Edward, I'm okay now. Some kids don't need mothers anyway. It's just gonna be me and my dad, just like always. All I need is my dad. And I want to go home now.'' That day Chandler had made a special trip into Charlotte to get his son to take him home.

"Mr. Stewart?"

Colby's voice invaded his memories of the past. "Yes?"

"You aren't eating."

He smiled. "I got lost in my thoughts for a moment, dear."

During the next half hour, they talked about a number of things, but Colby couldn't help noticing how Edward Stewart stayed clear of any conversations regarding Sterling. He suggested places for her to see while she was in town and provided her with the names of a number of good restaurants.

"I really enjoyed having breakfast with you," Edward finally said, when breakfast was over and they stood to leave the dining room. With a smile he took her elbow and started to guide her toward the elevator.

"Going back to what you said earlier, about certain decisions you have to make, I strongly suggest you think Sterling's proposal over very carefully before making any decisions. Once you sign that contract, there's no turning back. And trust me, it's airtight. Sterling made sure of it. He doesn't want to encounter any problems later on."

Colby nodded, knowing she wasn't going to get much more out of Edward Stewart than that little bit of advice. After all, his loyalty was to Sterling. When they arrived back on the tenth floor, he paused outside her hotel room door. A wry smile touched his lips.

"I happen to think, Ms. Wingate, that you could possibly be the best thing to happen to Sterling in a long time."

Colby was taken back. "What! How can you even think such a thing?" she protested.

Mr. Stewart held up a hand to silence her. "Just listen to what I have to say for a moment."

Colby conceded and he continued. "Have you ever heard the story of Sampson and Delilah?"

"Of course."

"Then I suggest you think about it. Sampson was bigger than life but all it took was a woman like Delilah who eventually had him eating out of her hands."

Colby frowned. "I don't want Sterling Hamilton eating out of my hands. I don't want to have anything to do with him, period."

"But to save your brother's company, you'll have to have something to do with him," he replied simply. "Goodbye, Ms. Wingate. If I don't get the chance to see you again before you leave California, I hope you have a safe trip back to Virginia." He turned and headed back toward the elevator.

An hour later, Colby found herself pacing the confines of her hotel room after reading the report once again. She'd hoped she had misread the document last night, but, unfortunately, that hadn't been the case.

Time was running out. Sterling would probably be returning to his room any time now and would seek her out for a decision. A decision she still had not made.

She paused long enough to take in a deep frustrated breath as she tried weighing her options. She had considered telephoning the president of Morton Industries to plead with him to leave Wingate Cosmetics alone, but deep down she knew Sterling was right when he'd said it wasn't all about money. The man also wanted to get even.

She began pacing the floor again.

Surely there was something someone could do. She refused to believe the situation was as hopeless as Sterling claimed. Wingate Cosmetics' Board of Directors consisted of a number of highly intelligent men. Surely one of them could come up with a solution; and the only way to find out was to come clean and tell James everything. Only then could he come up with a plan to save his company without Sterling's help, which was contingent on her agreeing to his proposal.

She picked up the phone and began dialing. There was a three-hour time difference between California and Virginia, so James would be at the office. Efficient as ever, his secretary, Shirley Timmons, picked up the phone on the second ring.

"Wingate Cosmetics, may I help you?"

"Hi, Shirley, it's Colby. Is James in?"

"No, Colby, he didn't come into the office today."

"What! Is something wrong?" she asked frowning. She'd never known her brother to miss a day from work.

"Not that I know of. He called this morning and asked me to clear his calendar and reschedule all of today's appointments. You may be able to reach him at home."

"Thanks, I'll do that."

After ending her conversation with Shirley, Colby quickly dialed the telephone number to her brother's home.

"Hello?"

"James, are you all right? Is anything wrong with Cynthia?"

She heard his soft chuckle. "No, honey, everything's fine."

Inwardly, Colby sighed. "Then why aren't you at work?"

"I decided to take the day off," he said. "The company can do without me for at least one day. Cynthia had a doctor's appointment and I wanted to be there."

Colby nodded. She was glad he'd finally put Cynthia before Wingate Cosmetics.

"I'm glad."

"So am I. All of my hard work has paid off and the

company is doing super these days. I'm at a point where I can finally relax and devote more time to Cynthia. She deserves that and more. I don't know how I could have made it the last couple of years without her."

Colby agreed. Cynthia loved James very much, and during the past few years she had been a patient and understanding wife while James devoted most of his time to making the company a success. "How's she doing?"

"The doctor said everything's looking okay, but she's not out of danger yet. The first four months are the most crucial, so she's at a delicate point right now."

Colby heard a tinge of worry in her brother's voice. "I'm sure things will be fine," she rushed in to assure him. She knew just how much having this baby meant to both James and Cynthia. It was Cynthia's third pregnany. All the others had ended with her losing the baby by the fourth month.

"All we can do is to continue to pray and hope for the best. I believe things will work out for us this time," he said.

"I believe that, too."

"How's California?"

"Nice."

"And how's that friend you went to see?"

His question reminded Colby of the reason she was here and the little lie she'd told him and Cynthia as to the reason she was coming to California.

"Just great." She took a deep breath. "Look, James, I have to go now, someone is waiting for me. Give Cynthia my love and tell her I'll call her back later today. Enjoy your day off work."

"All right, hon. You take care. Love ya."

"Love ya, too."

Colby hung up the phone knowing there was no way she could share any bad news about the company with James now. He had his hands full worrying about Cynthia.

She also knew what her decision would be and her heart sank.

Going into the bathroom, she undressed and put on her robe. She felt a slight headache coming on and decided to lie down for while. Walking across the room she dropped down on the bed and felt an unwilling trembling of her lips. She flopped down on her back when she felt tears clouding her eyes. Grabbing a pillow, she wrapped her arms around it and held it tight against her chest. She didn't want to cry but felt herself doing just that. In order to save Wingate Cosmetics she would have to go along with Sterling Hamilton's proposal. Clutching the pillow even tighter, she couldn't stop the tears from falling or stop her heart from aching. And having control over neither, she finally fell to sleep.

He had a problem.

And the seriousness of that problem was uppermost in Sterling's mind as he stepped off the elevator and headed toward his hotel room. He could barely remember the details of his early morning meeting with the producer of his next movie. Far too often, he'd found himself preoccupied with thoughts of Colby Wingate.

And that realization annoyed him immensely.

It had been far too easy for his mind to remember the things about her that had first caught his attention when he'd viewed the video he'd received with the investigator's report. It had not been the tendrils of brownish-black hair that covered her head, nor had it been her pretty oval-shaped face. Neither had it been her lovely full and enticing mouth, nor the sight of her rounded bottom in a tailored pantsuit.

What had caused him to study the video over and over again had been her compelling ebony eyes. He'd seen those same dark eyes, the ones that had glared him down yesterday, soften with love, care, and kindness while she'd held a crying child in her arms. He'd seen those same eyes light up with joy when one of her small students had handed her a wildflower he'd picked out of the school yard. That scene had touched him, and had stirred him in such a way that left him mesmerized, entranced.

But even as his mind had decided she would be the one, a part of him had rebelled immediately against the idea. It had been the part of him that didn't like the attraction he had begun feeling for a total stranger. It was also the part of him that had decided a long time ago to never succumb to the allure of a woman like his father had. Chandler Hamilton had gone to his grave still very much in love with the woman who had turned her back on him and their son.

Sterling's deep inner self had fought long and hard against the idea of bringing Colby Wingate into his life. But in the end, his mind had won.

As he entered his room, he thought of all the reasons the situation between them wouldn't work. First and foremost was the fact that she was totally against what he planned to do. Yesterday, she had told him in no uncertain terms just what she'd thought of his proposal.

He couldn't help but remember their meeting in Edward's office. She had reminded him of an eager child, so full of vibrancy and excitement, it had nearly taken his breath away. At least she'd been that way until she had discovered the reason she'd been summoned to California. When he had disclosed to her the real reason, her entire attitude had changed.

He'd seen the switch in the intensity of her expression. The sparkle in her dark eyes had disappeared immediately, and the look on her face had told him, before she'd said anything, that she wanted no part of what he considered a perfect proposition.

Deciding to find a woman who would agree to have his

child had not been a fly-by-night decision, nor had it been done on a whim. He had given a lot of thought to what he was about to do. He had reached a point in his life where he wanted to take on the responsibility of another person. More than anything, he was looking forward to raising a child—his child. He wanted to watch his child grow and be nurtured by his love, just like he'd been loved as a child. The desire to embark upon fatherhood had pulled at him for some time, and now he felt the time was right. And he would accomplish his goal with or without Colby Wingate.

But for some reason, he wanted it to be with her.

Sterling shook his head, suddenly feeling totally disgusted with himself for his lack of control and his uncharacteristic feeling of vulnerability. His mood darkened at the thought. He clenched his jaw. It wasn't like him to let any woman consume his every thought or get under his skin like Colby was doing. There was no excuse for it. He had seen firsthand what such a thing could do to a man. His past was littered with memories of the actions of a heartless and selfish woman. The only thing that would ever exist between him and Colby Wingate was a business deal, if she chose to go along with it. The arrangement, as far as he was concerned, was to be simple. For a set amount of money and his agreement to help her brother's company, she would give him a child and then disappear from their lives. That was the way he wanted it and that was the way he would get it.

For a little while, he had allowed himself to be taken in by a pair of beautiful dark eyes that were more overpowering than anything he knew.

But not anymore. Not ever again.

Chapter 5

Colby wasn't sure exactly what she expected when she stretched her body, opened her eyes, and became fully awake from her nap. But it definitely wasn't the rugged and virile sight of Sterling Hamilton sitting in a chair next to her bed like it was the most natural place for him to be.

She had to grudgingly admit he was the best-looking man she had ever seen. He was far more handsome than any man had a right to be.

Dressed in designer jeans and a pullover shirt that fully outlined a pair of masculine shoulders, his long legs were stretched out in front of him and crossed at the ankles. He held her eyes just long enough to make her squirm before directing his gaze to the locked connecting door. "You locked me out."

Colby ran her hands over her still sleepy eyes. Had he actually thought she wouldn't lock him out? She wondered if women locking their doors against him was another first. Appparently so if his expression was any indication.

"Obviously it didn't do any good, since you're in my

room," she informed him, sitting up. She pulled her short, skimpy robe together, not liking it one bit that he was in her room. And she had no idea how long he'd been there. "How did you get in here?"

Sterling slowly scanned her appearance. Even just waking up from a nap with tousled hair and very little makeup, she was still a breathtaking sight. Her dark eyes were compelling as ever, and her scent—it was so arousing, so seductive, so . . .

He clenched his jaw, not liking the way his thoughts were going. He forced his attention away from her and toward the main door. "I used that door. I have keys to both rooms."

His reply gave Colby pause and she realized this man was used to doing whatever pleased him. "What are you doing in here, Sterling? You have no right to be here."

He gave her a long, hard look. "I distinctly remember having this same conversation with you yesterday. I thought I clearly explained my rights to you."

"Don't you believe in knocking?" she asked as her eyes coolly met his.

"No. It's a bad habit of mine."

"One you definitely need to work on."

"Only if you insist," he replied politely.

"I do."

"All right."

Colby raised a brow at the quickness of his response. She had not thought he would agree with her. "Why?"

"Why what?"

"Why are you being so agreeable?"

"I can be a number of things when given the chance."

Colby ignored the implications in his soft, hoarse voice. "Well, how about being a good guy and leaving me alone to get dressed."

A smile tugged at the corners of Sterling's mouth. He

pulled himself out of the chair to stand. "Go ahead and get dressed. Don't let me stop you."

She glared at him. "But you are stopping me. I have no intentions of getting dressed while you're in here."

"In that case, I'll leave since we have some urgent business to discuss. The sooner we can get it out of the way, the better. Join me for lunch in my suite in half an hour."

Before Colby could give him the third degree for ordering her around, she heard the bedroom door close.

Colby downed the last of her iced tea under Sterling's penetrating stare. Although she didn't want to admit it, she thought that even his slashing black eyebrows couldn't downplay his dark beautiful eyes. And his beard made him appear even more handsome. "Thanks for lunch. It was delicious. I didn't think I'd be able to eat all of it since I had such a big breakfast," she said quickly, struggling to control the sudden attraction she'd felt for him.

"Did you enjoy having breakfast with Edward?"

"Yes. He seems to be a nice guy."

"He is. I've known him all of my life. He was a very good friend of my father's."

"Yes, he mentioned that," Colby replied. After Sterling poured some more tea into her glass, she asked, "Why did you send him here?"

"Who?"

"Mr. Stewart."

Sterling simply shrugged before replying. "You needed an escort."

Colby chuckled. "I didn't need an escort."

"I believed otherwise."

She sighed. She was in no mood to argue with him. "Suit yourself."

He smiled. "I did."

Colby became angry with herself when she felt momentarily mesmerized by his smile, feeling an instant attraction again. "Thanks again for lunch. Now if you'll excuse me, I—"

"What's your decision, Colby?"

She gave him a hostile glare. "Do we have to discuss this now?"

"Yes. Your decision is very important to me."

Colby inwardly fumed. How dare he make it sound like the decision was hers to make. He had her backed against a wall and he very well knew it.

"Before I give you my answer, there're some questions I'd like answered."

Black brows lifted. "Such as?"

"I want to know exactly just how you plan to stop Morton Industries."

Sterling sat back, relaxed. "It will be simple enough. During the next couple of weeks, Morton Industries will be so busy trying to take control of Wingate Cosmetics, they'll be overlooking something important."

Colby arched a brow. "What?"

"A certain company, one that I happen to own, Hamilton Enterprises, will be doing a corporate takeover of them. In other words I'll give them a dose of their own medicine."

Sterling met her gaze directly as he continued. "At this very moment plans are being developed to put the squeeze on Morton Industries. They'll either have to back off or they'll find the tables turned on them. All the Wingate Cosmetics stock they were able to obtain will be purchased by me and I'll sign them over to you, as well as controlling stock in Morton Industies, to ensure they stay in line. Everything is on hold, Colby," he said quietly, "just waiting for me to give the word to put a stop to the hostile takeover of Wingate Cosmetics. And if things go as planned, your brother won't even know there was ever such an attempt."

"What about the endorsements?"

"It will be stipulated in the contract that I'll be at Wingate Cosmetics' disposal for whatever advertising they deem necessary to get Awesome off the ground."

Colby nodded.

Sterling regarded her over his cup of coffee and asked. "Any more questions?"

She nervously ran her fingers through her hair. Shyness and embarrassment now plagued her over asking the next question. But it was something she desperately needed to know. "If I decide to go along with your proposal, how am I going to get pregnant?"

His eyes were contemplative when he answered. "What do you want me to do? Draw you a diagram or something?"

His unwavering gaze made her even more uncomfortable with this topic of conversation, and his flippant response didn't help matters. She glared at him. "For your information, Sterling, there are a number of ways for a child to be conceived instead of just the usual way."

He eyed her for a moment, then bestowed upon her a very sexy smile. "By the *usual* way I take it you mean conceiving during the heat of passion."

His steady gaze that held a spark of smoldering fire, and the smile that overtook his features, made Colby's insides tremor. "Yes, I suppose," she replied. She held his gaze for a moment as she tried to decide what about him attracted her the most, his seductive eyes or his heart-stopping smile.

"In that case, I like the usual way," he said.

"What about artificial insemination?"

He laughed and shook his head. "I don't consider that an option."

She looked at him in surprise. "Why not?"

"I've heard too many horror stories about the mistakes being made at those sort of labs. I don't want to take the chance of a possible mix-up or something. I want my child conceived the usual way, during the heat of passion. Ours."

Colby took a moment to collect her thoughts after sensuous images of naked bodies and silken sheets flashed across her mind. "Once," she said in a somewhat quivering voice.

Sterling lifted a brow. "Once?"

"Yes, once. Intercourse at the time of ovulation," she said, nervously twisting her fingers together. She was not at all enjoying this topic of conversation but felt these things needed to be discussed between them up front.

"There's a method where a woman can determine the best time of the month to conceive, due to her body's temperature," she continued. "Therefore, intercourse is only required once for her to conceive. I understand the method is rather simple and easy and—"

"Forget it. I don't plan on getting scientific with this. I'll have some time between filming, which I'll spend on my honeymoon. I won't take a chance on doing it just once. I have more to do with my time than waiting for the day your body reaches its hottest peak."

She glared at him. "So in other words, you'll be using my body whenever you feel like it, just for the heck of it."

His eyes held a faint flint of humor when he spoke.

"It won't be just for the heck of it. It will be for the sole purpose of conceiving my child. And I won't be exactly using your body, Colby."

His gaze became full of promises. "You'll enjoy it as much as I will. I'll make sure of it."

He exhaled a deep breath and continued. "In the end, we'll both have what we want. I'll have my child and you'll save your brother's company. I see it as a very satisfying conclusion for the both of us. Now, unless you have any further questions, I'd like to know your decision."

Colby said nothing for a long moment. *This is it,* she thought dazed. My actions will change my life forever. And as he pointed out, the terms of the contract would give her the means to save her brother's company, but she still had other concerns. They were concerns for the child she would agree to give to him. She wanted to make a counterproposal and it was one she had a feeling wouldn't go over well with him. But still she knew she had to at least try.

"I need to discuss something else with you first. It's an idea I've had about all of this."

Sterling studied Colby. "What sort of idea?"

"I know you want to raise the child alone but . . ."

"But what?"

Colby took a moment to collect her words. "But I think it would be better for the child if I were there, too. I don't think I should leave until the child is much older."

An uncomfortable silence settled over Sterling's suite. He had wondered where all this was leading. Now he knew. But he had no intentions of going along with what she was suggesting. However, merely out of curiousity, he asked, "And just how much older are we talking about?"

Colby shrugged under his direct gaze. "Twenty-one."

"Twenty-one! That's ridiculous. Why on earth would I want to keep you around for twenty-one years?"

In all actuality, Sterling thought, he could think of a number of reasons, but she would be the last to know of them. He was attracted to her. That in itself was a fact he couldn't, or wouldn't, deny. However, he would not let emotions enter into his relationship with her. The contract between them would rule their lives during the short time they would be together. He was determined not to let his emotions come into play.

His outburst, he now noticed, had been followed by dead silence. He looked into Colby's face and saw her hurt expression. Especially in her eyes—those same dark eyes he found so comeplling. It bothered him that he had put that look there, but he knew it was for the best. She would not be in his life any longer than necessary.

"One reason to let me stay is because my child will need me," Colby finally answered in a soft voice.

Her words, spoken with the confidence she evidently felt, agitated Sterling. *"My* child will not need you."

Colby frowned. "What about breast-feeding?"

Sterling raised an arched brow. "Breast-feeding? What about it?"

"Anyone will tell you breast milk is the best source of nutrition for a baby, and I have every intention of breast-feeding. Six weeks won't be long enough. Who'll continue after I'm gone? Surely you won't be able to."

"No, of course I won't, but—"

"And another thing," she went on, "you and I both know you travel a lot. Most of your time is spent out of the country. Who'll take care of my child while you're away? Even if you hired someone, no one will do a better job of taking care of it than me. I'll give it the best possible care."

Seeing that for the moment she had Sterling at a loss for words, Colby pressed on. "And what if you decide you want another child later? What will you do? Enter into a similar arrangement with someone else? And what about how things will look? If I leave too soon after the child's birth, the media will wonder why we got married in the first place. Remember the speculation regarding Michael Jackson's marriage and the birth of his son? Do you want to go through something like that? And then there's another thing."

She hesitated for a moment but his silence gave her courage to continue. "I could be a good wife to you," she said in a soft voice, her gaze holding his without flinching. "I know I'm not like a lot of the women you're used to, but I believe I could be a good wife." Colby wished she felt as confident about that as she sounded.

Sterling felt a deep stirring of unease. He had a feeling she probably could if given the chance, but he would not do that. He didn't want any woman to have a permanent place in his life.

"Have you ever been married before, Colby?"

"No."

"Then how do you know you could make me a good wife? You have no idea what I'd want in a wife if I were the least bit interested, which I'm not. I don't need a permanent wife nor do I want one. Our marriage will be a temporary one. And as far as being a mother, I must again repeat myself, my child will not need one."

"I'm sorry," Colby offered quietly a few minutes later.

Sterling frowned. "For what?"

"For whatever your mother did to make you hate the entire entity of motherhood."

"You have nothing to be sorry about, so save your pity for someone else," he said coldly. "And I don't hate the entire entity of motherhood. There're some good mothers out there. I don't believe all women are as cold and heartless as the woman who bore me."

"Name one."

"Name one what?"

"Give me the name of a woman you consider a good mother."

His response, to her surprise, was quick. "Kimara."

"Kimara?"

"Yes, Kimara Garwood. She's the wife of Kyle, my best friend, and the mother of my four godchildren."

Colby was silent for a moment, then she asked, "And you consider her a good mother?"

"Yes."

She lifted her chin and glared at him. "Do you want to know what I think?"

"Not really, but I have a feeling you're going to tell me anyway," he said, raising a fresh cup of coffee to his mouth.

Colby chose to ignore his barb. "I think on the issue of good mothers, you see Kimara Garwood as an exception and not the norm. As far as I'm concerned, you still think unkindly of motherhood. I wonder what some of your loyal fans, especially the ones who're single mothers without the help and support of the father of their child, would think of how you feel. I bet if you were to take the time to check, you'd find there're more men who shirk their responsibilities as fathers than there are women who shirk their responsibilities as mothers. Maybe that's something you need to think about, Sterling Hamilton.''

She looked at him a moment longer before saying in a pleading voice. "All I'm asking is that you at least think about allowing me to be a part of my child's life for more than six weeks.''

"No," Sterling answered without hesitation. "Agree to the terms the way I've offered them to you or don't agree to them at all. The choice is yours.''

Colby didn't say anything for the longest time. When she finally spoke, her voice sounded battered and defeated. It was as if his response had somehow broken her fiery spirit.

"I'll marry you, Sterling, for the sole purpose of saving Wingate Cosmetics." She stood. "If you'll excuse me, I'd like to be alone." She walked across the room to leave.

When she reached the door she turned back to him. "Edward Stewart was wrong. You're not a decent person. Earlier you referred to your mother as cold and heartless. In that case, you're definitely her son. You've turned out to be the same way.''

Then she walked out, closing the door behind her.

Chapter 6

Colby's words had cut him to the core.

The last person Sterling wanted to be compared to was Angeline Hamilton Chenault.

He stood from the table. His suite suddenly felt dark and empty; a lot like his life had been since the death of his father. Even with the constant flow of beautiful women in and out of his life, the huge box-office draw of his movies, and the financial success of his business ventures, he'd felt something was missing.

He had inwardly longed for something more. Something more substantial and meaningful. That's when he had made the decision to become a parent. He wanted to channel his energy into the happiness of his child—just like his father had done for him. After he'd made the decision, he had thought it would be enough, and that the arrangement would be simple, hassel-free with no complications.

But that was before Colby Wingate.

He shook his head. He had to give it to her, she was one gutsy woman. Never in his life had he encountered a woman like her. She'd even had the nerve to inform him at the beginning of lunch that, just to set the record straight, he wasn't her favorite actor; Denzel Washington was. In fact, she had continued to tell him that she had seen his latest movie and personally didn't think, like most women, it was all that.

At the time, he couldn't help but laugh at her frankness. In fact, he had laughed more since meeting her than at any other time in his life. He was a fool to admit it, but he was fascinated with her and that smart mouth of hers. She could give just as good as she got. He had a feeling that with her around, his life would never be dark and empty. It would always be bright and full.

But that was the crux of his problem.

That part of him that served as a protective shield against pain and rejection didn't want her in his life. That was the part of him that saw her as a threat to his very existence. He had learned a long time ago how to avoid setting himself up for disappointments. He knew women clung to him because of who he was. His status intrigued and captivated them.

He had given up all hope that there was a woman out there who would love him just for himself—who he was deep inside. His real mother hadn't. And she had proven it by abandoning him and never looking back. Then later when he'd seen her face to face for the very first time, she had wasted no time rejecting him.

As a child, the pain of that rejection had stayed with him for a long time. He had even gone so far as to believe the reason she hadn't wanted him was because she thought he was a bad boy. So he had done everything within his power to be good. He was the pride of his teachers, he excelled in school and sports, and was the kid around town that everyone liked. But all of that hadn't made his mother come back or want to love him.

He shrugged off the past and once again settled his

mind on Colby. He didn't want to, but he suddenly thought about twenty-one years with her. She had a lot of nerve to even suggest such a thing. Very few celebrity marriages lasted that long. Most couldn't survive the harsh reality of the media invading their personal lives. But he had a feeling to remain close to her child Colby would beat the odds or die trying. She would do whatever was necessary.

Already she had thrown factors into the equation he hadn't even thought about; like breast-feeding, for instance. She had raised some important questions. Who would continue to breast-feed his child once she was gone? And up to what age did you continue to breast feed?

Sterling rubbed the top of his head, clearly recognizing he had no answers about such things. Luckily, he knew someone who would. Crossing the room he picked up the phone and began dialing. Moments later a feminine voice came on the line.

"Hello?

"Kimara?"

"Sterling? How are you?"

"Fine and you?"

He could hear her soft chuckle. "Busy as usual. With the kids there's never a nonbusy moment around here. If you want Kyle, you just missed him. He left for the airport a few minutes ago."

"No, in fact you're the person I need to talk with."

"Oh? What's up?"

"I have a few questions about breast-feeding?"

There was a pause and Sterling could just imagine the curious look on Kimara's face about now. "Breast-feeding?" she finally asked.

"Yes, breast-feeding. Do you have a few minutes?"

"Sure, what do you want to know. I should consider myself an expert on the subject."

"First of all, is it absolutely necessary?"

"No, but medical and health reports have shown that

breast-fed babies are less likely to encounter childhood diseases and illnesses than those that aren't. And women who decide to breast-feed feel it's important to give their child that edge."

Sterling nodded. He remembered his father telling him how sickly he'd been as an infant. In fact, by his first birthday he had been hospitalized at least twice. He couldn't help but wonder if perhaps that could have been avoided if his mother had hung around to make sure he'd gotten the proper care as a baby.

"What's the normal period for breast-feeding? It's done up to what age?" he asked.

"It depends. Most mothers stop at one year. Some continue as long as eighteen months. Anything beyond that would be too risky."

Confusion lit Sterling's eyes. "Too risky? Against what?"

"Sharp teeth."

Sterling chuckled when understanding dawned. "I can see your point."

"Sterling?"

"Yes."

"Why are you interested in breast-feeding?"

"It's a long story. Look I have to go. I'll get back with you later. Give the kids hugs for me." He quickly hung up the phone before Kimara could ask any other questions.

He took a long, thoughtful breath. Sitting down he slumped back against the sofa, first staring up at the ceiling and then glancing down at his hands. A warm feeling touched him when he looked at the platinum ring he'd worn since his twenty-first birthday. It had been in the Hamilton family for generations and just like his father had passed it on to him, he wanted to pass it on to his son or daughter.

Sterling smiled good-naturedly. More than likely he would be passing the ring on to a son since there had not been a female born into the Hamilton family in over four generations.

Then he thought about his father. His dad had been a deeply caring and concerned parent with strong principles, who had tried raising him to be a man of integrity and honesty. Colby was wrong, he was nothing like his mother. Just because he didn't want a permanent wife in his life did not make him an indecent person. At present, his main concern was the the well-being of the child he desperately wanted.

And for that reason and that reason alone, he would extend Colby's time in his life from six weeks to at least a year. He wasn't too crazy about the idea, but there was no way around it.

Picking up the phone again, he placed a call to Edward Stewart.

Hours later Colby eyes were still red-rimmed and puffy from all the crying she'd done. Getting up off the bed, she knew she had no more tears left to shed. What good would they do anyway? Further crying wouldn't change her situation.

She couldn't help but think about what she had agreed to do. To save her brother's company she would marry Sterling. It was a decision she would have to live with for the rest of her life, and the impact of that decision left her shaking.

She took a deep breath and momentarily closed her eyes, willing her body to stay calm. Somehow she would get through this. She was known around school as the one person who could turn a negative situation into a positive one. She refused to let Sterling destroy her and all the things she held most dear. And the essence of marriage and motherhood were two on the top of her list. Although she hadn't had any immediate plans to engage in either, she'd always known that one day she would eventually settle down and become a wife and mother.

She stood and began pacing the floor. She couldn't help but think of her childhood while her parents were still alive, her life with James after they had died, her present life, and her future. She knew in her heart that if God ever blessed her with a child she could not give it away to Sterling or anyone else. She just couldn't. She had never felt more sure of anything in her life.

So how was she going to deal with Sterling Hamilton when that time came? Now that she had agreed to his proposal, no doubt he was fairly confident she would not cause problems and do everything stipulated in his iron-clad contract. But somehow she would try to work around that. In time, he would discover she was unlike any of the other women he'd ever been involved with. She was determined that somehow during their marriage she would convince him to keep her and not send her away. Ever.

A timid knock sounded on the door that connected her room to Sterling's, interrupting her thoughts. "Maybe if I ignore him he'll just go away," she mumbled to herself.

No such luck she found out moments later when he said. "Colby, I know you're in there so open the door."

"No. Just leave me alone. I told you I wanted to be by myself for a while."

"You either open this door or I'll let myself in," was his reply.

Colby rolled her eyes to the ceiling wondering what else was new. Seeing the lock on the door was firmly in place, she went into the bathroom.

When she came out moments later, she halted in her tracks. Sterling was standing leaning against the opened door frame. Her eyes narrowed at him.

"Why didn't you open the door, Colby?"

"I'm not in the mood for visitors, especially the likes of you."

Sterling's face didn't reveal a flicker of emotion, but Colby could tell he wasn't pleased with what she had said. He stood leaning against the doorjamb, his hands in the pockets of his pants. He had changed into a shirt that she thought clearly showed how well defined his physique was, especially his broad, muscular shoulders and upper arms. With great difficulty she tried not to concentrate on his well-built muscled body, but on the upheaval this man intended to place in her life.

He was glaring hard at her, so she decided to glare right back.

"Come here, Colby."

"Get lost, Sterling."

"We're going out to dinner."

His arrogant assumption riled her. "I'm not going anywhere with you."

"Suit yourself. I'll order room service then."

"Make sure it's just for you and that it's delivered to your suite not mine."

Sterling stepped farther into the room. Moving before her, he stood with his feet planted firmly apart and his hands resting on his hips. "Are you trying to be difficult?"

"You're supposed to have all the answers. What do you think?" By nothing but sheer willpower Colby kept her voice steady. Whether she liked it or not, the man standing before her had plenty of sex appeal and his dark, piercing eyes were totally unnerving.

Sterling stared at her for a while. She was an attractive woman. In fact, he'd discovered since meeting her that she was even more beautiful when she was mad about something. That thought made a genuine smile touch his lips. In that case, she would always be beautiful around him because he seemed to have a knack for setting her off.

"Yeah, I think you're trying to be difficult, and I have a certain way of dealing with difficult women."

Their eyes locked and Colby noticed the smile on his face slowly began fading. Then he lowered his head toward her. A part of her wanted to step back but another part wouldn't let her move. So she just stood there and prepared herself for the kiss she knew was about to take place. She smugly told herself so what if he kissed her, she wouldn't be affected by it, although her heart was pounding against her ribs and her pulse was beating erratically. The moment his lips touched hers she knew she had lied.

She was affected.

His mouth, at first, was gentle as he wrapped his arms around her, pulling her close against his hard muscled body. Then suddenly his mouth became rough with some sort of need that was more intense than anything Colby had ever encountered. She had never been kissed like this before. His tongue took total possession of her mouth, and she was helpless to do anything but respond by doing likewise with his, imitating his every intimate movement. She heard the sound of groans echoing through the room and didn't know if they were hers or his. And at the moment, she was too caught up in what was taking place between them to even care. His kiss was eliciting desires she had never felt or even known could exist. Of their own accord, her hands reached up and encircled his neck, and her long, neatly manicured nails rubbed against his hairline as her body pliantly molded itself to his hardness.

Sterling trembled at the feel of Colby's softness against him. Her body felt warm, cozy, enticing. It elicited a degree of desire from him he hadn't known possible. He'd known passion before, but never like this, not in all his thirty-five years. He was so out of control he couldn't focus on anything but the woman in his arms and how his tongue was foraging the deep sweetness of her mouth. Her hands that encircled his neck and her fingernails that were lightly touching his skin were pushing him over the edge of sanity. He knew he had to put a stop to this madness now.

With great effort he lifted his mouth from hers and slowly stepped back. Patting the top of his head, he inhaled a deep breath forcing himself not to reach out and touch her again. He had to put distance between them as soon as possible.

"I suggest you try not to be difficult again, Colby," he said harshly, attempting to regain control over the situation and feeling the need to kick himself in the butt for ever losing it.

"I'll be ordering dinner for the two of us in my suite. I expect you there in an hour."

Then he turned and left the room, firmly closing the connecting door behind him.

Chapter 7

Colby stood transfixed in place, staring at the closed door. With trembling fingers she touched her throbbing, swollen lips. The kiss she and Sterling had just shared had shaken her to the core. It had been smoldering with heated fire and blazing passion, and although she didn't want to admit it, it had been totally satisfying. Even her toes were still burning.

She hadn't known anything could make her feel that way. During her teen years, she had been so busy going to school day and night she hadn't taken the time to date much. And after she had left home for college, the guys she had met hadn't been particularly interesting.

The senior guys at college had hung around the girls' dormitory like panthers in heat, ready to pounce on the freshmen girls who were away from home for the first time. And some of the girls' naiveté made them easy prey.

Because she had been raised by an older brother who knew the score, and who had schooled her on what to expect from the hot-blooded young men on campus, she'd kept her virginity in tact, having no interest in being some guy's conquest. And with the risk of AIDS, she'd thought having sex just for the heck of doing so made as much sense as holding a loaded gun to your head.

Upon finishing college and moving into her own place she had begun dating, but even the older, supposedly more sophisticated guys hadn't impressed her. The only thing most of them wanted was easy sex with no thoughts of commitment.

So here she was at the age of twenty-six and still without her first sexual experience. She hadn't given much thought to that fact until now.

Momentarily closing her eyes, she recaptured the moment in Sterling's arms when she knew she had never before in her life felt so filled with desire for anyone.

But even with all of that heated excitement, she had felt something even more, something deeper. She had sensed some sort of primitive need in him that went beyond anything physical. There had been a strong undercurrent of something dark and forbidden. It was there in the way he had kissed her, and even though she was clueless as to exactly what it was, something told her that if only for a little while, he had lowered some sort of guard. It was as if he'd reluctantly allowed himself to be caught up in the moment.

Colby took a deep breath while she collected her thoughts. Now was not the time to start getting turned on and dreamy eyed over Sterling Hamilton like most women across the country were doing. The man was selfish and heartless, and it was best she remembered that. And if he thought for one minute she would show up in his suite for dinner, he had another thought coming. She was going out shopping just like she had planned.

Sterling leaned against the closed door and took a calming breath to steady the anger he felt with himself. How could he have let things get out of hand and kissed Colby that way? His sole purpose for seeking her out had been to discuss the change he'd made in the agreement. But her feistiness had gotten to him, and he'd felt driven to see if that smart mouth of hers tasted as good as it looked.

And unfortunately for him it had. Her mouth had been everything he'd imagined it would be and more.

Even now he could still taste her on his lips and the faintest hint of her perfume still clung to his skin. He couldn't ever remember kissing a woman with such passion as he'd kissed Colby. That single kiss had awakened sensations within him that had torn at his control and ripped it to shreds. And the thought of kissing her again aroused him to such a degree he didn't want to think what would happen if he were to take her in his arms, undress her, and make love to her.

He walked over to the bar in the room and poured a glass of scotch. He drank it down and felt something other than the hot liquid slowly burning his insides. It was the knowledge that he was behaving like a stupid, lust-crazed fool. He had no intention for any woman to turn his life inside out. He would never allow any woman to do that, especially the one who would soon become his wife.

When Colby returned to her hotel room a couple of hours later she discovered a table in the middle of the room with a number of covered dishes on it. Tossing her packages on the bed, she lifted the lids and was surprised to see Sterling had left dinner warming for her. There was even a salad and dessert.

Suddenly feeling quite hungry, she went into the bathroom to wash up. Moments later she sat down at the table, and after saying grace, she helped herself to a serving of smoked salmon, seasoned rice, and steamed broccoli.

She smiled. The food was totally delicious. Although she

didn't want to appreciate Sterling's thoughtfulness she couldn't help doing so. He could have just as easily sent the tray back to the kitchen when she had not shown up for dinner as he had asked.

She frowned. He hadn't asked, he had ordered and she hadn't liked it one bit.

"I prefer it when you smile."

She turned slightly to the sound of the masculine voice, not surprised to see Sterling standing in the doorway connecting their rooms. She hadn't heard him open the door.

"I thought you were supposed to try improving your knocking skills." She kept her voice slightly quiet but knew he could pick up on her irritation and annoyance.

"I tried that earlier today and it didn't work. You refused to be cooperative." He came farther into the room and stood across from the table.

Colby tried to ignore how good he looked in the dim lighting of the room but found herself conducting still another close study of his features. There was no doubt about it, he was a fine specimen of a man. For some reason, this evening his cheekbones seemed even more defined, but his dark eyes displayed the same things as usual, alertness, distance, and mistrust. She couldn't help but wonder about the reason. A woman would have to be very special to penetrate his hard wall and get to know the real man behind it. And a woman would have to possess the patience of Job to give him time to trust her enough to become emotionally involved.

Her gaze moved from his eyes to his lips. The sensual shaping of his mouth reminded her of how it had felt molded masterfully to hers while driving her mad with passion.

"Colby?"

Sterling had said something. Colby shook herself out of her distraction and back into awareness. "What did you say?"

"I said I hope you're enjoying dinner. I was somewhat disappointed that you didn't show up in my suite as I'd asked."

She lifted her chin. "You didn't ask, Sterling, you ordered and I didn't like that. I'm not a child but an adult. I would appreciate it if you remembered that."

His slight smile held no pretension of humor. "Are you being difficult again?"

"No, you are. Evidently it bothers you that, unlike most women, I'm not in total awe of who you are. I told you at lunch, I could care less for you as an actor and the more I get to know you, the less I care for you as a man."

Sterling's eyes sparkled with amusement. Colby had just put him down. "That's right you did mention you favored Denzel over me."

"Hands down," she responded, deliberately meeting his eyes.

His gaze continued to hold hers. "In that case, I'd better get busy doing something about that. As my wife, I can't have you preferring another actor over me, and I definitely can't have you not caring for me as a man."

"I doubt my opinion on either will change," she said smartly.

"But I can at least try."

"Yeah, go ahead and try," Colby replied, offering him a sweet smile. "And if you try with as much gusto as trying to learn how to knock, I can relax in knowing that a year from now my opinion of you will still be the same."

"Really?"

"Yes, really."

Sterling's fingers began toying with the stem of a wineglass that he'd picked up off the table. "Speaking of a year, I thought about what you said about needing more time to breast-feed my child."

It seemed that automatically Sterling's eyes lifted from his preoccupation with the wineglass and concentrated on the curve of Colby's breasts outlined through the blouse she was wearing.

"What about it?" she asked in a hoarse voice when it became evident just where his gaze was dead-centered. The room suddenly became quiet except for their uneven breathing.

His eyes met hers again, and from their intense darkness she could just imagine where his thoughts were. He gave her a slow smile, which indicated she probably was right in her deduction.

"I've decided to extend your time in our agreement from six weeks to one year."

The smile that lit Colby's face at that moment, to Sterling's way of thinking, was as sweet as wine and like a fool, he drank it up.

"Do you really mean that?"

"Yes. And I've already notified Edward of the change. He'll be by tonight to drop the papers off and give you a chance to look over them. He'll return tomorrow for our signatures."

Colby nodded. At the moment she was too happy to say anything else.

"I'll leave you alone now to enjoy the rest of your dinner."

He turned to leave the room but before closing the door behind him, he turned back around and said, "I think you'll discover this extension may not be such a good idea after all, Colby."

She lifted her brow. "Why?"

"The longer you stay around my child, the harder it will be for you when the time comes for you to leave. And you *will* be leaving. I don't want you to ever think otherwise. The only reason I extended your time was because I want the very best for my child, not because I need a permanent wife."

He turned and walked out the room, closing the door behind him.

Colby refused to let his words put a damper on how elated she felt. The Lord had answered her prayers and she'd been given more time. She was determined to use that time wisely. Somehow she had to convince Sterling that a permanent wife was the very thing he did need.

She stared blindly across the room at the closed door. For some reason, she wanted more than just the baby between them. An inner part of her wanted him to want her as well. That thought came to her unbidden. She knew he wouldn't be the easiest person to get along with, but she felt he needed something more in his life than what he was getting now. She could sense that even with all his riches and fame, a part of him held something back. There was something about him that hinted he was afraid to let go, afraid to reach out.

And as inconceivable as it seemed, she wanted to be there for him and not just for their child.

Chapter 8

Edward Stewart and his trusted secretary, Marva Webster, arrived at Colby's suite before noon the next morning.

"Are you absolutely sure you don't want to consult your own attorney before we get started, dear?" Edward asked Colby.

She shook her head. "No. The less people knowing about this the better."

"But there may be some areas of concern you may want—"

"No, I read over everything last night, and I'm fine with it."

Colby actually felt better today than she'd felt in the past few days. Knowing about the year extension had made her heart feel lighter and less burdened. No matter what the document said, she had no intention of getting out of Sterling Hamilton's life a year after the birth of their child.

"It seems Colby will be glad to get her hands on the money after all," Sterling said icily. His muscular body filled a wingback chair that sat across the room.

Colby's eyes narrowed at him. "For your information,

Sterling, I still have no intentions of getting that money—at least not for myself. I've instructed Edward to donate a portion of it to the school where I teach. It's an inner-city school that can use all the extra funding it can get. The money will go on record as a generous contribution from you to the school. The rest of it will be used to help other needy inner-city schools around the country."

A look of total disbelief was etched on Sterling's face as he stood and looked at Colby as if she had lost her mind. "You're giving all that money away?"

"No, *you* are. It's all being donated in your name. I told you in the very beginning my child wouldn't be bought. All I want is for Wingate Cosmetics to stay out of Morton Industries' hands. You've assured me it will, and I believe you."

Then she turned back to Edward. "Where do you want me to sign."

"Wait!" Sterling's single word echoed loudly in the room and everyone turned to him.

"What is it now?" Colby asked with annoyance in her voice. She wanted to sign the papers and get things over with so she could return home to Virginia. Somehow she had to find a way to break the news to James about her pending marriage without giving away the real reason she was doing it.

Sterling met her gaze evenly. "You are aware there'll be other papers for you to sign prior to the marriage?"

At Colby's confused look, he said, "A prenuptial agreement. I do expect you to sign one."

Colby released an exasperated sigh. Sterling Hamilton was getting on her last nerve. "Certainly," she flung back before turning to Edward. "Where do I sign?"

Sterling signed the papers after her, and Ms. Webster signed as a witness. After their departure, Colby found herself alone with Sterling.

"Hungry?" he asked, breaking the silence in the room.

She shook her head. "I've suddenly lost my appetite."

"It will eventually come back," he said smartly.

Colby opened her mouth to give him a tongue-lashing retort then immediately closed it. What good would it do anyway? Besides, she was not in the mood to argue with him.

"You're probably right," she said, knowing her response was not what he'd expected.

And it wasn't. Sterling lifted his brow at her reply. "What are your plans for the rest of the day?" he asked her.

"I don't have any."

He thrust his hands into the pockets of his pants. "Then there's no reason for us not to spend it together."

"Doing what?" Colby asked curtly.

He gave her a smooth smile. "Sightseeing. How about if I show you around the area. Then there's one more thing we need to discuss in detail before you leave California."

"What?"

"Our wedding plans."

First, Sterling took Colby on a personal tour of the major movie studios. From there, the places became unlimited. They toured The Boulevard, Hollywood, and Griffin Park. That was followed by lunch in Santa Monica at Palisades Park. The two-mile stretch of green provided a magnificent view of the ocean and beaches below. Later they took a walk along the Santa Monica Pier, which jutted out into the Pacific Ocean. He told her it was here where his action-packed movie, *Duncan's Revenge*, the one he'd made with Sylvester Stallone, had been filmed.

Dressed comfortably in shorts and both wearing sunglasses and big straw hats, they had blended in well with the numerous other tourists.

"Wow! This place is beautiful," Colby said of Jesse Owens Park. The twenty-acre park named in honor of the black olympic gold medal track star had a huge gym, a large indoor pool, basketball, volleyball and tennis courts, and a three-par golf course. Quite a number of people had chosen the park that day to have a picnic.

Leaning against a guardrail, Colby watched a group of teenagers play a serious game of basketball against a group of older men. Sterling, who was standing beside her, turned to her and began softly stroking her shoulder. At first she had stiffened at the contact but then she relaxed. His touch was both surprising and welcoming. She had done some heavy-duty walking that day and her entire body was beginning to get achey. His slow, gentle massage of her shoulder was helping to relieve the tightness lodged there.

She gazed up at him, her eyes filled with appreciation. "How did you know I needed that?"

His expression was soft as he gazed down at her.

"Somehow, I just knew. I think it's time for us to return to the hotel. You've done enough sight-seeing for one day."

Taking her hand in his, he led her back to the area where his car was parked.

They walked together silently. When they reached the parking area, Sterling turned and, placing light pressure on her hand, gently pulled her to him.

Colby fixed him with a mildly surprised look.

"Don't look now," he whispered, "but there's a photographer who's been following us for the last half hour. We may as well make his day and give him a picture worth taking," he said. He tipped her chin up to him and lowered his mouth to hers.

The kiss, although a lot gentler than the one they'd shared in the hotel room yesterday, was just as greedy, possessive, and passionate. Colby's heart pounded furiously in her chest, as her body shivered from the feel of his mouth taking hers with such breathtaking thoroughness.

She dismissed from her mind the rule against kissing in

public. She didn't understand exactly what she was feeling or the type of passion consuming her senses. And at the moment she didn't feel compelled to understand. She just wanted to enjoy what was taking place between them. So she clung to him with all the strength she possessed. And his hold on her was both protective and powerful.

When Sterling finally ended the kiss, he rested his forehead on the top of Colby's head as he fought for control. Again he had lost it. Kissing her always made him lose control; control he didn't like losing. Whenever he kissed her, an exquisite weakness seemed to take over his entire body, and all he wanted to do was to crush her against him and kiss her like there was no tomorrow.

He sighed heavily. Those thoughts were disturbing.

Colby was also absorbed in her own thoughts. She stepped back out of Sterling's arms, annoyed with herself for responding to him that way.

"I can't believe I let you kiss me here," she said, nervously running fingers through her hair.

Sterling leaned against a wooden post. Shoving his hands into the pockets of his shorts, he gazed down at Colby with an unwavering absorption that made his eyes appear even darker. "I really didn't give you a choice," he said huskily.

"No, you didn't," she agreed. *At least not in the beginning,* her mind taunted. *But you could have stopped him afterward anytime you wanted to.*

"Was that kiss necessary?" she asked, still reeling from the effects of it. His kisses left her feeling weak and vulnerable.

"Yes," he answered with quiet assurance. "It seems we've been forced into action."

Colby frowned. "What are you talking about?"

Sterling took her hand in his once again. "Come on. I'll explain things in the car. I've discovered that in some places even the garbage cans seem to have ears."

They began walking and when they reached the car

Colby turned to him. She stared up at him confused. "That was the second time you've kissed me. You can't go around doing that whenever you feel like it. It's not proper."

Sterling couldn't help but grin at her choice of such an old fashion word. "It's not proper, huh?"

"No, it's not, and you can't do it anymore."

"I can't?"

"No, you can't."

Out of the corner of Sterling's eye he saw that the photographer had disappeared. Evidently the man had been pleased with the shots he'd taken of him and Colby kissing.

"I'll try and remember that I can't kiss you anytime I want to," Sterling finally answered pleasantly, opening the car door for her. He closed it again after she had slipped inside.

"Yeah, just like you're supposed to try knocking before entering my room, and try changing my opinion of you," she said as he turned the ignition and backed the car out of the parking space. "As far as I can see, you aren't doing a very good job."

"I said I would try, Colby. You shouldn't expect miracles overnight," he said, smiling. She sat stiffly with her arms folded. He could tell she was teed off. And as usual, whenever she was angry, she was more beautiful than ever. A broad shaft of sunlinght shone through the car and seemed to concentrate it's golden rays just on her. It highlighted her flawless smooth brown skin and made her hair appear shinier, more silky.

After they had driven awhile Colby said, "All right, Sterling, I want an explanation of what happened back there."

When the car came to a stop at a traffic light he turned to her. "It's easy enough to explain. Evidently that photographer works for one of those tabloid magazines. It's my guess our picture will make the front page in a few days. Who knows? It may be out as quickly as tomorrow."

Colby's eyes widened. "The one of us kissing? In a public place?"

Sterling shrugged. "It wasn't all that public. There weren't many people around."

"But it was a park for heaven's sake."

He lifted a brow. "You've never been kissed in a park before?"

"No."

"That's interesting." For some reason that bit of information pleased him. "From here on out, we have to lay it on thick for the media."

"Lay what on thick?"

"Our absorption with each other. We have to convince them we're madly in love."

"Why?"

Sterling met the confused darkness of Colby's eyes. "My wanting to get married will raise a lot of questions, since I've gone on record on numerous occasions and said married life wasn't for me. And since neither of us want to draw any unnecessary speculation—especially from the media—as to why we're getting married, starting today we'll give them performances worthy of Oscars."

Colby couldn't help but think about the kiss they'd shared at the park. Did he mean there would be more public displays of them that way? She hoped not. She didn't think her body could handle too much of kissing him. Already it melted each and every time he took her into his arms.

"Will that be absolutely necessary?" she felt compelled to ask.

"Yes. If it was just me, I'd care less, but since we don't want my son to grow up with the stigma of being a surrogate child, I don't want to give—"

"Why did you just refer to the baby as 'your son'? Do you have a problem with the possibility of having a daughter?"

Sterling smiled. "No, but that's not a possibility. There

hasn't been a female born into the Hamilton family in over a hundred years."

"Not a one?"

"No, not a single one. Right now there aren't any women in the Hamilton family, period."

"Didn't you get females in your family when the Hamilton men married?"

"Not for long. There's a high divorce rate among Hamilton men. It's known as the Hamilton curse."

"That's awful that there weren't any females around."

His brow furrowed. "Why would you think so?"

"Because you lacked a female influence in your life. And why is there a high divorce rate among Hamilton men?"

"For the longest time the Hamiltons, including my own father, were lumberjacks who resided in a small logging town in the wooded mountains of North Carolina. Because of the nature of their work, they were away from home living in logging camps for extended periods of time, so it wasn't advantageous to have a wife. And those who were married discovered the wives they left behind eventually got bored waiting for them to return home. Most of the women decided a logging town was no place to live for the rest of their lives, so they up and left."

"Is that the reason your mother left?"

Sterling's mouth tightened and the words he spoke were cold and emotionless. "I've told you I don't have a mother, and I would appreciate it if you'd try not to forget that fact again."

The rest of the ride to the hotel was in silence. Colby could not stop wondering why Sterling's mother had left. Whatever the reason, he had not forgiven her for it and from the way he sounded he never would. She could not imagine ever having her child grow up feeling that way about her. That was why she was determined not to let

Sterling send her away. She would always be a part of her child's life.

She smiled at the thought of one day having a baby. In her mind, she could picture a bouncy baby with black curls and dark eyes to match. And a part of her just knew it would be a girl.

She grinned to herself. So there hadn't been any girls born into the Hamilton family in over a hundred years? Well, she hoped Sterling was ready for "sugar and spice and everything nice" because their child would be a girl.

She just knew it.

Chapter 9

Colby looked at herself in the full-length mirror. She ran her hands under the thick hair flowing past her bare shoulders, letting her fingers tangle in the curls there.

She wasn't the type to stand in front of a mirror checking herself out, but the impression she would give tonight would be an important one. Sterling was taking her out to dinner and would announce their engagement to the media.

After they had returned to the hotel from sight-seeing, he'd explained their plans and how important tonight would be. Then indicating he had a number of things to do before they left for dinner, he had departed, leaving her alone.

She had wasted no time rushing to her closet in search of something to wear. Unfortunately, she had not brought anything fancy with her to California. At least nothing fancy or sophisticated enough to be seen out with Sterling Hamilton.

Seeing she had no other choice, she had left the hotel, caught a cab, and gone shopping. Upon entering a number of the stores she had been taken aback by their high prices, but she then remembered the stores' usual clientele were the rich and famous. A number of the shops indicated you could only shop by an appointment, and at others you were assigned your own personal salesclerk—or clothing representative assistant—who assisted you on an one-on-one basis while you made your selections.

Colby's afternoon spent on Rodeo Drive had been fun. Some of the names of the shops she had recognized as ones that supplied clothing for major network television shows. Their names often appeared among the credits at the end. And others, such as Gucci, had a worldwide reputation. She herself owned one of their purses.

She considered herself a person who liked nice things and dressed accordingly. However, she thought paying two hundred dollars for a pair of stockings a bit too much. Her eyes widened at the underwear prices that began at four hundred dollars. But she was soon forced to bite the bullet, and pulling her paid-up charge card from her wallet she proceeded to go shopping wild.

Three hours later she had walked out of the expensive shop with an outfit she felt would be perfect for tonight, along with all the accessories she would need. She had even purchased a couple of casual outfits and a bathing suit that had cost more than she had paid for the sofa in her living room at home. She cringed when she thought of the amount of money she had spent. The balance on her charge card would probably take her the next fifty years to pay off.

But now as she stood in front of the mirror admiring the raw silk dress she had purchased, she knew it was well worth it. Everyone always told her she looked good in red and as she gazed at herself, she had to agree with them. She liked what she saw and hoped Sterling would, too.

She would find out soon enough, she thought, when

she heard his knock on the connecting door to their suites. When she opened the door she took a step back as Sterling's imposing height and stature filled the doorway.

The man looked absolutely gorgeous.

He was dressed in a black dinner suit that was immaculately tailored to fit his broad frame. His crisp, designer white shirt and the black bow tie he wore made him look so devastatingly handsome that a lump suddenly lodged in Colby's throat. The man who stood before her, the son of a lumberjack, whose strikingly handsome features often graced the pages of numerous magazines as well as the big screen, exuded a physical magnetism that was awesome.

Awesome.

Colby released a sigh. That was the one word that could describe him. Sterling Hamilton was awesome. He would do justice endorsing her brother's new cologne. Awesome would perfectly describe the man promoting it.

"Hello, Colby. You look nice. Very nice."

Sterling's words, spoken soft and husky in a deep-timbered voice, brought Colby back to full awareness. She knew he'd been observing her close scrutiny of him. Evidently he felt now it was his turn to do likewise with her. He gave her a deep penetrating stare with clear and observant eyes. Awareness flowed through her body as she watched his open and unbidden gaze begin at the top of her head and slowly work its way down.

His gaze met hers and she saw something in the dark depths of his eyes that made her slightly wary. She felt like a canary caught by a cat, and somehow felt he knew it. She tried to relax but discovered she couldn't. The only thing she was capable of doing was standing there and returning his stare as he gave her a heated appraising look.

Then after holding her gaze, much too long to Colby's way of thinking, his eyes slowly moved down and settled dead-center on her mouth. And it stayed there.

* * *

He had a problem.

That thought occured to Sterling for the second time in two days, as he stood before Colby with his gaze fastened on her mouth. It was a mouth whose lips had been pampered with glossy red lip color. He inhaled sharply when she nervously swept her tongue across those red lips to moisten them. Desire, hot as volcanic lava, suddenly rushed through his body.

He forced his gaze down. The dress she was wearing could have been made just for her. It showed off her figure to a degree he found enthralling. His eyes consumed every sensuous detail, including the way the t-straps left her shoulders partially bare, and how its simple cut bodice emphasized her generously rounded breasts and small waist. But it was the front slit in the dress that captured his full attention. It provided him a tantalizing glimpse of a dark silk-clad thigh.

He was quite taken with her appearance. Most people wouldn't consider her drop-dead gorgeous, but her attractiveness definitely made a statement. And he knew without a doubt that to him, tonight, she was the most beautiful woman he'd ever laid eyes on. And that was a strong conclusion to make considering that his profession placed him in the company of many glamorous and beautiful women.

But Colby Wingate's beauty stood out. It was different, it was unique, and like the perfume she wore, the only way he could think to describe it was to simply define it as Colby. Even with her feistiness, there was a rare innocent quality that seemed to radiate from her. He had felt that way ever since their first kiss yesterday. Initially, he had dismissed such a notion as ludicrous. After all she was twenty-six years old. But then after their kiss today in the park, he wasn't too sure anymore. Although she had returned his kiss with a hunger so intense it had fueled his own out of control, it had been a curious hunger, an uncertain hunger. It was as if she'd been unsure just what kind of hunger had overtaken her. And it had made him want her more than he had ever wanted a woman before.

"You look nice, too, Sterling."

Colby's words penetrated the silence in the room. She watched as Sterling's gaze returned to her mouth. And there it lingered once again. The suite suddenly appeared smaller and Sterling's height and breadth became larger than life. Thinking more of her self-survival than anything else, Colby forced a quick smile and took a step back into the room.

"I'm ready. I just need to grab my purse," she said almost breathlessly. She tried to sound calm and composed but knew she'd failed miserably under the intense perusal of his eyes.

"This is for you," he said in a deep masculine voice as he handed her a small box.

Colby raised a brow as she took the gift-wrapped package from him. She had been so engrossed in her appraisal of him that she hadn't noticed him holding anything in his hand. "What is it?"

He shrugged with indifference. "Why don't you open it and see."

Colby didn't miss the silky timbre that suddenly appeared in his voice. She met his gaze. "All right." She slowly opened the box.

She gasped. There inside the box on emerald green velvet was a five-carat diamond solitaire ring. "Sterling!"

He took the box from her still-shocked fingers. "It's your engagement ring," he said, placing the huge ring on the third finger of her left hand. "This officially makes us engaged."

"B-but you didn't have to get anything so . . . so extravagant. I didn't expect it."

He released her hand. "Maybe you didn't, but the media will. I've never been engaged before, so they'll expect the woman I've chosen to become my wife to have some huge glittering representation of my esteemed affection," he said. "If you're ready, we can leave now. I've made reservations."

Colby wasn't given the chance to ask where they were going as she found herself quickly ushered from the hotel to a beautiful sleek red Jaguar. Sterling opened the car door for her.

"This is a beautiful car, and it's my favorite color," she said, lowering herself inside the polished leather of the expensive vehicle.

"I'm glad you like it," Sterling replied as he got under the steering wheel. "For some reason I knew you would look good in red," he said.

Colby assumed the comment had been made in reference to her outfit until Sterling added.

"It will be shipped to you in a few days."

"What will?"

"This car."

She thought she must have heard him wrong. She sat upright. "Excuse me?"

Sterling had expertly eased the car out into traffic before he responded. "This car. It's an engagement present from me to you, and I'll send it to you in Virginia."

Colby was aghast. "You can't give me this car!"

Sterling raised a brow. "I can't?"

"Of course, you can't."

"Why not?"

"It's not proper and you can't do it."

Sterling shook his head. She was the only woman he knew who seemed to care about what was or was not proper.

Most of the women he dated didn't give a flip. In fact, they thrived on doing improper things.

"Colby, I can do anything I want to do, and you're getting the car."

"Well, I don't want it!"

He frowned. "Of course, you want it. You're a woman. All women like expensive presents. Why should I believe you're any different?"

Sterling regretted saying the words the moment they had left his mouth. Deep down, a part of him knew in actuality, she *was* different. Although he wasn't sure to what degree, he believed Colby Wingate was different from any other woman he had ever come in contact with. He had reached that conclusion after watching the video that showed her interacting with her class, and then meeting her. But still, a part of him would never fully trust her or any woman. And although he had all intentions of marrying her, their marriage would not be forever. It was a business deal and nothing more. He had spent too many years with his emotions locked up deep inside of him. And he wasn't about to unleash them now. More than ever, he would have to keep his guard up around Colby. She had a way of getting next to him and if he wasn't careful, he would find her suddenly embedded right under his skin.

Colby sat in brooding silence. Sterling's words had hurt her in a way he would never know. Evidently most of the women he knew walked around with dollar signs in their eyes and placed money above everything. If that was the case, then she *was* different.

Her parents had been two hard-working, God-fearing, middle-class Black Americans who had provided her and James with a good and loving home, and had instilled in them good moral values and a firm belief in doing what was right. Even after their deaths when James had become her legal guardian, he had continued to provide that strong foundation for her. No matter how much studying he had to do on the weekends, he had carved out precious time for her and spent a part of his Saturdays doing fun things with her; and then on Sundays he had taken her to Sunday school and church.

She knew like Reverend Johnson often said, money was not the root of all evil but the love of it was. Even when James had worked hard putting all his time and energy into his business, she and Cynthia had known it hadn't been about money. It had been about accomplishing a goal in life and making the best out of a talent God had given you no matter what the odds.

"We're here."

Sterling's words invaded Colby's thoughts. She looked out the window and was not surprised he had taken her to a restaurant she could immediately tell was frequented by the elite and wealthy.

Most of the cars lining the parking lot were very expensive. A valet dressed in a short-waisted white jacket and dark trousers greeted them. No sooner had they alighted from the car than they were thrust upon by a swarm of reporters surrounding the establishment. They suddenly found themselves caught in the firing line of flash bulbs.

"Who's your new lady this month, Mr. Hamilton?" a lanky reporter asked as he held his miniature tape recorder in his hand.

"Where's Diamond Swain? Does she know she's been replaced? Or has she really? When was the last time you saw her?" another reporter asked.

Then there came a question from a third. "How long will your fling with this one last, Hamilton? Considering your track record, I'd say a week or two."

Sterling laughed. "Gentlemen, can't the lady and I enjoy a nice evening without your endless questions?"

"Hey look at the size of the rock on this broad's hand," the lanky reporter exclaimed, getting the attention of the others.

Sterling gave the lanky reporter a leveled stare. "The lady isn't a broad and don't ever call her that again."

Then he turned his gaze on the other dozen or so reporters who seemed to have all gone temporarily speechless. He knew the reason. He rarely came to the defense of any women he was with.

"I think it's time I set the record straight," he replied smoothly, sliding a possessive arm around Colby's waist and pulling her closer to his side. Colby came to him willingly although he could tell she was somewhat nervous from all the attention she was getting.

"This is Colby Wingate, and as of this afternoon she became my fiancée."

This was news and what followed Sterling's statement was an explosion of more questions, one fired right behind the other. One reporter drowned out his colleagues as he unceremoniously raised his voice above the others. "Where did you come from, Ms. Wingate? And exactly what do you do for a living?"

Acute nervousness churned inside Colby. She looked at Sterling and to her surprise he gave her an assuring wink. That wink somehow gave her the inner strength she needed to answer the reporter's question in a rather calm voice. "As you can tell, I'm not a model. I've got too much hair for it," she said, jokingly placing the blame on her long, thick hair and not her size-ten figure. Her comment elicited laughter from all, including Sterling.

"I'm from Richmond, Virginia, and I'm a school teacher. I teach third grade."

"A teacher! Sterling Hamilton is marrying a school teacher and not a Hollywood glamour girl?" Someone in the crowd shouted out.

"But take a good look at this teacher. They never looked like that when I was in school. If I would have had one who looked like her, I would've volunteered to stay back in third grade another year or two," another reporter shouted. His statement got chuckles and nods of agreement from the others.

"Now that you've gotten your story, do you mind letting us enter the restaurant in peace?" Sterling snapped. He was becoming slightly irritated at the number of reporters who were more interested in Colby's outfit than getting a news-breaking story.

A reporter then asked, "When is the wedding?"

Sterling answered as he ushered Colby toward the restaurant. "As soon as possible in a very private ceremony. So don't any of you wait on invitations."

"Why the rush with the wedding, Hamilton?" the same reporter asked. "Could it be Miss Wingate is expecting a bundle of joy in the very near future? Like less than nine months from now?"

Sterling stopped and turned around. His deadly gaze lighted on the short, plump reporter. Removing his hand from Colby's waist, he stood in a threatening stance. The stormy expression on his face radiated the fact that Sterling Hamilton was a man to reckon with when angered.

"For the record, Colby and I very much want a child one day. However, at the present time we aren't expecting one. The only reason we're marrying quickly is for my own selfish reasons."

Colby reached out and placed her hand on Sterling's arm. She felt his tensed muscles relax with her touch. Their eyes met as he returned his hand to her waist. And then to her complete surprise he lowered his mouth to hers. Oblivious of the cameras flashing around them he kissed her. The kiss was soft, warm, and tender. And although it only lasted mere seconds, the feel of his lips on hers, as always, totally consumed Colby.

"As I said, gentlemen," Sterling stated in a husky voice as his eyes continued to gaze into Colby's, "my reasons for rushing into marriage with Miss Wingate are purely selfish ones. Goodnight." Then he tenderly gripped Colby's elbow and led her into the restaurant.

Once inside, Colby noticed that heads turned and curious glances followed them as they made their way to their table. "Well that's over," she stated as Sterling pulled out the chair for her.

"Don't count on it," he replied gruffly.

Colby tried to dismiss the brief kiss they had shared. She knew it was all a part of the playacting they had agreed to do, but as usual, it had left a whirlwind effect on her. He had looked at her so intensely, so tenderly, and so caringly. His words had seemed so genuinely sincere, so believable, that for a brief moment she had felt . . . what? A fraction of truth in them? Of course, they were the truth, she realized as she accepted the menu from the waiter. He really hadn't actually lied. They were rushing into marriage for his own selfish reasons. He wanted a baby and was using her as a means to get one.

She glanced around the beautiful establishment. Across the room she could have sworn she saw Will Smith dining with his wife, Jada Pinkett. Colby suddenly wondered how many times Sterling had brought Diamond Swain here with him. She immediately dismissed the thought, convincing herself she cared less. She would not let her mind dwell on one of the questions a reporter had asked him about Diamond Swain that he had not answered.

They studied the menu in silence. Unable to make up her mind on a selection, Colby, ended up letting Sterling order for her. She was not disappointed. Both the meal and the wine were exquisite. She didn't know which of the two she could credit with relieving the tension from her body, although she leaned more heavily toward it being the vintage wine he had ordered. She was surprised that just like earlier that day at the park, she was enjoying his company.

He asked her numerous questions about her job while

they ate. He also shared tibits with her about the movie he had just finished filming in Paris and the one he was scheduled to begin shooting next month in Spain.

He told her about his home in Malibu and the one in North Carolina, saying the latter was the one he considered his real home, although he commuted back and forth between the two while filming. He briefly mentioned his father's death, and the tone of his voice and the flash of pain that appeared in his eyes confirmed just what Edward Stewart had told her, Sterling and his father had been close.

Not once did he mention his mother and after his acrid words earlier that day, she knew it was not a safe topic for discussion. But still she couldn't help being curious. She also noted he didn't bring up anything associated with Wingate Cosmetics or the subject of a baby. She was very appreciative of that.

"We can leave now," Sterling said, calling for their bill.

"I'm surprised you didn't have a cup of coffee before leaving," Colby said as he escorted her out of the restaurant. "You appear to be someone who'd love to drink a cup after such an enjoyable meal."

"Really?" Sterling asked, raising a darkened brow as he led her outside and waited as the valet brought them their car. "You're right. A meal such as that should be followed by a good cup of coffee. But I would like to have my coffee without an audience even if I wasn't so lucky with my meal. Whether you realized it or not the two of us were the center of attention tonight."

"Yes, I noticed," she answered. *And you gave them a performance worth watching,* Colby thought, remembering his attentiveness during dinner. To anyone looking at them, they appeared to be a couple very much in love. She had hung onto his every word, and he hers. Several times he had reached across the table and had captured her hand in his. His touch had been warm, gentle, assuring.

It had stirred feelings in her she'd only been introduced to since meeting him.

When they arrived back at the hotel they again found themselves caught in the midst of reporters. Colby noticed they were not the same ones from the restaurant. Evidently news traveled fast. Once again, Sterling provided them with the same information he had given the others. Nothing more, nothing less.

Afterward, he ushered her across the hotel's plush carpet and well-lit foyer to the elevator and up to their rooms. Colby was mildly surprised when he followed her inside her suite.

"Would you like to join me in a cup of coffee?" he asked.

She felt tired, but more than anything she felt the need to distance herself from Sterling. If nothing else, the reporters tonight had reminded her of just who he was. Sterling was a Hollywood superstar, an acclaimed macho man accustomed to a glamorous lifestyle that included beautiful women who would jump at the chance to be a part of his life, including sharing his bed. And like he had told her on their way to the restaurant, he could do anything he wanted. She knew that included taking advantage of her if she let him. But she had no intention of letting him do that.

"No, thank you, I don't want any coffee," she declined hastily.

Sterling nodded then picked up the phone and ordered coffee to be delivered to her suite. Afterward, the room was quiet for several minutes before Colby finally spoke.

"If you don't mind, Sterling, I want to call it a day. I'm tired and have a plane to catch in the morning."

He met her gaze. "No you don't."

"Excuse me."

Sterling ignored her question as he walked away to open the door for room service. When they were alone once more Colby again asked what he had meant by his earlier statement. It wasn't until after he had poured a cup of coffee and had taken a few sips that he answered her. The silence had been unnerving.

"You don't have an early plane to catch. I'm taking you home day after tomorrow. In my private jet."

"You're what!"

"I said I'm taking you home."

"Wait a minute. This is the first I've heard of this. And just who made that decision?"

"I did."

"And who gave you the right? I don't need you to take me home."

Sterling's cool gaze held Colby's and knew she was angry. He watched as she crossed her arms under her breasts. The gesture made her breasts swell against the fabric of her dress. He got so caught up in looking at her, that for a minute he had forgotten she was waiting for his response. She soon reminded him, however.

"I asked you a question, Sterling."

"Aren't I the lucky one," he responded smartly, annoyed with himself for finding her so darn desirable that at times he couldn't think straight. He placed his coffee cup down and walked over to where she stood in the center of the room. When he spoke, his voice was soft but very clear.

"First of all, you and I are officially engaged. You are the woman who will become my wife and you're also the woman who will give me my son. You can chalk it up to masculine possessiveness or just plain arrogance on my part, but from the moment you agreed to marry me, temporarily binding our lives together, I claimed you as mine. And what's mine, Colby, I protect."

Colby felt a soft tremor pass through her body with Sterling's statement claiming her as his, but still she was determined to stand up to him. Squaring her shoulders she said. "But I don't need your protection."

He released a deep breath before he continued. "Yes, you do. Because of our engagement, you'll now find yourself hassled unnecessarily by reporters who'll want a story, and the paparazzi who'll want pictures. They will badger you relentlessly. You wouldn't even make it to the airport."

"But you've given them a story. Surely they won't bother to ask me anything else."

"Yes, they will. And although I think you handled yourself remarkably well tonight with those reporters, the paparazzi can be relentless, thoughtless, and inconsiderate. You do remember what happened to Princess Di don't you? Think about it, Colby. The news of our engagement is now a hot item. Your life as you used to know it is virtually gone. I'll try to protect you from the media as much as I can and taking you home is one way."

Sterling then chuckled throatily. "Besides, if anything I believe your brother will expect me to bring you home. I'm sure he'll want to talk with me."

Colby nervously wrung her hands together. "But I haven't had the chance to tell him about you yet."

"Then I suggest you do so as soon as possible. News of our engagement will hit the newspapers in the morning. It may even make the late night news on television tonight. I believe your brother is a good and decent man to have taken the responsibility of raising you after your parents' death. I highly respect such a person, and it wouldn't be right if I sent you back alone. Especially if he thinks the two of us are sleeping together while you're here."

"Why would he think anything like that!"

"Why wouldn't he? You've been in California three days already and no doubt those reporters will release information indicating the two of us stayed together at this hotel. People will speculate about how we spent our time here. We know we haven't been intimate but others won't."

"James will if I tell him so. He knows me. He knows I have all intentions of remaining a ..." Colby stopped talking mid-sentence and decided not to finish what she was about to say.

Unfortunately for her, Sterling had no intention of not letting her finish it. "Remaining a what?" he asked, quietly, intently.

She shrugged. "Nothing."

"What were you about to say, Colby?"

"It's not important."

Sterling stared at her. "If it's what I think it is, it's very important. Is it?"

She didn't reply immediately, she just shrugged her shoulders again. "I have no idea what you think it is."

Sterling was silent for a moment as he looked at her. The red dress she wore molded itself to her body with such allure, it gave an image of her being a seductress and temptress—unmistakably so. But deep down he had a gut feeling that image was false and far from the truth.

"I think you've never slept with a man and that you had all intentions of saving yourself for marriage," he finally said.

She met his unwavered gaze. "I still plan to save myself for marriage."

Sterling controlled a smile at the determination in her tone of voice. "I can give you a good reason why you shouldn't, but I'm sure you've heard a number of them from other men."

"Yes," Colby answered. Her eyes suddenly shone with silent laughter as she recalled a few of them. "I've heard that the longer I put if off, the more it will hurt when I do try it. I've heard men no longer want virgins for wives, they prefer more experienced women in their beds. And I've heard that men will appreciate you even more if you let them try you out first."

She looked up at him with amused fascination. "I even had one guy tell me my mother had been wrong and that a man will still buy a cow after getting the milk free."

Sterling grinned. He adored this side of her, her gentle camaraderie, her subtle wit. "I'm sure you had a good reply for all those reasons you were given."

"Yes, especially the one about the cow. I asked him would the cow be just as valuable to him after he had used it."

"What did he say?"

"Of course, he said yes, but I knew he was lying. He worked as a new car salesman and I knew right away his words couldn't be trusted. Besides, he was the one who had sold me my first new car, and as part of his sales pitch he'd given me a number of reasons why a new car was better than a used one. He kept saying that a new car would hold its value longer than a used one. Can you believe that?"

Sterling threw his head back and let out a great peal of laughter at the seriousness in Colby's voice and the expression on her face. For whatever her reasons, he was glad she hadn't allowed a man take advantage of her. He knew he could probably thank James Wingate for that. Evidently the man had schooled his sister on handling the players out there.

"So, Sterling, what reason do you want to tell me as to why I shouldn't wait?"

His expression suddenly became serious, determined. He took a few steps that brought him closer to her. Reaching out he lightly traced his finger softly up her shoulder. Her skin tingled from the contact.

His words were soft when he spoke, and his soft breath felt warm and moist against her face. "I could tell you how our bodies will connect in mindless passion and ecstasy as I make you a part of me and me a part of you. And that when I make love to you, I will give you a glimpse of heaven. Our coming together will be one special moment, and we don't need a marriage license to enjoy such a spiraling experience."

Colby trembled under Sterling's words and touch. For a while she wasn't capable of speech. Her insides jangled with an unwelcome surge of excitement. But somehow and from somewhere, she found the strength to deny what she was feeling.

She managed to pull herself together to say. "Not bad. In fact, that line was better than most. However, my response to that is for you to think of just how much more special the moment will be knowing you'll be doing all those things to your wife and not just another woman. You'll be making me yours in the most intimate way. And I won't just get a glimpse of heaven, I'll become a part of it, with you. That in itself will make the experience even more special."

Sterling's lips parted in an astonished smile. She had thoroughly and completely turned the tables on him. Her eyes, so serious and calm, dared him to refute her words. And he knew he couldn't.

"Not a bad comeback," he said.

She smiled. "I'm usually quicker with my responses."

He shook his head and an amused grin touched his lips. "Yeah, I bet you are."

He wondered now that he knew the truth about her, how in the world was he going to keep his hands off her until after they were married. It wasn't going to be easy. He was a man used to getting what he wanted whenever he wanted it. But that would not be the case with Colby.

"Now getting back to our discussion regarding me taking you home Friday," he said, not wanting to dwell on his dilemma anymore.

"All right, Sterling, I'll call James tonight and tell him. And I'll agree to let you take me home. But why wait til Friday? Why can't we leave tomorrow? Once I tell James about us, he'll want me to return home to talk to him immediately."

"I'm sure he will, but I have an important business

meeting scheduled tomorrow, and I want to check on our progress with Morton Industries.''

Colby nodded. She had almost completely forgotten about Morton Industries and the real reason behind her marriage to Sterling.

Sterling walked back over to the table to get his coffee but knew it had gotten cold. He took a sip anyway and studied Colby over the rim of his cup. She was moving around the room, unnecessarily tidying up. He could tell from her movements she was tired. They had spent most of the morning sight-seeing and then over dinner she had told him of her shopping adventure.

He set his cup down when he saw her smother a yawn. Walking over to her, he pulled her to him. "I think it's bedtime."

She pushed herself out of his arms. "Look, Sterling, evidently you didn't understand—"

He placed his fingers to her lips to silence her. "Lighten up. I didn't mean it the way you took it. What I meant is that it's bedtime for you."

She tinted, embarrassed she had jumped to conclusions. "I need to call James first."

"Then I'll leave so you can do that. It's getting late and there's a three-hour time difference between here and the East Coast."

"Yes, I know."

A faint smile touched his lips. "It's my guess reporters will be camped out front in the morning, but the sooner we can leave here and go to my home in Malibu, the better. Things are more secure and private there. We won't be hounded by any reporters."

"All right."

"Good night, Colby."

"Good night, Sterling."

Unhesitantly, Sterling lowered his head and brushed his

lips against hers. He wanted to do more but didn't. Instead he walked out of the room, closing the door behind him.

Colby walked over to the table and picked up the telephone. Taking a deep breath she began dialing numbers.

"Hello," a deep masculine voice answered sleepily.

"Hello, James, it's me."

She could hear his soft, sleep-filled chuckle. "How are you doing, Me?"

She grinned. "I'm fine." A lump then formed in her throat. "I'm sorry to call so late but I have something very important to tell you."

"Oh? What?"

"Remember that friend I told you I was coming here to see."

"Yes, what about her?"

"I deliberately led you to believe it was a she."

There was a pause. "And she's not?"

"No, *he's* not."

There was another pause. "Colby, are you trying to tell me that your friend is really a *he* and not a *she*?"

Colby took a deep breath. "Yes."

There was another pause. "I think I can handle what you're telling me, Colby. After all, you're twenty-six years old. Cynthia told me a long time ago I was too overprotective where you're concerned. And she's right. You're out on your own and have been since completing college. You have a good head on your shoulders, and I trust you to make the right decisions in life. You've never disappointed me, Colby, and I'm proud of you. I know I don't say that often enough, but I am proud of you. And I want you to know that no matter what, I'll always be here for you. Cynthia will, too."

Tears blurred Colby's vision. "Thanks."

"Are things serious between you and your friend?"

"Yes, very serious. I wouldn't have traveled all this way to see him if they weren't."

"When will I get to meet him? And why haven't I met him already?"

"You'll get to meet him soon, and the reason you haven't met him yet is because we were sort of conducting a long-distance relationship and weren't sure how things would work out between us. Now we're sure."

Colby closed her eyes. She hated lying to him and knew she was about to do so even more. Crossing her fingers, she added. "We have decided to get married."

"What!"

"I know it comes as a surprise, but we love each other and want to get married."

"Colby, don't rush into anything. Come home and we'll talk about this. Marriage is such a big step. How long have the two of you known each other?"

"We met two months ago."

"Two months ago? Colby, it's too soon to think of getting married. People date for years before marriage. Cynthia and I dated for almost three years before we decided to get married."

Colby smiled. "The two of you should have gotten married a lot sooner. You were driving each other, as well as me, crazy."

She heard her brother chuckle. "Well, yeah, but let's get back to you, young lady. Just how well do you know this guy?"

"I know him well enough to know he's the man I want to spend the rest of my life with. He's the man that I want to father my children."

"But why the rush?"

Colby couldn't help but shake her head. Nothing in life had prepared her for this type of conversation with her brother. He was the type of person who had to know everything and had to understand every little detail especially when it concerned her. After their parents' death, he had tried wrapping her up in a covering of protection so thick it had taken Cynthia's emergence into their lives to rip it apart.

Cynthia, a mere twenty-two years old and fresh out of college, had been Colby's Spanish teacher in her first year of high school. She had gone head-to-head with the handsome James Wingate when he had refused to let Colby go on a field trip with the Spanish club. That had only been the beginning. Somehow through teacher versus guardian constant battles over her, James and Cynthia had discovered they actually liked each other. And much to Colby's delight, her favorite teacher and brother had begun dating.

"Colby? Are you still there?"

"Yes."

"Well, answer my question. Why are the two of you rushing into marriage when you've only known each other a couple of months?"

"Because we don't want to wait any longer to . . ."

There was a pause. "To do what?" James asked.

"To become intimate. You know my feelings on sex before marriage."

"So you're marrying him just so it'll be all right for the two of you to sleep together?"

"No, of course not. I told you, we love each other and we want to do the right thing; and it's getting harder and harder for us to stay apart that way. He's a good person and wants to do the right thing. You should admire him for that."

"If he's such a good person why hasn't he made it a point to meet your family? I would think he would have if things are this serious between the two of you."

"We didn't think it was a good idea. Because of who he is, we had to keep things a secret."

"A secret. Just who is this guy?"

Colby took a deep breath and plunged forward. "Sterling Hamilton."

The pause on the phone was so long that for a moment Colby thought the line had gone dead. Then the explosion came. "Sterling Hamilton! *The* Sterling Hamilton! The actor?"

"Yes."

"Colby, you can't be serious!"

"I am serious, James."

"Colby, honey, listen to me. I want you to come home immediately, baby. We need to talk about this."

"Sterling is bringing me home day after tomorrow and we'll talk then."

"Listen, baby. I think you should come home now. Alone. Tonight. How on earth did you get involved with the likes of Sterling Hamilton? I read the papers and the magazines. The man is a nationally known playboy. He's into women, lots of them. Besides, he's almost ten years older than you. Colby, think about what you're getting yourself into."

"I have thought about it, and I want to marry him. I wanted to let you know that Sterling and I became engaged yesterday. Chances are an announcement of our engagement will make tomorrow's papers. I wanted you to hear it from me first."

"Colby, don't, baby. Listen to me for a—"

"No, I have to do this. I want to do this. Sterling is bringing me home on Friday. We'll talk then. Tell Cynthia I'll call her tomorrow. Good night, James."

"Colby, wait!"

"Yes?"

"I love you, sis."

Colby's eyes became misty again. "And I love you. I know you want what's best for me, but you have to take my word for it that right now Sterling is it."

"I'll expect to see you on Friday and we'll talk; me, you, and Mr. Hamilton."

"All right, James, good night."

Colby hung up the phone. Tears she couldn't control flowed down her cheeks, and sobs she couldn't contain racked her body. For the first time in her life, she felt alone.

Chapter 10

Colby's eyes were glued to the scenery outside the car window as it moved along a canyon road. It provided an unforgettable and breathtaking view of Santa Monica Bay with mountains on one side and the San Fernando Valley on the other.

She knew they were headed to Sterling's home in the Malibu Beach Colony, a residential community of beach homes. She had read enough magazine articles to know it was a haven for numerous celebrities who wanted to get away and find peace and quiet.

And today she needed to get away.

Just as Sterling had predicted, a ton of reporters had camped outside the hotel. There had been even more of them than last night, with more cameras and more questions. Sterling had summed up an answer to their inquiries in one statement.

"Yes, Colby and I are are getting married, and yes, we are very much in love."

Colby sighed deeply. *Lies, lies and more lies. She was now living the life of a lie.*

She thought about her telephone conversation with James. He had not been completely satisfied with the information she'd given him. He had more questions and he would demand more answers. She leaned her head back against the seat and closed her eyes. At the moment all she wanted to do was to think about pleasant things and she couldn't help remembering yesterday and the time she and Sterling had spent together. She had really enjoyed herself when he had taken her on a tour of the city. For some reason she felt torn by conflicting emotions. There were times the man actually got on her last nerve with his arrogance. But then at other times, he fascinated her with the way he handled things, like his handling of those reporters. She couldn't help but admire his strength and control.

Sterling couldn't help but notice Colby was unusually quiet. And from the look of things, it appeared she hadn't gotten very much sleep. He could think of only one reason for both.

"I take it you talked to your brother last night."

Colby opened her eyes and glanced over in his direction. "Yes."

He gave her a searching look when the car momentarily came to a stop on the two-laned roadway. "And?"

"And even with my story, which I thought sounded pretty convincing, he still had a lot of questions. He has a big problem with the fact I told him we'd just met two months ago."

"We both know the reason we decided on that."

Colby nodded. Sterling had explained that his activities were usually monitored by one tabloid or another seeking a story. But two months ago he had outsmarted them and spent two weeks in a secluded lakehouse belonging to a friend in Virginia. Coincidently, the place was less than an hour drive from Richmond. They decided to use that to their advantage and tell everyone it was during that time their paths had crossed.

"I take it he doesn't believe two people can meet and fall in love within two months," Sterling said. "The media bought our story easily. What's his problem with it?"

Colby gave him a wan smile. "Oh, he knows two people can fall in love in a relatively short period of time. He and Cynthia did. James just doesn't think that I can."

"Why not?"

"Because taking the time to fall in love wouldn't fit into my hectic schedule. I don't date much and most weekends I spend my time doing lesson plans or trying to come up with creative ideas to become more effective as a teacher. And when I do date, the men are usually other teachers who share my love for teaching. James definitely can't see me falling in love with a well-known celebrity. It's just not me, and of all people he knows it."

Sterling reached out and gently touched her cheek. A strange, faintly tender look flashed in his eyes. "Then I guess I'll have to convince him that I swept you off your feet."

Once again Colby felt that deep feeling of heat flow through her with his touch. "Yes, I guess you will, tomorrow. He definitely wants to talk with you."

Sterling chuckled. "I'm looking forward to our meeting."

Colby almost said she wouldn't be overly anxious if she were him, but she refrained from doing so. "How much longer before we get to your home?"

"Not much longer. We'll be there in less than ten minutes."

"Who're your neigbors?"

Sterling looked over at her and smiled. "Barbara Streisand lives on one side of me and Morgan Freeman lives on the other. Neil Diamond and Johnny Mathis live across the street."

A short while later Sterling brought the car to a stop in front of a huge wrought iron gate. Seconds later, after keying in a special code, the gate opened allowing them passage.

They pulled into the driveway of an enormous two-story structure nestled among cacti and palm trees, and gardens that included numerous exotic flowers. The sweet smell of the surrounding botanical landscape and the strong salty scent of the ocean assailed Colby's nostrils.

"You're on the beach!" she exclaimed. A huge smile curved her lips.

Sterling couldn't help but smile at her excitement. "Yes, I live on the beach. It's a private beach owned by the people who live here. But that doesn't mean you're allowed to go skinny dipping any time you want," he teased.

"I don't skinny dip," she said, opening the car door and getting out before he had a chance to come around and assist her.

"I really like this place, Sterling."

"I'm glad. Come on and let me introduce you to Simon."

"Simon?"

"Yes, my housekeeper. He's been with me for quite a while. You'll like him."

No sooner had the words left Sterling's mouth than a tall, thin elderly man opened the door for them. "Welcome home, Mr. Hamilton."

"Thanks, Simon," Sterling replied as he and Colby stepped into the foyer. "I'd like you to meet Colby Wingate, my fiancée."

Simon smiled. "Yes, sir, I heard all about it. It's in the newspapers, and it was announced on the *Today Show* this morning. I must say you and Miss Wingate have caused quite a stir."

Then he gave his undivided attention to Colby. "I'm happy to meet you Miss Wingate and congratulations."

"Thank you."

"Simon, I have some business to take care of, and then later today I'm expecting Kyle Garwood. I'd appreciate it if you took care of Colby for a while. See that she's settled into one of my guest rooms."

"Yes, sir. I'll be glad to." He turned to Colby. "Let me show you to your room, Miss Wingate."

"All right, Simon."

"Colby?"

She turned and gazed up into Sterling's dark eyes. "Yes?"

"Because of my business meeting with Kyle, I won't be joining you for lunch. However, I'd like for us to have dinner together. And Kyle will be joining us."

"Okay."

Colby watched as Sterling turned and walked across the hall and into a large room. She caught a glimpse of the expensively decorated room with its thick carpet before he closed the door behind him.

"Not only is Mr. Hamilton a dynamic actor, he's also a top-notch businessman," Simon said proudly of his boss.

Colby nodded. She followed the man as he led her up some large, sweeping stairs. "I have quite a few messages for you, Miss Wingate."

She looked up at Simon, surprised. "Messages for me? Are you sure? Who would know to call me here?"

"Didn't Mr. Hamilton tell you he had all your calls forwarded from the hotel to here ever since early this morning?"

Colby shook her head. "No, he didn't mention it."

Simon shrugged. "I guess he forgot. Well, here we are."

Colby found herself in a room too beautiful for words. It had a bay window facing Malibu Beach. The view was magnificent. "It's lovely, Simon."

"I'm glad you like it. I'll leave you to get settled and will bring your luggage up in a minute. If you need anything just call me. The messages for you are on that table over there.'' Then he left, closing the door behind him.

Colby walked over to the table and picked up five slips of paper. One was from *Ebony Magazine* requesting an interview. The other was from *People Magazine* requesting the same thing and the other three messages were from Cynthia.

She picked up the phone and immediately called Cynthia. A soft voice answered.

"Hello, Cynthia, it's me.''

"Colby! Is it true!''

Colby smiled. She could just imagine her sister-in-law's excitement. "Is what true?''

"Don't play games with me, Colby Wingate. Is it true you're actually engaged to Sterling Hamilton? *The* Sterling Hamilton?''

"Yes. I guess James filled you in on everything.''

"Are you kiddin'? Your brother has told me very little. I think he's still in shock himself. In fact he didn't even mention it until breakfast this morning. And that was mere seconds before I opened the newspaper to discover it myself. He claimed the reason he didn't tell me sooner was because he didn't want me getting overly excited in my condition.''

"Yeah, that's a thought.''

"Colby, you made the front page here today.''

"The front page?''

"Yes. It's not every day a local girl snags a Hollywood superstar. There're a number of pictures of you and Sterling in very interesting poses.''

"What sort of poses?''

"Poses of the two of you kissing. Obviously you and he enjoy doing that.''

"Oh.''

"Yes, oh. James nearly hit the ceiling when he saw them, but he soon calmed down after reading the newspaper article that came over the wire service. Sterling Hamilton did an outstanding job of upholding your reputation. In fact, he made it very clear you mean a lot to him. At this moment, you're probably the envy of every woman in the country.''

Colby frowned. "I really don't understand why."

"Well, according to this article, and I quote . . . *The mighty Sterling Hamilton has fallen . . . undeniably in love. At least that's this reporter's opinion who saw the couple together last night as they entered the Paradise Cove Restaurant. The woman on his arm, who he proudly presented as his fiancée, was a beauty and deserved all the attention and unselfish affection being lavished on her by Hamilton. Colby Wingate of Richmond, Virginia, whose career is in education (she's a third-grade teacher) has accomplished something many thought was an impossible feat. She is bringing Sterling Hamilton to the altar and without any underhanded tactics, as one fellow reporter discovered when he boldly asked the couple if by chance they were expecting a baby. That reporter (and I won't give his name) found himself under Hamilton's famous belligerent stare, and his reply left all in attendance satisfied a baby is not on the way, and the reason for the soon-to-take-place wedding is for purely selfish reasons. Hamilton merely wants the woman he loves by his side as his wife. I for one believe his story. I'm no romantic fool, but I've seen Hamilton with numerous female companions in the past, and I've never seen him display so much open attention to one before. And that includes Diamond Swain. In my rap up, I can only say that Colby Wingate has evidently tamed the beast. Hamilton may have put a ring on her finger—and a huge one at that—but she's gone one step farther and put an even bigger one in his nose. The man is definitely smitten. But as they say, the bigger they come, the harder they fall, and it definitely appears to this reporter that the mighty Sterling Hamilton has fallen, and fallen hard.''*

"Well, what do you think of the article?"

"Interesting."

"Is that all you have to say?"

"Afraid so."

"I can't believe you kept your involvement with him from me. You've known for years that I'm an avid fan of his. You owe me all the details. How did the two of you meet?"

Colby swallowed and tried not to let anxiety cool her thoughts. She was prepared for the question and had actually rehearsed the answer that morning. However, she still felt uncomfortable with the lie she was about to recite.

"Sterling happened to be in Virginia, and I ran into him at the library."

"The library? You actually met Sterling Hamilton at the library here in Richmond?"

"Yes. He'd been using a friend's winter home in some secluded place and had gotten bored and drove into town to get a good book to read."

"Wow! Did you recognize him right away?"

"No."

"No?"

"No. I didn't recognize him right away. He came up to me and asked where he could find a particular book and I told him."

"For Pete's sake, Colby, how could you not recognize Sterling Hamilton!"

"Well, I didn't. I knew he was an attractive man but I didn't know who he was. He had a beard and I'd never seen Sterling Hamilton with a beard before."

"So you fell in love with him, Sterling Hamilton, the movie star."

Colby thought about her actual first meeting with Sterling in Edward's office, and the time she had spent with him since. Although there were a number of things about him she didn't know, like his relationship with his mother and the full truth behind his relationship with Diamond Swain, a part of her felt that over the past couple of days, she had gotten to know him in a way deeper than she would have by just reading about him in newspapers and magazines. She had gained more insight into Sterling Hamilton, the man, more so than Sterling Hamilton, the actor.

"No, I didn't fall in love with Sterling Hamilton, the actor, but I have fallen in love with Sterling Hamilton, the man," she said simply, regulating her tone when she realized the words she had just told Cynthia were true.

She almost stopped breathing and a tight knot formed in her stomach. How in the world could she have allowed herself to fall in love with Sterling Hamilton! She felt as if a heavy hand was closing around her heart, squeezing it. How could she have let herself fall under his spell like a zillion other women?

Colby clenched the phone in her hand until it hurt and slowly eased up. She took a deep breath and tried not to panic. Somehow and some way she would find a way to deal with this.

A sound behind her caught Colby's attention. She turned to find Sterling standing in the doorway. She could tell by the way he was looking at her that he had been privy to her conversation with Cynthia; specifically he had heard the part where she had said she loved him.

She quickly turned back around. "Cynthia, I have to go," she rushed out. "Someone just came in."

"Who?"

Colby rolled her eyes upward. "Look, we'll finish this conversation later, I promise."

Out of the corner of her eyes Colby saw Sterling walking toward her. Before she had a chance to react, he was standing right in front of her.

"May I?" he asked.

Not giving her a chance to respond, he took the phone out of her hand. "Hello, Cynthia. This is Sterling."

There was complete silence on the other end. Sterling quirked a brow and covered the mouthpiece of the phone with his hand and whispered to Colby. "She won't say anything."

"She's probably fainted," Colby stated calmly.

Sterling frowned and put the phone back to his mouth. "Cynthia? Are you there?"

Seconds later, Cynthia's happy and excited voice came back on the line. It was so loud even Colby could hear it. Evidently her sister-in-law had recovered from shock.

"Yes," Sterling laughed. "I'm really Sterling Hamilton, and yes, I'm marrying Colby."

He laughed again. "I'm looking forward to meeting you, too."

He nodded. "Yes, I assure you Colby's in good hands."

Another nod. "And yes, we'll be arriving in Richmond around noon tomorrow."

Colby shook her head. Cynthia was as bad as James at times. She wanted to know everything, every little detail.

"You have one more question?" Sterling asked Cynthia. "All right, what is it?"

Whatever Cynthia was asking made Sterling look at Colby. His dark eyes held hers as he studied her intently. "Yes, I fell in love with Colby the moment I saw her." A few moments went by then he said. "All right, Cynthia. Goodbye."

He hung up the phone. His expression was mildly humorous. "I take it she's a romantic," he said.

"Of the worst kind."

Dipping his head slightly, he said. "I guess the more people we tell our little story, the more believable it will seem. Just listening to you tell Cynthia how we met almost had me believing it myself. You're a good storyteller."

Colby leaned toward him, seething with mounting anger. "Is that a nice way of saying I'm a good liar?"

Sterling raised a brow at the fury he saw lighting her eyes. "No, that's not what I meant at all. There's a difference between being a good storyteller and being a good liar. I consider a liar as someone who makes a habit of not telling the truth to serve their own purpose. I think of a storyteller as a person who has the ability to weave magical, believable tales and fables for the enjoyment of others. I bet you do that a lot for your students."

The lines of anger in Colby's features dissolved. Sterling's comment had not been the put-down she'd assumed. Instead he'd said it as a compliment.

"Yes, I enjoy telling stories to them," she said, annoyed with herself for overreacting. She didn't like these new emotions assailing her senses. How could she suddenly have such strong feelings for Sterling? A couple of days ago she was convinced she totally disliked him.

She walked over to the window wondering why he was there. She'd thought she wouldn't be seeing him again until later that day. "Is there something you wanted?" she found herself asking him. She wanted to be left alone for a while to think.

Sterling looked past her and out the window at the beautiful ocean view before meeting her gaze. "I thought you'd be interested to know the squeeze we put on Morton Industries is working. Already my people have received calls from them."

Colby became instantly excited. "Oh, Sterling, that's wonderful."

"But it's not over yet."

"I know, but that's still good news. Thanks for telling me."

He continued to look at her, thinking how beautiful she looked with the sun's rays highlighting her features. He suddenly became annoyed with himself for having such thoughts.

"Why shouldn't I share it with you?" he asked curtly. "That's all part of the deal, isn't it? I'm to save Wingate Cosmetics and you're supposed to give me a child. And no matter what romantic tale we've fabricated for others, you and I know the truth.''

He quickly turned and left the room.

Colby sighed deeply. Sterling's words had seared her heart because they had painfully reminded her of her place in his life. A place he considered to be only temporary.

Now she had a new problem to deal with, an even bigger one than before. How was she was going to deal with the fact she had fallen in love with Sterling Hamilton?

Chapter 11

Colby inhaled the salty smell of the ocean. It was invigorating, stimulating, and soothing. Its gentle breeze ruffled her hair, tantalized her tender skin and at the same time it beckoned her to enjoy the awe-inspiring beauty of her surroundings. It lured her to relax, unwind, and appreciate the mystic effect of the lush blue-green waters that touched the sandy shores.

And so she did.

The salty spray of the ocean seemed to slowly wash away the troubles that plagued her mind. She didn't want to think about why she had suddenly fallen head over heels in love with a man who didn't love her in return, a man who saw her place in his life as only temporary, and only as a means to an end.

She opened her arms, closed her eyes, and inhaled deeply. The smell of the ocean, the feel of silken sand beneath her bare feet, and the warmth of the sun on her skin consumed her senses. She opened her eyes, leaned her head back to stare up into the clear blue sky, seeking comfort and relief from her tormented mind.

And from somewhere she received the inner peace she sought.

She was suddenly entrenched with a feeling that somehow things would be all right. It endowed her with the belief that there was a reason she had been placed in Sterling Hamilton's life and he in hers. And it bestowed upon her a promise that in time the answers would come and the purpose would be made clear.

She took another long, deep breath of the clean, salty air and felt her anxieties and tension slowly disappear. She smiled and like a small child filled with an abundance of energy and full of life, she ran toward the beach to enjoy the waters.

"You're so busy enjoying the view outside that window, you haven't taken the time to notice my presence."

Sterling's gaze slid from the window to the man whose imposing height and stature nearly filled the room. "You're early, Kyle."

Kyle Garwood smiled. "My grandfather used to say the early bird catches the worm." He walked over to where Sterling was standing in front of the window. Curiosity made him gaze out of it to see just what held Sterling's attention.

Kyle's smile widened, "But I guess I can say in your case, Hamilton, the early bird catches you standing at the window ogling your future wife," he said chuckling. "From the news I've read in this morning's paper, I assume congratulations are in order."

"Yes, I guess you can assume that," Sterling answered before turning his attention back to the window. He ignored the fact Kyle was watching his actions with keen interest. And frankly at the moment he didn't care. He couldn't remember another time the sight of the ocean looked so breathtaking. And he knew it had a lot to do with the fact Colby was out there enjoying it.

She was wearing a bathing suit that some would think was conservative, considering most women enjoyed parading around in bikinis or even less these days. But it was what Colby's one-piece swimsuit didn't reveal rather than what it did that heated up his imagination. It fitted snugly around her hips, and her full, generous breasts were well defined by the soft material. Even from a distance his gaze was able to travel the perimeter of each and every delectable curve of her body.

Sterling heard a chuckle beside him. "Don't mind me," Kyle was saying. "I'll just take a seat over there until you're finished gawking at your fiancée."

The beginning of a smile tipped the corners of Sterling's mouth. He doubted he would tire of watching Colby any time soon. "It might take a while," he said.

"Take your time," Kyle replied, crossing the room and easing his muscular frame into a chair that sat across from Sterling's desk. "And when you're through, I want answers, Hamilton. Lots of them," he said with a friendly grin on his face but a firm tone in his voice.

Sterling's smile turned into chuckle. He wasn't surprised Kyle wasn't buying the story that had appeared in the newspaper that morning. And with good reason. Kyle Garwood knew him better than anyone.

He and Kyle had been good friends ever since their early teen years. They had met the year Sterling's father had delivered all the fresh-cut lumber needed to build an addition to Special K, the Garwood family cabin retreat in the North Carolina mountains. Although Kyle had been born to wealth, and Sterling was the son of a lumberjack, the two teenagers had forged a deep friendship. Over the years, one had always been there for the other, and deep down they both knew it would always be that way.

Both the room and it's occupant faded from Sterling's

mind as he turned his attention back to Colby. He couldn't help but grin as he watched her repeatedly dodge the waves. She was frolicking to and fro behaving in a frisky, playful way. He thought her movements were fluid, lithe, and even sensuous. Her gay and lighthearted antics reached out to him and a part of him was tempted to join her outside. He couldn't remember the last time he had enjoyed the beach the way Colby was doing now.

A soft knock sounded at the door seconds before Simon entered. "Will Mr. Garwood be joining you for lunch, sir?"

"Yes, he intends to feed me," Kyle answered the man before sinking back against the chair's cushions.

Sterling lifted a brow at his friend.

Kyle merely gave him an apologetic smile. "I thought I'd answer for you since you were somewhat preoccupied."

Sterling frowned at the humor he saw in Kyle's eyes. He turned to Simon. "He'll also be joining us for dinner," he said.

After Simon had left Sterling turned his attention back to Kyle. "My apologies for being somewhat preoccupied."

"Apology accepted. I know how it is when you're in love."

Sterling raised a dark brow. "And what makes you think I'm in love?"

Kyle shrugged his broad shoulders. "According to the newspapers, you are." He then leaned forward in his chair. "In fact, I'm a little anxious to see that ring in your nose."

The look Sterling bestowed on Kyle was totally lacking humor. In fact, it showed signs of tightly held annoyance. "I don't have a ring in my nose. You should know me better than that."

Kyle's grin was one of amusement. "Yes, I should, but when I talked to Kimara yesterday she happened to mention your sudden interest in breast-feeding. Then in this morning's paper, I read an announcement about your engagement. And today I show up early for our meeting to find you standing at the window gawking at your fiancée, and not even trying to hide the fact you were doing it. So what am I to think, Sterling?''

Sterling looked at Kyle thoughtfully for several long seconds before answering. One corner of his mouth pulled into a slight smile. ''You're to think that I never do anything without a purpose. And that's all I'm going to say right now.''

Kyle digested Sterling's words and he couldn't help but notice the agitated expression on his face. ''All right, but do you want to know what *I* think?''

Sterling lounged casually against the window frame. ''Not really, but I'm sure you're going to tell me anyway.''

''I think that whatever your purpose, you may have gotten yourself in a little too deep.''

For some reason Kyle's observation clawed at Sterling's insides. ''Let's change the subject shall we.''

He walked over to his desk and took a seat. ''I take it everything is going well with Kimara's pregnancy.''

At Kyle's nod Sterling shook his head. ''I can't believe she's pregnant again. Kamry was just born six months ago.''

Kyle shrugged. ''What does that have to do with anything?''

Sterling was barely able to keep the laughter from his voice. ''To you and Kimara, obviously nothing.''

He bent his head to make sure he had Kyle's undivided attention. ''But the way I see it, you have four kids and haven't been married four years yet. Can't the two of you find something else to do with your time other than make babies?''

Kyle's eyes glowed with unhidden warmth at the thought of his children, Kyle VI, the twins—Kareem and Keshia, and the newest member to the Garwood household, another beautiful daughter, Kamry. They were his and Kimara's four special Ks. He leaned back in his chair and let his gaze meet the probing inquiry he saw in his best friend's eyes. "Kimara and I want a house full of kids."

"At the rate you two are going, you'll meet your goal in no time," Sterling interjected.

The curve of Kyle's mouth deepened into a grin. "That's a very good possibility. We found out a few days ago we're having twins again."

Sterling's mouth dropped open. Intense astonishment lined his features. "Twins again! Is that normal?"

"I'm sure it's a rare occurrence for most people," Kyle replied calmly.

Sterling's mouth curved in pensive humor. "But then you and Kimara aren't like most people are you?"

"No, we aren't," Kyle answered in a deep, jovial tone. His grandfather's will had forced him and Kimara to marry. Now he couldn't imagine his life without her.

"I hope you realize that every time you and Kimara have another baby, I take on another godchild," Sterling stated as his mouth twitched with amusement. "That can get rather expensive."

Kyle's laughter was a full-hearted sound that vibrated throughout the room. "Then I guess it will be to your advantage, Hamilton, to stay gainfully employed."

A few moments later Simon arrived with their lunch.

"Has Miss Wingate been taken care of, Simon?"

"Yes, sir. However, she declined lunch. I think she's having a good time on the beach."

Sterling nodded and glanced back toward the window. "Yes, I totally agree with you."

"You and your wife are expecting a second set of twins! Why that's absolutely wonderful, Kyle."

Awareness flowed through Sterling's body as he leaned back in his chair and watched Colby conversing with Kyle as the three of them enjoyed an after dinner drink.

Unbidden, his gaze was drawn to her mouth. He couldn't help but remember how good it tasted and how soft it had felt beneath his as he plied it with languid strokes of his tongue.

Almost instantly, as if she'd been able to read his thoughts, Colby's gaze turned and met his.

"Isn't that right, Sterling?" she asked.

Sterling blinked when he realized both Colby's and Kyle's eyes were on him. It suddenly became apparent he'd been asked a question. "I'm sorry, what was the question? My mind was elsewhere."

He frowned when he saw Kyle's grin. He'd been caught gawking at Colby again.

"I was just telling Kyle that we're having girls."

"Girls?"

"Yes, all our babies will be girls."

Sterling released a deep agitated sigh. Thinking Colby was apparently laying it on thick for Kyle's benefit, when he himself didn't want to do so because of the smirk he saw on Kyle's face, he met her gaze directly and said, "You and I will have only one child and it will be a boy. I've told you there aren't any girls born into the Hamilton family."

Colby turned to Kyle and said, "In that case, when our daughter is born it will truly be one special moment, don't you think?"

Smiling widely, Kyle nodded in agreement. "I don't see how it won't be, Colby."

Sterling raised his eyes to the ceiling. It was apparent that Kyle was quite taken with Colby and had been ever since introductions were made before dinner. The fact that his best friend had taken an immediate liking to Colby had been surprising. To most people, Kyle was not a man of many words and by nature he was usually guarded, restrained. But that wasn't the case tonight. Somehow Colby had managed to wiggle her way through Kyle's shield and engage him in the topic he loved best—his wife and children.

After a few more minutes of conversation, during which Sterling felt like an outsider, Colby stood and said, "Well, I know you two have additional business to discuss so I'll leave you now."

When both men stood, she turned to Kyle. "Although Sterling and I haven't set a date for our wedding, I hope that both you and your wife will be there."

Kyle's smile deepened. "Oh, I plan to be there. Sterling and I agreed a while back that if he ever got married, I'd be his best man."

Colby smiled. "That's wonderful, and I'll look forward to seeing you again. And I hope to one day meet your wife and children."

"I'm sure you will."

"Good night, Kyle."

"Good night, Colby."

Then she walked over to Sterling. On tip-toe she leaned up and kissed his cheek. "Good night, Sterling."

Not waiting for his response she walked out of the room and up the stairs.

The room was silent for a minute or two before Kyle spoke. "Do you know what I think?"

Kyle's voice pulled Sterling from his thoughts. He'd been thinking that tonight Colby had played her part as the loving fiancée to a tee. "No, but as usual I'm sure you're going to tell me anyway."

Kyle grinned. Then he walked over to Sterling and patted him on the shoulder. "I think that somehow you've found yourself a jewel. Colby Wingate is one precious gem."

She couldn't sleep.

Colby's mind was busy playing possible scenarios of how

things might go when they saw James tomorrow. What would he say to Sterling? Would the two of them get along?

Throwing back the covers, she climbed out of bed and went to the window. She couldn't help but smile as today's memories flooded her mind. She'd had so much fun on the beach. It had been the most fun she'd had in years. And then later, after meeting Sterling's friend, Kyle, he had kept her entertained throughout dinner. Sterling, for the most part, had ignored her, so she had been grateful for Kyle's company.

The urge to walk on the beach tugged at her. Sterling had said it was a private beach so chances were it was pretty safe at night. In a matter of seconds, she slipped out of her thin, spaghetti-strap night gown and into a pair of shorts, a T-shirt and her sandals.

She quickly ran down the stairs and was about to exit through the back door when the sound of Kyle's raised voice stopped her. It sounded like he and Sterling were having a disagreement about something. Curiosity made her move closer to the closed door where the two men were.

"I just don't understand your attitude, Sterling. You're an astute businessman with a sharp eye for good investments. You've read the report. Why on earth would you not want to be included in on this deal?"

Sterling's hand tightened on the glass of wine he held in his hand. His eyes were dark; as dark as the liquid in the glass. "I have my reasons."

Kyle gazed long and hard at him. "Then how about sharing them with me. You know as well as I do this deal is a steal. Nicholas Chenault has done an outstanding job with Chenault Electronics since his father's death. And at the age of thirty, he's already proven to be an even better businessman than his father was. At the rate he's going, there's a good possiblity Chenault Electronics will become the largest Black-owned electronic business in the country."

"Then why does he need our help?" Sterling asked, slowly taking another sip of wine.

"Because of necessary expansion and further research. Chenault's development of that mangolid chip will move them into the twenty-second century. That fact is a given. He just needs more capital to back him. I think it will be a worthwhile investment."

"I don't want any part of it, Kyle. End of discussion," Sterling said angrily.

Kyle stared long and hard at his best friend. He then came and sat across from him. "No, Sterling, it's not the end of discussion. I want to know what you have against Nicholas Chenault."

Sterling's eyes clashed with Kyle's. His body began executing an emotional somersault as pain he thought he'd buried long ago resurfaced. He inclined his head in silent acknowledgement.

"I've never really told you everything about my mother have I, Kyle?"

Kyle frowned. He wondered why Sterling was deliberately changing the subject. "You told me she walked out on you and your father when you were only six-weeks old."

Sterling nodded. He suddenly felt tired and drained. "Yes, but what I never told you is that after she left us and divorced Dad, she moved to Florida and married a very wealthy man a few years later. I only saw her once as a child and that was purely by accident. I was six years old at the time and had accompanied a youth group to Charlotte. She happened to be there and was staying at the same hotel I was."

Sterling sighed deeply. "She was there with her new husband and their one-year-old son."

He paused briefly before continuing. "I recognized her

immediately. Dad never removed her picture from his bedroom dresser so I knew how she looked. Not knowing any better, I walked over to where she was standing alone holding her little boy and asked when she was coming home to me and my dad.''

There was silence in the room before Kyle asked softly, "What did she say?"

Sterling chuckled. It was a deep heart-wrenching sound. "At that instant she recognized me, too, not as the little boy she had given birth to six years before, but as a threat to her new life with her husband and child. She denied even knowing me and went so far as to summon hotel security. She told them I was harrassing her and her son. I got a good tongue-lashing from the security officer in front of all of my friends. That day my mother denied my very existence, and it hurt like hell.''

Anger swept through Kyle. He could not believe anyone could be that cruel and heartless to a child. Even now he could feel Sterling's pain, his anger, his hurt.

"But what does all that have to do with Nicholas Chenault and Chenault Electronics?"

Sterling met his gaze directly. "It seems Nicholas Chenault and I have something in common.''

Kyle frowned in confusion. "What?"

"The same woman gave birth to the both of us."

Kyle was shocked. He stood and began pacing the full length of Sterling's office. Then he stopped and met Sterling's gaze. "You mean to tell me Nicholas Chenault is your half brother? He's the little boy your mother was holding that day you saw her?"

Sterling nodded his head. He stood and walked over to the window. This time when he looked out he didn't see Colby. All he saw was darkness. It was the same darkness that had plagued his life since finding out as a child that his mother hadn't wanted him. He turned back to Kyle.

"Yes, so to bring it all home to you, Angeline Chenault,

the widow of Alan Chenault is my mother, and Nicholas Chenault, their son, is my biological brother."

"Does he know?"

"I doubt it. I doubt even Alan Chenault knew about his wife's past."

Sighing, Sterling took another sip of wine. "So for personal reasons, Kyle, I have no desire to enter into any type of relationship, business or otherwise, with Chenault."

The ache in Colby's throat kept her from swallowing.

She knew she was wrong to have listened in on Sterling and Kyle's private conversation, but once she had heard Sterling's heart-wrenching words, she couldn't move.

No wonder he felt the way he did about his mother. The woman had had two sons. She had turned her back on Sterling, but Nicholas Chenault had grown up surrounded by her love. Love that Sterling had been denied.

Tears misted Colby's eyes. No longer wanting to take a walk on the beach, she turned and softly tiptoed back up the stairs. Back in her room, she took off her clothes and slipped back into her gown. Getting back in bed, she punched her pillows a few times as she tried to settle in, but it was useless. She couldn't push Sterling's words out of her mind, nor her heart. Reliving that part of his life had effected him deeply. She had heard the pain in his voice when he was talking to Kyle. Tears flowed down her face. The man she loved was hurting and there was nothing she could do about it.

In the distance she heard a door closing and knew it was Kyle leaving. He had told her at dinner that he would be catching a plane that night to return home to his family.

A little while later, Colby got out of bed and slipped into her robe. Without giving much thought to what she was doing or why she was doing it, she left her room and headed downstairs in search of Sterling. She didn't know what she would say to him when she saw him. All she knew was that she had to see him.

He was not in his study. She walked quietly through the rest of the large house, and when she didn't see him anywhere, she slipped outside the back door.

The smell of the ocean was even more potent at night, she thought, inhaling the salty scent. She remembered how earlier that day the beach had soothed her troubled mind and had helped her put a number of things in perspective.

The moon's glow led her way as she took several steps forward, feeling the soft, silky sand beneath her bare feet. She stopped when she came to a cluster of palm trees and took the time to enjoy the cool, gentle breeze.

"What are you doing out here?"

Sterling's deep, masculine voice startled Colby and she swiftly turned around. "Sterling, you scared me."

She leaned back slightly against a palm tree and looked up at him. The light from the patio didn't reach far enough to light his dark features, but the soft light from the moon did. Colby's breath caught in her throat. His chest was completely bare and the only thing that covered his body was a pair of black shorts.

Her eyes took in every vivid detail of him. His broad shoulders, steel-muscled chest, and muscular thighs and legs indicated he kept himself in great physical shape. The heat of his body seemed to heat her own, and the scent of him was undeniably all male. She noticed his eyes, which were looking at her, cold, distrustful, and filled with anger.

"I asked what you're doing out here, Colby." His voice was hard and tight.

"I was looking for you," she said.

"Why? Did you think Kyle was still here and you would seize the opportunity to eavesdrop on our conversation again?" he snapped.

Colby was stunned speechless. She'd never given

thought to the possibility that he would know she'd been listening at the door. She had barely made a sound. She was sure of it.

"But how did you know I was there? I was quiet."

Sterling lifted a brow mildly surprised at her admission. He thought she would have denied his accusations. Her honesty deflated his anger somewhat, but not completely. He narrowed his eyes at her. "Your scent gave you away. When I left the study to walk Kyle to the door, I picked up on it. Traces of your fragrance still lingered in the hallway. The perfume you wear is unique and has your name on it. I would pick up your scent anywhere and at anytime."

"Oh." Colby unconsciously gnawed at her lower lip. "Well, I didn't mean to listen, it was sort of an accident."

"An accident?" At her nod he said. "Deliberate eavesdropping isn't an accident."

She slightly raised her chin. "It wasn't deliberate. You told me earlier today you thought I was a good storyteller. Well, listening to your story tonight sort of pulled me in," she answered truthfully.

Sterling's eyes hardened. "Everything I told Kyle was the truth."

"I know and that's what's so sad."

Sterling grabbed her wrist and pulled her to him. Colby looked into his eyes and they appeared cut from stone. "I don't want your pity," he snarled.

Colby jerked her hand away from him. Her anger flared instantly and her spine became ramrod-stiff. "Pity? I don't pity you, Sterling Hamilton," she said placing hands on her hips. "Why should I pity you? At least you did have one loving parent, so the way I see it, you should count your blessings."

She took a step forward and Sterling unconsciulsy took a step back. He had been around Colby enough times to know what that firey look in her eyes meant. She was about to give him hell.

"Let me tell you about pity. I save my pity for Otis Marshall, one of my students. He doesn't know his father, and his mother is somewhere strung out on drugs. She has never bothered to come and see him since the day he was born. He was lucky enough to have a grandmother that cared, but unfortunately she recently had hip surgery and her medical bills were so enormous, they can barely make ends meet right now."

Colby took another step forward. "Then there's Maria Martin who earlier this year confided to me that her step-father was sexually abusing her. She has my pity because her mother chose to believe her husband's denial instead of her own daughter's accusations. Fortunately, we were able to get her in a foster home for now, but the authorities haven't been able to locate her natural father."

Sterling met Colby's furious stare with a seemingly composed expression and that made her even madder. "You, Sterling Hamilton, don't need my pity because you have more than enough pity for yourself. For once, you need to take a look around you. You aren't the only person whose parent has walked away and not looked back. So get over it."

"Have you finished?" Sterling asked in a hard, cold voice, crossing his arms over his chest.

"Not quite," Colby replied lifting her hand to her hair and pushing the thick mass of curls away from her face. "I want to leave you with something to think about."

Her features became gentle and her voice became soft when she said. "A real mother would never have just walked away and not looked back. That incident you experienced as a child only proves one thing. You were better off without her in your life. Not being there was her loss and not yours. You made something of yourself. Just look at all of your accomplishments. I know your father had to have been very proud of you, and any woman with a lick of sense would be proud to claim you as her son. Good night, Sterling.'' Then she turned to leave.

Sterling reached out for Colby and pulled her to him. Before she could draw breath, his lips captured hers. He had only meant to kiss her good night, at least that's what he'd convinced himself, but the moment his lips took possession of hers, blatant desire took control of him. This time he was not surprised by it.

As if it had a will of its own, his mouth latched onto hers wanting to see if she still tasted as good as the last time, knowing deep down that she did. But once he delved into finding out, he couldn't stop. Especially when he felt her mouth melt beneath his and sensed a hunger in her as strong and keen as his own.

And he became a victim to it.

He used his tongue to brand her, and his arms held onto her tight. He hadn't realized how badly he needed to hold and to taste her until that very moment. Reliving that part of his life with Kyle had left him torn and feeling bruised. Although he didn't want to admit it, Colby felt so right in his arms and was filling a void he hadn't known existed.

Colby let her hands wander over the firm muscles of Sterling's bare back and shoulders. She liked the way his skin felt underneath her fingertips. When his lips suddenly increased their pressure and demand on hers, her body shuddered with pleasure. He was holding her so close, she could feel his heat, his strength, and even the evidence of his desire for her.

She caught her breath when he released her mouth, and began placing a trail of butterfly kisses around her nose, ears, and neck. And when his hand pushed the robe from her shoulders, she almost drowned in the sea of desire that shone in his dark eyes.

Sterling breathed in Colby's scent as he looked at every

detail of her. The thin, white, spaghetti-strap gown she wore was short and skimpy and didn't come close to fully covering her. Slowly, his fingers reached out and touched the gentle curve of her waist to the small of her back. When his fingers moved upward to graze the soft swell of her breasts that were pressing against the thin material, he heard her release a passionate groan.

These were the breasts that would one day nourish his son, he thought as his fingers gently caressed each one. Wanting her in a way he had never wanted another woman, he leaned down and kissed her again, wanting her taste to fill him completely. This kiss was hungrier, more urgent, and more full of strained passion. He pulled her even closer to the hard length of him. The feel and taste of her were all-consuming.

Thunder rumbled overhead and with the turbulent sound, Colby's control returned. She had allowed Sterling's kiss and fondling to render her mindless, and knew she had to put a stop to what they were doing. Things were getting out of hand. She had a will of her own and was determined to use it. She had given him liberties she'd never given another man because she loved him, but she had to remind herself he didn't love her. And at that moment when he whispered in her ear just what he wanted to do to her tonight in his huge bed, it reinforced her resolve.

She broke off their kiss and moved out of his arms. "I'm sorry, Sterling. Please don't think I'm a tease. I never meant for things to go this far, but you make me lose myself," she said truthfully. "We can't continue to do this any longer. It's not—"

"Proper," Sterling ground out, finishing the statement for her. Frustration clearly lined his features and was evident in his voice.

"Yes," she said, nodding and putting her robe back on. "I'm glad you agree."

"I don't agree with anything, Colby." The set of his jaw was firm and the darkness in his eyes was intense. "Do me a favor and go to bed."

She cast a glance at him and saw his frustrated features. "We have enough to deal with in our relationship without the complications of sex before our marriage, don't you think?"

Sterling looked at her like she had completely lost her mind. "No. I don't think that way at all," he snapped.

There was a gentle quietness in her voice when she replied. "Then it's a good thing I'm thinking clearly for the both of us. Good night."

Sterling watched as she quickly walked away toward the house. When she was no longer in sight he removed his shorts and raced off toward the beach. For once he was in dire need of the cold ocean waters.

Kyle was right, he was in way too deep.

Chapter 12

"Sterling, promise me you'll try to get along with James."

Sterling sat leaning back in the seat of his private jet with his eyes closed. Colby's words, which had been whispered softly in his ears, made him cock one eye open and look at her. The gaze that met his was so serious he couldn't help but open both eyes.

"Colby, your brother is the least of my problems right now," he replied truthfully, in an irritated tone. He was tempted to tell her his main problem was having endured a sleepless night, and he wasn't in a good mood because of it. His late night swim in the ocean had done little to quench his desire for her. The wanting he felt was strong, urgent, and needy. It was like a deep ache straining against the zipper of his pants. And it wasn't helping matters sitting this close to her tempting body.

"If anything he better try to get along with me," he added in an agitated voice.

Thinking he had ended all conversation between them for the time being, Sterling closed his eyes again. However, he discovered that wasn't the case when she said, "I take it you're still upset about last night."

Without opening his eyes he answered. "I really don't want to talk about last night."

"All right, but one day you'll thank me."

He felt the chronic ache against his zipper and said, "I doubt it, and I'm curious as to why you would think so." He shifted in his seat. Her scent was nearly driving him insane.

To his dismay, she leaned closer to him and said, "Well, the way I see it, I did you a favor by not letting things go too far. I'm not on any type of birth control so there would've been a strong possibility of something happening."

Sterling opened both eyes and arched one brow at her. "Something happening like what?"

She leaned even closer and whispered. "An untimely pregnancy."

He rolled his eyes heavenward, wondering where she came up with her logic at times. As far as he was concerned, she looked at things too seriously, too maturely. She had the ability to think things through too much to suit him. The women he usually was involved with just rolled with the flow. They agreed with whatever he thought and didn't make waves. Unfortunately for him, Colby didn't agree with whatever he thought, and as for making waves, she was right up there with Martha Reeves and the Vandellas. Heat waves were becoming a specialty of hers. Even now he wanted to drown in the lush hotness of her body.

"Why would you concern yourself with an untimely pregnancy? You're going to have my baby eventually," he pointed out to her, relaxing in his seat once more. "Timing would not have to be an issue."

"Yes, it would. If I get pregnant before our marriage the terms of the contract won't apply. It clearly states the terms apply to a child conceived *during* our marriage."

"Is that so?" Sterling asked thinking about that slight technicality. He studied Colby with curious intensity. As usual, she looked beautiful and the outfit she had on, a printed skirt and matching blouse, looked good on her. Her hair was pulled back away from her face and the style openly displayed all her flawless facial features.

"Yes, that's so."

"Then thanks for bringing it to my attention. I'll try real hard not to knock you up before the wedding."

He then leaned over and whispered in her ear. "But I can guarantee you this, Colby, having you in my bed will be the number one thing on my mind after the wedding, so I hope you're up to it, because I plan on keeping you there for days and days and days."

Sterling leaned back in his seat and closed his eyes, satisfied for the time being that his frank and true statement had rendered Colby totally speechless.

"What's taking them so long in there, and why wasn't I included?" Colby asked Cynthia as she nervously paced the living room floor. Sterling and James had been closed up in the study for well over an hour.

"Just relax, Colby, everything's going to be fine. You know James, he needs to know that Sterling's intentions are honorable," Cynthia said as she went about setting the table. It was evident she was in hog heaven because Sterling had consented to stay for dinner.

"Why would James think otherwise? He's marrying me isn't he?"

"Well, yes, but you know James. He has to know every little detail when it concerns you."

Colby nodded as she nervously gnawed her bottom lip. Knowing about James inquisitiveness was what really had her nervous. Her brother rarely took things at face value. She had been able to talk him out of meeting them at the airport by telling him Sterling had made prior arrangements for a rental car to be waiting for them. But they hadn't counted on half the city being there for their arrival. Everyone, including many of her coworkers, had shown up to welcome her back to town. She knew the media's leak that Sterling would be returning with her had a lot to do with the reception she got. The California reporters had been mild compared to the mob of reporters that met them at the airport and began firing one question after another. Although she could tell Sterling was annoyed by it all, he had taken it in stride and had played the part of the loving husband-to-be.

"Colby, please sit down and relax. They'll be out in a minute," Cynthia said.

No sooner had the words left Cynthia's mouth than the study door opened and both men walked out. Colby couldn't help but notice that James and Sterling equaled one another in size and height. They were also equally handsome. "Is everything all right?" she asked immediately.

Sterling raised a brow. "Of course. James and I just had to reach an understanding."

Colby tossed a questioning glance at them. Neither of their expressions revealed anything. "What sort of an understanding?"

The two men glanced at each other before glancing back at her. It was James who spoke. "An understanding regarding you."

"What about me?"

This time it was Sterling who spoke. "James thought we should wait for at least six months to marry, to get to know each other better, and I told him that was out of the question. The wedding will take place in three weeks. I prefer getting married next week, however, since you prefer waiting until this school term ends, I'll agree to three weeks."

Colby's cheeks became warm when she remembered what Sterling had whispered to her earlier that day about just what he intended to do once they were married.

"James also felt that until the wedding took place, you were his responsibility," Sterling continued. "I convinced him since your life will be turned upside down because of our engagement, I had every right to share in that responsibility. And after much discussion, we both agreed."

"Agreed on what?"

"That we're both responsible for you."

Colby slanted a very readable look at both men. "Excuse me, but I'm old enough to be responsible for myself."

"Under normal circumstances that would be true, Colby," Sterling said smoothly. "But not with this. End of discussion."

Colby looked at him as her anger flared. "It's not the end of discussion. I don't need you or James being responsible for me."

Sterling cast James a questioning look. "Was she this difficult as a kid?"

James shook his head. "No. She was an easygoing child who did what she was told. Personally, I get the impression she likes giving you a hard time, Hamilton."

Colby didn't miss the grin the two men exchanged. Somehow, during the time they had been behind closed doors, they had done more than come to an understanding about her. It appeared they had also gained respect for one another.

"The key word is 'child,' which I am not anymore," she said. Then she turned and walked out of the room, confident she had set both men straight. She would not be told what to do. The thought of James and Sterling working together and being responsible for her was enough to give her a headache. Dealing with James at times was bad enough. She refused to add Sterling to the equation. Things would never add up. It was time they realized that she could handle things on her own.

She hadn't set them straight at all, Colby discovered later. She glanced across the dinner table at James. "I'm not moving in here with you and Cynthia. I have my own place, thank you very much," she said.

"Colby, be reasonable," James said, helping himself to more of his wife's candied yams. "You heard what Hamilton said. Your apartment building is probably swarming with reporters."

"I am being reasonable, James. Reporters or no reporters, I see no reason why I can't stay in my own apartment."

"I do," Sterling said when he saw that James wasn't getting anywhere with his sister. "Until the frenzy of our engagement wears off, you'll receive a lot of attention. You saw the reporters at the airport, Colby. The decent ones will probably leave you alone after a while, but the others, the relentless ones will be ill-mannered and lacking any kind of scruples. At least living here will provide you with the security of a gated community."

Colby frowned. She was used to coming and going whenever she wanted. She didn't like the thought of being confined. "But you can't expect me to be kept locked away behind some gate twenty-four hours a day. I have a job, Sterling. I took a week's leave to go to California but I have to return to my classroom on Monday."

"I don't think you should return to work."

Colby looked away from the intensity of Sterling's gaze and returned to eating her food. "I'm going back to work." She looked back up at him. "The school is secured so there shouldn't be any problem."

"And I'm going to make sure of it. Mac will be here first thing in the morning."

She lifted a brow. "Who's Mac."

"The man who handles my security."

Colby released a deep sigh. She thought James and Sterling were getting worked up for nothing.

Cynthia, forever a diplomat, smoothly shifted the conversation when she said, "Sterling, Colby mentioned you wanted a small wedding."

Sterling took a sip of his iced tea. If it was left up to him they would fly to Las Vegas, but Colby had insisted on having a wedding. So he had agreed to a small, simple one. "Yes, I want it small, simple, and private in exactly three weeks from tomorrow."

After dinner, Sterling urged Colby to call her landlord to make sure there was not any activity at her apartment.

"Reporters are all over the place," Mrs. Foster informed her in an agitated voice. "And it's annoying the other tenants. I think it would be a good idea if you were to stay some place else for a few days until this blows over. I'm sorry."

Colby hung up the phone feeling sorry, too. She hadn't actually expected this degree of media mania.

"I still can't stay here," she said after telling the group of her conversation with Mrs. Foster. "You and Cynthia need your privacy. I'll check into a hotel for tonight. Hopefully, tomorrow things will be better."

Sterling shook his head, knowing they wouldn't. "You can stay with me tonight," he said.

"No she can't," James said with righteous indignation. "It wouldn't be proper."

Sterling frowned. He was beginning not to like that one particular word. "Look, Wingate, Colby and I have practically spent the last four days together anyway, so what's one more day? I'm only going to be there tonight. I'll be leaving tomorrow and won't return until a couple of days before the wedding. The condo my attorney was able to find for me here is completely secured, and with Mac overseeing everything, Colby will be safe."

"Fine. She can stay there beginning tomorrow—after you leave—but she'll not stay there with you tonight," James said.

Colby rubbed her forehead, feeling a headache coming on. "All right, all right. I'll stay here tonight and then tomorrow I'll move into Sterling's condo temporarily while he's gone, until things get back to normal."

Both men looked pleased with her decision.

Later, Colby walked Sterling out to the car when he was ready to leave. "Will you be returning to California?"

"Yes. I have some business I need to take care of there. Then I plan on spending a few days in Texas visitng my friend, Jake Madaris. When I leave Texas, I'll be returning here."

Colby nodded. "Call and let me know in advance when you're coming back so I can move out of your condo."

Sterling nodded. "It seems so far everyone is buying our story and that's good."

At the moment Colby didn't want to think about the real reason they were getting married. She loved him and no matter what he thought, she had no plans to ever leave his life. After their marriage she intended on proving to him that he did need a wife and that their child did need a mother.

"Will you miss me?" she impulsively asked.

Sterling was mildly surprised by her question. He thought about it for a moment and knew that although he didn't want to miss her, he would. He would miss her feistiness, her perky personality, and her straightforward approach on things. But most of all, he would miss her scent, her taste, and the feel of her in his arms. In the four days they had spent together, he had gotten used to having her around. "Yes, Colby, I'm going to miss you. Will you miss me?"

She looked up at him. A grin tugged at her lips. "No, not really."

Sterling tipped his head back and laughed. Once again it occurred to him that he had laughed more in the past four days than at any other time in his entire life.

"I want to kiss you," he said, bringing her closer to him. Deep down he knew he should back away. Things weren't going as he'd originally planned. His relationship with Colby was to be all business and nothing more. But whenever he was around her, business was the last thing on his mind.

"I want you to kiss me, too, but I know for a fact James and Cynthia are at the window watching us."

Sterling smiled. "Let them watch. They would expect us to kiss goodbye, wouldn't they?"

"I suppose so," Colby said.

Sterling lowered his mouth to hers. The kiss, to his way of thinking, was just as sweet as all the others had been, only too brief. Way too brief.

Afterward, he hugged her to him, knowing he would indeed miss her and that very thought bothered him.

It bothered him a lot.

Chapter 13

Seven days.

That's how long it had been since he'd last seen Colby, Sterling thought for the hundredth time that day. He was trying to concentrate on the script that had been delivered to him that morning. And he couldn't keep his mind on what he was doing.

It had been seven whole days.

Seeing his concentration level was at an all time low, he stood and went to the window and looked out. The view of the ocean was beautiful, but not as beautiful as it had been that day he had watched Colby rousting about in it.

Sterling knew he ought to get back to the script. Filming would begin in five weeks; that was two weeks after he returned from his honeymoon. The last thing he wanted to do was think about Colby, but that was the very thing he was doing.

He had refused to call her by convincing himself of out of sight, out of mind. And he wanted to get her out of his system. But to his utter dismay, that hadn't worked with him, which was very confusing. Never before had a woman effected him the way Colby had. His past affairs with women had always been a way to release his lust. They had been brief and meaningless liaisons. But Colby touched him on a different level, one that wasn't just physical.

He had tried desperately to close his mind and thoughts to her, needing distance to get his mind back in focus, and to reinforce the reason for her place in his life. He kept telling himself that she was just another woman, like all the others, whether they were fashion models, other movie stars, or star-crazed groupies. He wanted to believe there was nothing about Colby that was so special. But deep down he knew that in itself was a lie.

He pulled in a ragged breath as he shifted his gaze from the ocean to the sun that was blazing bright in the sky. Why did things with Colby have to be so complicated? Getting through each day was hard enough, but his nights were even harder. He would lie awake during all hours just thinking about something she'd said or something she'd done, and would find himself smiling or laughing out loud like a fool. He was no longer able to take a walk on the beach without thinking of that night when their passion had nearly flared to the point of no return. While his better judgment told him she had done the right thing by calling a halt to things between them before they had gotten out of hand, another part of him still ached for something only she could give him. He needed to find complete release in her arms.

In the midst of his thoughts, he looked around and saw Simon enter the room. "Yes, Simon, what is it?"

"Security just called, sir. You have a visitor at the front gate."

Sterling went over to the table to pour a glass of wine. He wasn't in the mood for company. "Who is it?"

"A woman by the name of Angeline Chenault."

The glass froze in Sterling's hand midway to his mouth. His body stiffened. "Who did you say?"

Simon heard the sharp hardness in Sterling's tone and didn't understand the reason for it. "Security said the woman identified herself as Angeline Chenault. Can she be admitted?"

Into Sterling's mind sprang the image of him as a six-year-old boy approaching his mother for the first time, the harsh words she had spoken to him that day, and how they had hurt. He'd felt devastated, betrayed, rejected. But then another memory stood out. It was the recent memory of Colby and the words she had spoken that night on the beach. She didn't know how much he had truly needed to hear them. She had read him the riot act and had made him realize that regardless of the fact his mother had not been a part of his life while he'd been growing up, Chandler Hamilton had more than made up for it. Colby had been right, he had been blessed to have had at least one loving parent.

"Sir?"

He suddenly remembered Simon's presence. He didn't know why Angeline Chenault had made a trip from Florida to see him, but he was going to find out. "Tell security it's okay to let her through."

She hadn't heard from Sterling in seven days. Not that she was counting, Colby told herself as she slipped into a pair of black leggings and a colorful T-shirt that promoted Wingate Cosmetics. It was Saturday, and she was getting dressed to go spend her weekly hour at the gym. Mac would be picking her up any minute. She smiled when she thought about Mac.

Earl MacFadden hadn't been what she expected. She had expected someone a lot younger than the fifty-five-year-old man who had shown up the day Sterling left. But she soon discovered what Mac lacked in the way of youthfulness, he more than made up for in the way of competence. He was good at what he did. Thanks to him she was no longer unnecessarily hounded by reporters.

Mac took her to school each morning and picked her up in the afternoons. At first she had resented him being her personal chauffeur and watchdog. But after that first day, when she returned to school, she had been very appreciative of him and his ability to protect her from the media's unnecessary hassles. She knew he had been instrumental in having the police ban the reporters from hanging around the school. Sterling had been right, some of the reporters had been outright jerks. Their questions had been relentless. Most of them wanted to know how she felt about Sterling's past involvement with movie actress Diamond Swain. Her "no comment" had not appeased their curiosity. The more she refused to be baited by their questions, the more they tried making Sterling's past involvement with Diamond Swain an issue.

Colby wished she could say this week had been pretty much uneventful, but she couldn't. It started out with the arrival of the sleek red Jaguar that Sterling had shipped to her. She hadn't been too happy about that.

Then she smiled. But at least two things had occurred to make her happy. And both incidents had been the result of Sterling's thoughtfulness.

The first happened the second day after she had returned. Otis Marshall's grandmother was standing outside her classroom door waiting for her. She wanted to thank Mr. Hamilton for being so kind and paying off all her medical bills. The hospital had informed her that Sterling Hamilton had taken care of all her unpaid bills. With tears in her eyes, the older woman could not thank Colby enough for Sterling's act of kindness. Colby had downplayed her shock and accepted the woman's thanks.

The next incident happened when she was called out of her classroom to the principal's office on the fourth day of her return. Again she had been taken back by what she had discovered. Sterling had accomplished what the authorities hadn't been able to do, and that was to locate Maria Martin's natural father by using his clout and friendship with Jay Leno, David Letterman, and Oprah. All three of the popular talk show personalities had agreed to periodically flash a message across the television screen asking if anyone knew the whereabouts of Frank Martin, and to have him call the toll-free number given. The plan worked. Within less than twenty-four hours, Maria's father had phoned in. The sad thing about it was that he, too, for the past two years, had been working with the authorities in Connecticut, to help him locate his daughter. Maria's mother had taken the child after their divorce and fled to parts unknown. The authorities, although they had tried to help, had been unsuccessful in their attempt to locate his daughter.

Colby sighed. She couldn't believe Sterling had actually listened to anything she had said that night on the beach when she'd gone off on him like a raving lunatic. But he had done more than just listen to her, he had taken it upon himself to make the lives of Otis and Maria a lot better.

She had called Sterling to thank him for what he had done for her two students, but Simon had told her he had gone out and that he would give him the message when he returned. She was sure he had done so, but Sterling had not bothered to return her call. But she knew for a fact that he checked in with Mac every day. He was making it very clear that whatever harmony that had existed between them during the last days they'd spent together was over. He was now taking the same position he had taken in the beginning. Their relationship was strictly a business deal and nothing more. And by ignoring her, he was reinforcing that fact.

And he was doing a pretty good job of it, Colby thought as she moved around the room keeping herself busy until

Mac showed up. But she was just as determined not to be ignored. She picked up the phone and began dialing his number when she heard a knock at the door. She hung up the phone knowing it was probably Mac to take her to the gym. She would try calling Sterling again when she got back.

Sterling took a deep breath when he heard the soft knock on the study door. "Come in."

He braced himself when Angeline Chenault walked in, convincing himself that how she felt toward him no longer mattered. She had chosen not to be a part of his life nearly thirty-five years ago, and like Colby said, it was her loss and not his.

The woman who entered the room had dark hair and delicate features. She didn't look the age of a woman who had a thirty-five-year-old son or a thirty-year-old son, for that matter. The years evidently had been good to her.

"Hello, Sterling."

Sterling nodded. "Mrs. Chenault. This is a surprise. Why are you here?" He frowned. To his way of thinking, she looked calm. Too calm. Like it was an everyday occurrence to pay a visit to a child she had walked out on thirty-five years ago. "Is there something I can do for you since I'm sure this isn't a social call."

Angeline Chenault sighed appreciatively. "You inherited more from Chandler than just his good looks, Sterling. And I'm glad of that. You're upfront and to-the-point like he was."

"My father was a hard-working man, so am I. He didn't believe in playing cat and mouse games and neither do I. So I'm going to ask you again. Is there a reason why you're here?"

He watched the coloring slowly drain from Angeline Chenault's face. She dropped her head and closed her eyes before lifting her head and looking back at him, meeting his gaze directly. "I'm here to try to right a wrong. Turning my back on you was the worst thing I could ever do, and I know that before I leave this earth, I'll pay for how I treated you that day when you approached me in North Carolina. You weren't any older than—"

"I frankly don't want to talk about it," Sterling said with a definite hardness in his voice.

"But I have to. I want to apologize for the pain I caused you that day. I called you the day after the incident, but Chandler wouldn't let me talk to you. He said if I ever hurt you again, he would tell Alan all about my past. And at the time, I thought I would lose Alan if he found out. So I never contacted you again. I don't want you to hate me any longer."

Sterling rubbed his hand across his forehead, feeling a tension headache coming on. "Lady, I don't hate you. In fact, I have no feelings for you whatsoever. Now if that's all you came here to say, I'm through listening. I have work to do and would appreciate it if you left. Please have a nice trip back to Florida."

Angeline Chenault nodded. When she spoke again her voice was subdued. "I also wanted to congratulate you, Sterling. I read in the papers that you're getting married. I wish you the very best, I sincerely mean that. I hope you'll be very happy."

She sighed deeply and Sterling saw tears cloud her eyes. "Hopefully one day you'll forgive me for being a seventeen-year-old girl who thought money was everything and was willing to sacrifice anything to get it, even the love of a good man and my newborn child. I made a mistake, and I know that before I die I'll have to pay for it. I'm paying for it right now."

Her voice was soft and quivering when she continued. "My doctors informed me a few days ago that I have a blood clot on my brain that's causing the headaches I've been having lately. They don't think there's anything they can do, and surgery may not even be an option at this point."

She took a hankerchief out of her purse and dabbed at the corners of her eyes. "I want to get things right in my life, and more than anything I want to bring my two sons together. If anything were to happen to me, you'll be the only blood relative Nicholas will have. I plan to tell him everything. I just wanted to let you know that. And whether you choose to believe it or not, I regret not being a part of your life. I realized that many years ago, but then it was too late. The damage had already been done. I did tell Alan the truth before he died, and he was very understanding and supportive. I was a fool not to have told him sooner. If I had, maybe things would have been different. Like Chandler, Alan was a good man."

Her mouth trembled at the corners when she said. "No matter what you may have thought over the years, I've always been proud of you and all of your accomplishments, Sterling, and I do love you. I just hope and pray that one day you'll believe that. Goodbye."

Sterling didn't say anything as he watched her walk out of the room.

Colby sat curled up in the huge rocking chair in her brother's office trying to be quiet as she watched him go over some business reports. It brought back memories of her sitting in this very chair as a child doing homework while he studied at that same desk. Even now his concentration was just as intense.

Cynthia was upstairs taking a nap and had been ever since Mac had dropped Colby off here instead of taking her back to the condo. She had decided to pay James and Cynthia a visit after her workout at the gym.

She released a deep sigh, which James heard. He looked up concerned. "Are you all right, honey?"

"I'm fine. Sorry, I didn't mean to disturb you."

"You never do that. You ought to know that by now." He pushed aside his papers. "How are the wedding plans coming along?"

"Okay, I guess. There really wasn't a whole lot to do since Sterling wants a small, private ceremony. I've already bought a dress to wear, the flowers and cake have been ordered, and since I'm getting married here, Mac said that will eliminate the need for security from those pestering reporters who'll want pictures."

James nodded. "What about the honeymoon?"

Colby shrugged. "According to Mac, Sterling is working on those details."

"So you have no idea where you're going?"

"No, none."

James smiled. "Maybe I'll wheedle the information out of Sterling the next time he calls me."

Colby jumped out of her chair and went to stand in front of James' desk. "Sterling calls you?"

James laughed. "Yes, he calls me. I talk to him every day."

"Why?"

"He calls to see how you're doing."

Colby was livid. "I don't believe this!" she said throwing up her hands. "He calls both you and Mac every day to check to see how I'm doing, but he doesn't bother to call *me.*" She began pacing in front of James' desk. "It doesn't make sense."

James nodded. "I admit it didn't to me either at first. Then he explained things."

Colby stopped pacing. "By all means, please explain things to me."

James sat back in his chair. "He misses you, Colby. He

misses you a lot and if he were to hear your voice, he'd miss you that much more."

"Sterling told you that?"

"Yeah, he told me that."

Colby shook her head. Sterling was some actor. "And you believe him?"

James frowned and looked at her with a bemused expression on his face. "Why wouldn't I believe him, Colby? Is there any particular reason why I shouldn't?"

Colby tinted. She had almost given something away. "No, of course not. I'm just surprised he would admit something like that to you, that's all."

"Well he did admit it. And although I still have reservations about him being a lot older than you, I have to admit he's doing everything in his power to look out for your welfare, and I like that. I really was prepared not to like him."

Colby nodded knowing that was an understatement. At that moment the phone rang and James picked it up.

"Hello." His smile widened.

"You were just being discussed, Sterling." James laughed. "Yes, she's here." James nodded. "Sure, hold on." He handed Colby the phone, got up from behind the desk and walked out the room, quietly closing the door behind him.

Colby scooted into the seat James had just vacated. Excitement rushed through her veins. She wouldn't fuss, she wouldn't complain, and with heaven's help, she wouldn't let him know she'd been upset that he hadn't called. She took a deep breath, and with a calm, controlled, and nonpersonal voice she said, "Yes, Sterling? What can I do for you?"

"I miss you and you can let me make love to you over the phone. Is that possible?" he asked huskily.

Colby closed her eyes and took another deep breath. Her calm, controlled, and nonpersonal manner went flying out the window with Sterling's words. She wanted to cry, she missed him so. He could say some of the most unexpected things at times.

"Is it?" he asked in a deeper, huskier voice.

"Is it what?" she managed to somehow choke out.

"Possible for us to make love over the phone?"

Colby tightened the phone cord around her hand. "I don't think so."

"Can I try it?" he asked, crooning smoothly in her ear.

She hesitated briefly before saying, "Yes." A huge lump formed in her throat.

"Is James still there?"

"No, he's left the room."

"What about Cynthia?"

"She's upstairs taking a nap."

"All right. We'll pretend it's the day after our wedding. That will make it proper won't it?"

Colby couldn't help but smile. "Yes."

"Then just imagine it's the day after our wedding night. I made love to you all night and it's morning. I want to make love to you again. Is that all right?"

Colby could barely get a response out. "Yes."

"Good, because this is what I'm going to do. Now close your eyes and listen very closely."

In a voice that was light, soft, and more sexy than any voice had a right to be, Sterling told her in explicit detail just what he was going to do to her. Colby's body became heated and aroused. Her breathing quickened.

"Colby, are you still with me?" Sterling asked in a deep, sensuous voice.

"Yes," she managed to say. She felt hot all over. Her body literally felt like it was on fire. Her lips were sizzling from his description of all the ways he was kissing her, and her breasts were smoldering from all the things he said he was doing to them.

"Colby?"

"Hmm?"

"Can you feel my touch?"

"Yes."

"Can you taste my kiss?"

Colby flicked her tongue across her lips, remembering the taste of him from their last kiss. "Yes."

"That's good, because I can taste you, too. It's a sweet, delectable taste. And I can inhale your scent. It's a scent that's exclusively yours."

By the time Colby ended her telephone coversation with Sterling, the only thing she wanted to do was to go home and sleep for the rest of the day. She didn't know that talking on the phone could be so stimulatingly draining. If just talking to him about making love had this sort of affect on her, she didn't want to think about how the real thing would be.

The afternoon sun slanted across the ocean as Sterling jogged along the beach. Sweat poured from his body and his muscles ached, but he kept on running.

He had been a fool to break down and call Colby and confess that he missed her. But after Angeline left, he had desperately needed to hear her voice. He needed a touch of the soothing calmness she seemed to be able to give him. His mother had hit him with some heavy stuff. The mere fact she could be dying had caused deep emotions to flare up within him. They were emotions he hadn't wanted to deal with. To his surprise, he had felt compassion for the woman who had turned her back on him. The very idea that he could feel such a thing for Angeline Chenault made him run faster and made him push his body harder. He raced across the sandy beach at relentless speed trying to get rid of the emotions raging within him.

After his conversation with Colby, his turbulent emotions had been soothed. But talking to her had made him desire her that much more, causing him to want to play out one of his fantasies and by the time their conversation had ended, he couldn't help but anticipate their wedding night.

But his common sense was kicking back in and and warning him that more and more he was getting himself in deeper and it was time to pull up and pull back.

He must not forget that Colby's time in his life was temporary, and that someday he would have to send her away, out of his life forever.

Chapter 14

"Oh, Colby, you look so beautiful," Cynthia said, dabbing at her eyes.

"Thanks, and I want to thank you and James for letting me have my wedding here. I know you went to a lot of trouble to pull this together when you should have been taking it easy in your condition."

Cynthia frowned. "Don't you dare try making me an invalid like James wants to do. I'm doing fine, and the doctor says this pregnancy is progressing along nicely. I have tests scheduled at the end of next week. I hope the results are good."

Colby smiled. "Me, too, and I believe they will be." She glanced over her shoulder. "Do you know if Sterling has arrived yet?"

"Umm, I don't think so, but don't worry he'll be here. He called James this morning from Texas."

Colby nodded. Something must have come up to make Sterling stay in Texas longer than he had planned. He was supposed to return to Virginia a couple of days before the wedding. But he hadn't done so. In fact, she had not heard from him since that Saturday he'd called nearly two weeks ago. Their sensuous and steamy phone conversation still made her blush whenever she thought about it. Although he hadn't called her, she knew he still checked in with Mac daily and called James periodically.

"Kimara Garwood is a beautiful woman," Cynthia was saying, breaking into Colby's thoughts. "She and her husband make such a stunning couple. And to think they already have four kids and are expecting another set of twins. That will make six kids all under the age of four. That's what I call having guts."

"Or a need to have my head examined," Kimara said, coming up to them from behind. A huge smile was on her face. "I came to see if I could be of any help."

"No, I'm ready and just waiting for Sterling. Thanks anyway," Colby said smiling. Cynthia was right. Kimara was a beautiful woman and she looked gorgeous. For a woman who was having a second set of twins she appeared rather calm about it. She and Kyle had arrived that morning and Colby had taken an immediate liking to her. She was a very nice person who was truly genuine. There was nothing pretentious about her. No wonder Kyle Garwood simply adored his wife.

At that moment, James walked over. "I just got a call from Sterling. He's on his way from the airport and should be here in twenty minutes or less." He chuckled. "I have a feeling it will be less."

Colby nodded, suddenly feeling nervous. "Thanks for telling me. Will you let the others know?"

James nodded and left.

"If you're sure you don't need me for anything, I'll go back to my husband. Kyle's been watching that wedding cake very closely, and I don't want him to sneak a slice before he's supposed to," Kimara said smiling. "Sterling is very special to me, Colby, and I thought he would never settle down and get married. And after meeting you today,

I can see why he's doing so. I think you're special, too, and I wish the both of you much happiness. Kyle and I both do."

"Thanks."

Kimara gave Colby a hug before turning and walking away. Colby glanced around the huge room. Sterling had wanted a simple, small, and private wedding and that was exactly what he was getting. The only persons present other than herself, James, Cynthia, and the minister were the Garwoods, Mac, two of her coworkers whom she was close to, and a formal photographer for the media's benefit. Edward Stewart was also present. He had arrived yesterday to get her signature on the prenuptial agreement. She had kept that information from James. He would not have agreed with her decision to sign such a document.

The living room had been decorated with Cynthia's special touch. The flowers arranged around the room were beautiful and the dining room was elegantly prepared for the small reception that was to follow.

Colby sighed. She still had no idea where Sterling was taking her on their honeymoon. All she knew was that they would be gone for a week, and then he would take her to his home in the North Carolina mountains for another week. After that, he would be leaving for Spain to begin work on his next movie.

Since North Carolina was closer to Virginia than California, she had mentioned to Sterling that she preferred living there instead of California while he was in Spain. Because of Cynthia's pregnancy she wanted to be as close to James and Cynthia as possible. Sterling had understood and had said that would be fine with him.

Colby checked her watch. Sterling should be arriving any minute now and she felt butterflies in her stomach. The thought of spending the next week with him was fire to her mind. If he did anything to her like he had described that day on the phone, she doubted she would be able to survive the experience. Sterling Hamilton was something else, and for her he was a dream come true.

The moment Sterling entered the house he quickly scanned the group of people present before targeting his sight on Colby. He nodded brief greetings to James, Kyle, and Kimara before making his way across the room where his future wife was standing with Cynthia. He thought she looked absolutely gorgeous in her tea-length white lace dress. She saw him and he noticed her eyes light up. The thought that she was glad to see him made him smile.

He closed his fingers around hers and carried her hand to his mouth. He kissed her palm. "I apologize for being late, but something unavoidable came up."

Colby was glad to see him. She hadn't realized just how much she had missed him until now. And she hadn't been sure she had made the right decision to marry him until now. In her heart, she felt that whatever problems she faced in the future with this man, she'd be able to deal with them. She would be the kind of wife he needed, and soon she hoped he would come to appeciate her and would want her to remain with him and their child always.

"You're not late," she said, smiling up at him. "The wedding isn't supposed to start for another forty-five minutes or so."

"I know, but I wanted to get back two days ago."

Colby nodded. "I understand you had business to take care of. That's all right, you're here now and that's what matters most."

Sterling gazed deep into her eyes. "I'll make it up to you, I promise."

Colby sighed deeply as the warmth from his eyes touched her.

"Since I'm here is there a reason to wait any longer? Can we get things started now?" he asked.

She nodded.

His smile came easy. "Good. I'll let James and the minister know." He kissed her palm again before walking off.

Cynthia began fanning herself with her hands. "Whew, honey, I just hope you're ready for tonight because I have a feeling Sterling definitely is," she teased. "He is one hot-blooded male. Did you see how he was looking at you?"

Colby watched Sterling walk across the room to James and the minister. She had never known a man with a more graceful and masculine stride. "No. How was he looking at me?"

"Like a man who's very hungry and you're going to be his appetizer, main course, dessert, and late night snack. If the two of you don't want kids right away, I hope one of you thought about birth control."

Cynthia's words snatched Colby back into reality. And with it came the knowledge of why she and Sterling were getting married. She couldn't look at Cynthia when she said, "There won't be any birth control. We want to start a family right away. Come on, I think they're ready for us now."

"Mom and Dad would have been so proud of you, today."

Tears burned the back of Colby's eyes as she lovingly gazed up at her brother. "Thanks, James. And they would have been proud of you, too."

A look of confusion wrinkled James' forehead. "Proud of me? For what?"

Colby tried to smile but couldn't. She could not . . . she would not make light of what she was about to say. "They would have been proud of you for taking care of me the way you did, putting my needs before you own, and for finishing what they started by making sure I always felt loved and protected."

James shrugged. Colby could tell her praise was some-what embarrasing him. "I just did what any brother would have done."

Colby shook her heard. "No. Any brother would not have done what you did. Only a special brother, a loving brother, and a caring brother would have done what you did." She leaned up and kissed his cheek. "And this sister thanks you from the bottom of her heart."

At that moment the music began playing for the wedding ceremony to began.

Sterling took Colby's hand in his the moment James walked her to him. Then together they faced the minister and began reciting their wedding vows. Sterling's face was carefully schooled and Colby had no idea what he was thinking as he said the words that, in the sight of God and all those present, were supposed to bind their lives together forever.

She stared up at him and listened as he repeated the words the minister had instructed him to repeat. She smiled when he glanced down at her and she knew then, at that very moment, that she would love him forever. She knew in her heart she was truly pledging her life to him, and unlike him, she was not pretending. She intended to keep each and every vow she was saying.

Kyle passed Sterling the ring to put on her finger, and moments later, Cynthia gave her the one to place on his. Not long after that, the minister announced they were man and wife and told Sterling he could kiss his bride.

Sterling reached out and tenderly stroked her bottom lip with his thumb. His gaze was gentle as he lowered his head and kissed her. Then suddenly he began kissing her with a fierceness that surprised her. All of a sudden, it seemed that all the barriers he had ever erected between them came crashing down in that one kiss.

Colby felt the stirrings of desire that Sterling could arouse in her so quickly and so easily. She returned the kiss with all the love she felt in her heart. She felt happy, elated, and renewed. And no matter what he thought his plans were for their future, their lives were being joined forever.

She knew she wasn't like the other women he had been involved with, some more beautiful, worldly, and sophisticated. But she believed she had something to offer him that a lot of them did not. She would give him her undying love, devotion, and trust. And one day she would give him a daughter. In her heart, she truly believed that.

"Do you have any idea how beautiful you look today?" Sterling whispered to her as they moved around the room dancing. James had cleared back the funiture to make room for them to share their first dance together as husband and wife.

"No, but thanks for telling me," she said, smiling at him.

"Chandler would have liked you." Pain flashed across Sterling's features. "That's the only sad part about today. I always assumed he would be there whenever I did get married."

Colby nodded as she gazed deep into Sterling's eyes. "But he is here. I can feel his presence, and I know you can, too. And as always, he is very proud of you."

At that moment, Colby's words touched him. Once again they had been the soothing calmness he needed. He suddenly forgot about the promise he'd made to himself on the drive from the airport to remember to stay focused and to be mindful of the reason he was marrying her, and to not forget that she would not be a permanent fixture in his life. But from the moment he had entered the house and had seen her, his entire world had brightened up.

Despite everything, especially the contract their marriage was based on, he knew the woman he held in his arms was special. He pulled her closer to him.

"Are you ready for the honeymoon?"

Colby tinted when she remembered what Sterling had once told her he planned to do to her during their honeymoon. "It depends on where we're going."

Sterling smiled. "I guess I should tell you so you'll pack accordingly. How does Barbados sound?"

She smiled. "Wonderful. Is that where we're going?"

"Yes. I've rented a very secluded place on the ocean. It will be our fantasy hideaway for a week."

At that moment, the music stopped and their dancing came to an end. The photographer approached them for more pictures and they happily obliged him.

A few hours later after changing into travel clothes, Colby and Sterling were ready to leave. They had prepared themselves for the chaos they knew awaited them at the airport. The photographers would have questions and the paparazzi would want pictures. Sterling had deliberately kept where they were going on their honeymoon a secret from the media so they wouldn't be pestered once they got to Barbados.

After Colby gave everyone hugs and kisses, she and Sterling were on their way.

Chapter 15

Colby fell in love with the beach cottage the moment she walked through the doors. It was a huge single-story house that had two connecting bedrooms, two bathrooms, a living room, an eat-in kitchen, and a screen-enclosed patio on the back that faced the ocean.

"Oh, Sterling. It's beautiful. How did you find it?"

Sterling leaned back against the door. He couldn't help but share Colby's excitement. "A friend of mine told me about it, and I knew I wanted to bring you here."

Colby walked back over to him. She curved her arms around his neck and kissed him on the cheek. "Thank you for this and for everything. Today has truly been special."

"The best is yet to come," he said, pulling her closer to him. "I missed you," he said truthfully.

"And I missed you, too," she whispered, loving the feel of being in his arms.

Sterling lowered his mouth to hers and at the same time his arms drew her hard against him. There was very little gentleness in his kiss. It displayed the deep need he felt.

It was a need that had nearly driven him out of his mind during the last three weeks.

Colby had felt his desire for her the moment he had pulled her against him and she'd come into contact with his thigh, and it had sent her over the edge. She couldn't help the moan of passion that escaped her lips. He was making love to her mouth, just like he had described that day on the telephone.

He slowly lifted his head and slackened his hold on her. He smiled when he looked down at her mouth. "I think you have now been properly kissed."

Colby smiled back at him. "I think so, too." Suddenly feeling nervous, she stepped back out of his arms. "You didn't eat much at the reception, and you didn't have anything on the plane. Are you hungry?"

"Yeah, I'm starving. Are you going to feed me?"

"Sure, what would you like? I noticed the refrigerator is stocked with all kinds of—"

Sterling laughed.

Colby frowned. "What's so funny?"

An impish smile curved Sterling's lips. "Food is not what I'm starving for, Colby." He pulled her back closer into his arms. "A man can be hungry for more than just food, baby. In my case, I'm starving for you. I want my body to feed off yours."

Colby tinted. "Oh."

"Yes, oh. Do you have any idea of just how tempting you are?"

She lowered her head. She had never thought of herself as tempting. "No."

"Colby?"

Sterling's voice was soft as silk. Her name on his tongue felt like a warm, velvet caress. She looked up at him and met his gaze. He was staring at her. The look in his eyes was indeed hungry. It elicited a shudder of arousal in her. Swallowing slowly, she answered.

"Yes?"

"You are a very beautiful woman. In fact you're the most beautiful woman I know."

His words surprised her. They also disappointed her because she knew he wasn't being completely honest. She lowered her eyes and grasped for composure before letting her eyes meet his again. She raised her chin a notch. "Thanks for saying that, but it's really not necessary."

"What isn't necessary?"

"For you to say I'm beautiful."

Sterling lifted a brow and studied her, taking in the significance of her response. She evidently didn't think he was being truthful. "You don't think you're a beautiful woman?"

She frowned. "I think I look okay, but beautiful would be stretching it a bit. I know you told me that earlier today and I thanked you for it because all brides look beautiful on their wedding day. But saying I'm the most beautiful woman you know is really going overboard," she said. "Beautiful is women like Vanessa Williams, Tyra Banks, and," she nervously stroked the ring she now wore on the third finger of her left hand, "someone like Diamond Swain."

Sterling's dark eyes were hooded as he watched her face. He reached out and lifted her chin so their eyes could meet. "Beautiful is also Colby Wingate Hamilton."

She lifted a shoulder in a self-conscious little shrug. "If you say so."

Sterling shook his head. Other than Kimara Garwood and Diamond Swain, most of the women he knew were shallow and thought too much of themselves at times. Colby, he had discovered long ago, was just the opposite. Although she didn't lack any self-esteem, she didn't have a clue of just how beautiful she was, or more importantly, just how beautiful he thought her to be. Feeling the need to kiss her again he leaned forward, opening his mouth over hers with drugging urgency. Although incredibly tender and painstakingly seductive, his tongue pledged promises of more things to come.

He gave up all control as her mouth moved under his with a passion so ravenous he thought he would not survive its fire. And when she pressed her body deeper against his, he released a groan from low within his gut. He tuned out everything around him as he again explored and tasted her mouth. Cupping her bottom, he brought her even closer to him, pulling her hard against his hips, kneading her backside and grinding against her, letting her feel the hard length of his arousal. He felt her squirming against him, trying to get even closer to him. Without realizing it, her body was instinctively seeking out that part of him that was more than ready for her.

It was that part of him that was hungry for her. It was starving for her.

"Sterling."

He heard his name escape her lips in a passionate, agonizing plea. Slowly, he lifted his mouth from hers. His control shot to pieces.

She opened questioning eyes to him and the look of desire in them nearly took his breath away. For a moment, he wanted to believe they were the only two individuals on the island. He wanted to believe she was a temptation he could yield to, and that she could bring more joy to his life than pain. He regretted that tonight would be just a fantasy—an awesome fantasy the two of them would share.

Each time they came together would be for a purpose, but tonight, against his better judgment, he wanted more pleasure than purpose. Tonight he wanted their coming together to be one special moment. Just like she'd said it would be. And for her, tonight, he would make it so.

Unable to help himself, he slowly lowered his head to hers again at the same time he swept her off her feet and into his arms. He headed for the bedroom. Once there he placed her on her feet beside the bed.

"Tonight, Colby, we're not going to remember the purpose we're here together or the reason we got married in the first place. Tonight I need you in a way I've never needed any woman. I don't understand it, and I don't want to question it. At least not now. All I know is that you're an ache inside of me and have been from the moment I saw you on that video."

Colby tipped her head to him. "What video?"

"The one my investigator sent me of you. It was from watching that video that I made my decision to choose you as the mother of my child."

A confused look touched Colby's features. She didn't understand. She had known nothing about a video, but tonight, like him, she didn't want to understand. She had a need, too. She needed him as much as he needed her.

Her body shuddered with desire when he reached out and began removing the clothes from her body. He enjoyed inhaling her soft scent, and when he had her naked before him, he began to remove his own clothes.

Colby looked at Sterling, his body intrigued her and challenged her to touch it. So she did, surprising herself more than suprising him. His body felt hot to her touch and it felt hard.

The more she touched him, the more fascinated she became with his body. She continued to let her hands gently move across his chest and shoulders, down his arms and around his midsection.

"You want it?" he asked, huskily. He felt his heart beat faster with her touch.

She looked up at him and saw desire in his eyes and knew it matched her own. "Yes, I want it."

"There will be pain," he pointed out, at the same time sucking in a deep breath when he felt her hand move lower over his body.

"You know what they say, no pain, no gain."

Her sensuous reply sent trickles of sensations racing over Sterling's body. His eyes narrowed at her playful challenge. "For your sake, I hope you really believe that, baby. There's nothing we can do now that won't be proper."

He then pulled her down on the bed with him. Pulling back the spread he placed her on the silk sheets. "Feed me," he growled in her ear. It was a gutteral sound from deep within him. "I'm starving for you. Feed me, Colby. Feed me, now."

He laced her fingers with his and angled his body over hers. He kissed her again, hard and urgent at the same time the lower part of his body entered her in a long, explosive thrust that rocked his entire world. His body began trembling. He took one deep breath, never feeling so out of control with desire as he did at this very moment. He reined in his control to look down at her to make sure she was all right.

"How do you feel?" he asked in a voice he couldn't even recognize as his own.

Colby looked up at him and smiled. She had done the right thing by remaining untouched all these years, she thought. This was how it was supposed to be the first time, joining as one with her husband, the man she loved and the man she had committed her life to before God.

"I feel this moment is very special, just like I told you it would be when we came together as husband and wife," she whispered. "And nothing would make me happier than for you to put your baby inside of me now."

Her words made him lose it.

In the past he had done everything in his power, whenever he made love to a woman, to make sure his seed never reached fertile ground. But tonight, for the first time in his life, he was not using any sort of protection. Tonight he would willingly release his seed into Colby's body. That very thought pushed him forward in rapt anticipation.

His mouth found hers and he made love to her with his mouth and his body. He made love to her in a way he had never made love to another woman, giving and sharing a part of him he had never shared with anyone. And when he felt her moving beneath him, lifting her hips to receive him, branding his back with her fingertips and holding him tight within her, he knew he couldn't last much longer. When he felt her body shudder in pleasure beneath him, he knew it was time for him to let go.

And he did, spilling into her body the very essence of his being and somehow believing in his heart that at this one special moment, he was giving her his child.

Chapter 16

Sterling eased from the bed, careful not to awaken Colby. He stood for a moment and watched her sleep. Her features were calm, relaxed, satisfied.

He backed away slowly. Unlike her, he couldn't sleep. He needed time away from her to think and to put things back in perspective. Making love to her had shaken his world more than he thought was possible.

He walked out of the room into the other connecting bedroom. Pulling back the covers, he got in the bed. The moment the cold sheets touched his naked skin, he couldn't help but remember the warmth in the bed he had just left. His mind was filled with Colby's body heat wave and how time and time again he had literally drowned in it.

Unable to sleep, he propped his body up on the pillow. Colby's scent, that special fragrance of hers, was all over him and he knew there wasn't any place he could go without some reminder of her.

He leaned back against the headboard and closed his eyes. He couldn't help but think about the softness of her skin, the heat of her body, and the sweetness of her smile after the first time they had made love.

Her smile.

Tonight, each time she smiled at him he felt like a man on top of the world. A man with a very special woman. And he had gotten more than just a glimpse of heaven. Just as she had predicted, he had become a part of it. He had found heaven in her arms.

Sterling reopened his eyes and raked a hand across his face, releasing a deep gutted breath. "What is she doing to me?" he asked himself quietly. Before the question had fully left his lips he knew the answer.

She was breaking his resolve, messing with his mind, and undermining his determination to keep things on a business level between them. She had taken advantage of a weakness he hadn't known he had, and as much as he didn't want to admit it, it went beyond mere physical desire. She was easing her way into his very soul.

His hands balled into fists. *I don't want this in my life! I don't need this! All I want is my child! Not a mother for my child nor a wife for myself! I want my original plan, where she's history a year after my child is born. I want her out of my life!*

But as his mind thought those things, another part of him ached with different emotions. His breath thickened in his throat, almost making it impossible to breathe. A turbulent war was going on within him, and he fought desperately for control of the situation. The last thing he wanted was to become a victim to love like his father had done. He didn't want his life dictated by the whims of a woman who might not be there for him when he needed her most. But he couldn't stop his thoughts from drifting back again to earlier that night. Colby had made love to him in a way no other woman had before. He had felt her sincerity in everything she did. There wasn't a pretentious bone in her body.

At that moment, Sterling heard the sound of the connecting bedroom door opening. Moonlight washing in through the curtains made out Colby's form in the darkness. She stood in the center of the room wearing a short, skimpy silk robe. The sight of her barely clad body and the floral scent of her assaulted his senses. The silk robe showed off her long, slender legs, the feminine curve of her hips, and her high, rounded breasts.

His breathing thickened even more and the hands, which were balled into fists at his sides, trembled. She stood in the room, a few feet from the bed with the same expression on her face that had been there when she had been underneath him while they had made love. It was a look of total trust and surrender. She was again offering him peace and calm from the turbulent storm raging within him. He knew he should rebel at the pull she had on him, and fight her all the way. He shouldn't let her get any closer to his emotions than she already had.

But when she took another step into the room, coming closer to him, the only thing he could think about was keeping her even closer. He released a deep breath and gave up the fight. At this moment, he wasn't strong enough to fight her and what she was offering him: a sweet, steamy sexual healing of his mind and body.

He extended his hand to her, and unhesitantly she took it. Her hand felt warm in his larger one. He eased the robe off her shoulders and he pulled her to him, making room for her in the bed.

"I woke up and you were gone," she whispered as he cradled her close to him. "I missed you."

He didn't say anything. At the moment he couldn't say anything. He just continued to hold her in his arms. He didn't want to think about what she was doing to him and how she was making him feel. He only wanted to savor this moment. This very special moment with her. Tomorrow he would face the reality that she was not a permanent part of his life. Tomorrow he would remember the contract existing between them. But for now, for tonight, he wanted to find the pleasure he knew awaited him in her arms.

It was early morning when Sterling wakened to find Colby still sound asleep in his embrace. Her position next to his body caused a deep ache in his groin. And when she sighed and snuggled even closer to him, bringing her backside even closer into the cradle of his hips, all he wanted was to wake her up and make love to her.

He gently moved his hand along her body, touching places he had discovered last night were her erotic zones. Just touching those places made her heated, aroused and filled with desire. And he was determined to concentrate on all of them.

He let his thumb move across her breasts, before moving lower to tease her belly button. She moved against him in sleep, her back arching as he let his hand move lower. She slowly opened her eyes and looked up at him with sleep-filled eyes.

Raising up on his elbow, he gazed deep within her eyes. His gaze shifted to her mouth, then slid lower to her breasts. He saw a shiver pass through her and watched as her nipples hardened beneath his gaze. He pushed the covers aside and his eyes were slow in their appraisal of the rest of her body.

He closed his eyes in an attempt to force himself to get a grip. But when he reopened them and saw her watching him with the same intensity, he lost it again. And when he leaned down, her lips eagerly met his. He felt her body tremble when his mouth clung hard to hers, his tongue exploring her mouth relentlessly.

His kiss dared him to ask himself why he couldn't get enough of her. He'd never had a problem controlling his sexual desires before.

But now he did.

If making love to her last night had been a unique experience for him, then making love to her again this morning was doubly so.

He almost lost control when he felt her body respond to him, taking everything he was giving her and at the same time, giving him all of herself. He had no idea a wife could be so passionate, so exciting, so giving. And he had no idea a wife could completely satisfy all his needs. The sound of her moans of pleasure pleased him, making his desire for her spiral totally out of control.

He lifted his head and looked at her. "I want you, even more than last night," he whispered before taking possession of her lips once more. And with gentle hands and techniques born from his experience, he slowly and completely brought her to flaming readiness.

"Please, Sterling. Now!"

Sterling shifted over her and gently eased into her body, once again joining them as one. He groaned at the pleasure he felt being inside of her, and when he felt her body once again stretch to accommodate him, he slowly began moving within her. He didn't want this time with her to end. His eyes riveted to her face and stayed there, watching her watch him. Her need and want of him was there plainly in her features for him to see.

Not able to hold back any longer, he groaned aloud his pleasure at the same moment he felt her shudder, lifting her hips and locking her legs around him.

He bent his head and took her mouth in a deep, hungry kiss, holding her tighter until her body had taken all the essence of him, and then more.

Afterward, Sterling held her in his arms. Her dark eyes were still glazed with spent passion. And he could smell the warm intimate scent of their lovemaking. It surrounded him and pulled at him, making him feel calm, soothed.

A few minutes later Colby spoke. Her voice was a soft whisper in the room. "You know what I think?"

"Mmmm," he murmured, not having the strength to say anything more.

She lifted her head and looked down at him. "I think we're good together."

Sterling didn't give a response to her comment. But deep down, although he didn't want to think so, he thought the very same thing. But at that moment, he could not . . . he would not admit it to her.

Chapter 17

"How does your food taste?"

Colby glanced up from her meal. Her eyes locked with Sterling's and she drew a deep breath. Why did one man have to look so good?

Since arriving in Barbados three days ago, they had remained at the cottage, venturing out only to take short walks on the beach in the early mornings or late afternoons. But today they had taken a grand tour of the city.

Sugar was the primary crop in Barbados and many, many years ago, the British colony's numerous sugar plantations were worked by African slaves. Most of the residents of Barbados were direct decendants of those workers. While out and about today, she had enjoyed the Barbados people as much as she had enjoyed the island's scenery. The Bajans, the name the residents of Barbados called themselves, were very friendly, and as she discovered, the best educated in the Caribbean. At the marketplace she had conversed with them on a variety of subjects. She had been amazed at how easily they could blend their West Indian identity with a heavy British influence. One of the islanders had recommended this restaurant as an exclusive and sophisticated place to enjoy some of the caribbean's cuisine.

She had looked forward to coming here, but now the only thing she could think about was getting back to the cottage, being in Sterling's arms and feeling his bare skin against hers. For someone who had just discovered her passionate side only days ago, she was constantly anxious at the thought of them making love.

All she had to do was watch his mouth at work doing something as relatively simple as chewing his food, and she would remember that same mouth leaving trails of tender kisses over her body. He could arouse her to the brink of mindless ecstasy with that mouth.

"The food's fine," she replied silkily. "How's yours?"

"It's okay."

"Do you think you'll want dessert?" she asked after several minutes had passed and he was still staring at her with a seductive look in his gaze. The heated desire she saw in his eyes made her pulse jump.

"Yes, I'll want dessert. But the dessert I want isn't on their menu," he answered huskily

Colby couldn't help staring at him as the meaning of his words became clear in her mind. A warm, melting sensation rushed through her already heated veins. She briefly closed her eyes and inhaled deeply. Her nostrils didn't pick up the smell of the spicy food before her, instead it picked up the scent of him, all male, arousing and enticing.

"Let's finish our meal and get back to the cottage," he suggested softly.

Colby nodded. She returned to eating her meal.

Sterling forced his attention back to his own meal. Suddenly his mind became overloaded with chaotic emotions. It was so unlike him to get caught up in a woman. But that's all he'd been doing since meeting Colby. He had somehow gotten caught up in her very existence.

He ate absently, his mind and thoughts were in turmoil. Why was she so different from all the others? He lifted his gaze and looked at her again. No matter what she thought, she was indeed beautiful. Her long, thick, black hair was wrapped upward, away from her face, clearly emphasizing her prominent features. Her makeup hadn't been heavily applied like that of a lot of the women he'd dated. And for some reason, he couldn't stop focusing on her lips. Those same lips he enjoyed tasting time and time again.

Sterling returned to eating his meal. There was more to Colby than her physical attributes. She was also a person you could talk to. She was a person who knew how to listen.

He lifted his head and again looked at her. She would make any child a good mother, of that he had no doubt. That very thought made him think of his own mother and her visit a few weeks ago. Even though he had tried not to think about it, he had. Angeline Chenault's visit weighed heavily on his mind at some of the oddest times. Like now.

"She came to see me," he said simply, as if Colby would immediately know who he was talking about.

Colby lifted her gaze to his, arching an eyebrow. "Who came to see you?"

He shrugged. "Angeline Chenault."

For a moment, she looked like she couldn't place the name, then she gave him a surprised look. "Your mother came to see you?"

He nodded before lifting the glass of wine to his lips. "Yes."

Colby stared at him, wondering if he was going to tell her any more than that. When moments passed and he didn't say anything else, she asked bluntly, "What did she want?"

He met her gaze. "My forgiveness." He took another

sip of wine before telling her the entire story of his mother's visit and everything that was said.

"Colby," he said raggedly after he had finished. "I don't know if I can forgive her for what she did to me, and most importantly, for what she did to Chandler. He loved her until the day he died."

A part of Colby was touched that he had shared this with her. It was something personal, and she knew he was not one to openly share himself with too many people. She reached out and took his hand in hers. "You can't hold it against her for how Chandler felt about her, Sterling. It was his choice to continue to love her. But as to what she did to you, how you handle this is up to you. Forgiving someone isn't really the hard part. Forgetting what they did is. But you have to be able to do both. Forgive and forget."

He felt her fingers tighten around his. Her words and her touch were what he needed. But there was something else he needed and wanted even more. He needed to lose himself in her.

He closed his fingers urgently around hers. "Come on, baby. Let's get out of here."

He signaled the waiter for their check.

The trees outside the window stirred gently in the breeze and a fine mist of rain suddenly blanketed the island. None of these elements of nature were noticed by the man who eased the woman down on the bed, letting her naked body absorb the coolness of the sheets beneath her.

"Colby," Sterling whispered her name softly in the darkened room as he moved over her. He kissed her the moment he entered the depths of her, joining their bodies as one. This is what he wanted, this is what he needed, being one with her, moving deeper and deeper into her, and with the rhythmic movements of their bodies being so much a part of her.

She had the ability to reach him on a level no other woman could and in a way no other woman would. When the heated waves of passionate desire tore through him, he thrust deeper, wanting to touch the very core of her being and wanting her to feel the very core of his. He wanted to forget about all the upheaval in his life and just concentrate on making love to her.

Her soft moans became music to his ears, and the movements of her body beneath his continued to drive him over the edge. He was always amazed by the degree of her passion. He lifted his head, their eyes met, and he thought he saw something flicker in their dark depths moments before the force of their shattering release shook them both.

Long moments later when she lay in his arms asleep, he reached out and brushed a tangle of hair back from her forehead. A silent question formed in his mind.

When the time came, how on earth was he going to let her go?

Chapter 18

"Don't give me that look."

Colby smiled innocently at the man sitting across from her. They were in his private jet as it flew them high across the Atlantic Ocean, returning them from Barbados. "What look?" she asked.

Sterling grinned. "You know what look." He studied her, something he'd done a lot for the past seven days, and had reached the conclusion there was nothing about her that didn't turn him on.

"Looks are usually deceiving," Colby replied, widening her smile. "But in this case, you're right. I am giving you *that* look. So what are you going to do about it?" she asked seductively.

Sterling couldn't help but grin again. "Obviously you think there's nothing I can do about it. Well, that's where you're wrong. I'm a person who believes that the sky's the limit."

Colby's eyes gleamed with laughter with Sterling's play on words. Her expression suddenly turned serious when he stood and began pulling his shirt out of his pants.

"What do you think you're doing?" she asked, watching him remove his shirt and then his shoes.

He smiled down at her. "I'm going to teach you a lesson about tempting me when you think I can't do anything about it."

She sat up straight in her seat. "Sterling, you can't. Your pilot's up front. He'll know what we're doing. We can't just—"

"Oh, yes we can. I'll lock the cabin door to assure our privacy. John's concentration is on flying this thing and not on what we're doing in here."

"But he'll know." Colby's heart began beating a mile a minute at the recklessness of her actions. If nothing else, she should have learned by now that Sterling Hamilton had a passion that was all-consuming. All it took was her smile or her touch to set him off. And whenever she gave him *that look,* where her eyes became dark as a raven's wing and emitted secret, seductive overtures and promises of steamy passion, he would take her then and there. No matter where they were. He had made love to her in every room in their honeymoon cottage at least once, sometimes twice. And she didn't want to think about the number of times they had made love on the secluded beach. He had proved that when it came to passion between a husband and wife, everything was proper.

Their week in Barbados had been beautiful. It didn't take long for her to realize he didn't know the meaning of moderation. The word meant nothing to him. She'd discovered that reality the *hard* way, she thought, looking at the huge bulge pushing against the zipper of his pants. He had a voracious sexual appetite and throughly enjoyed making love.

Colby immediately got out of her seat when he began removing his pants. "Sterling, wait!"

He smiled that sensuous smile she had come to love. "I

am waiting. I'm waiting for you to take off your clothes, too."

She quickly glanced around, expecting John to appear any minute. She didn't care that he was supposed to be flying this jet. She knew there was such a thing as autopilot.

At that moment, John's voice came over the intercom. "Mr. Hamilton, you have a call."

Colby released a huge sigh of relief. Sterling, however, had a huge frown on his face.

"Who is it, John?"

"It's Kyle Garwood. And he said it's important."

Sterling slipped back into his shirt and pants. "It better be," he mumbled. He looked at Colby. "It seems you've been saved by the bell for just a little while. I'll be back in a minute so don't think you're out of the woods yet because this wolf has every intentions of mating when he returns."

Colby shook her head as she watched Sterling leave the room, pulling the door closed behind him. She knew he had all intentions of doing just what he claimed he would do when he got back.

She sat back down in her seat and thought some more about the past week. Although they had enjoyed the time they had spent together, in all reality, nothing between them had changed. She was still operating under the time clock he had established. She knew that as far as Sterling was concerned, the contract between them was still valid. Although he had shared the information with her about his mother's visit, he had given her no indication during the past week that her position in his life had changed. And that thought bothered her more than anything because she knew she had fallen even more in love with him.

Colby straightened in her seat when she heard the sound of Sterling returning. When he opened the door, she took one look at the expression on his face and knew something was wrong. She stood and immediately went to him.

"Sterling, what's wrong?"

He didn't say anything at first, and for a moment she wondered if he would.

"That was Kyle," he finally said, pulling her into his arms. "Nicholas Chenault contacted him to see if he could locate me."

"Why?"

"The blood clot on Angeline's brain burst and she was rushed to the hospital. She had to undergo emergency surgery and is now in critical condition. They're not sure she's going to make it."

"Oh, how awful."

Sterling sighed. "I'm surprised Nicholas Chenault wanted me to know."

Colby pushed herself out of his arms and looked up at him. "Why wouldn't he want you to know? Angeline Chenault is your mother, too. Evidently she told him the truth, and he feels you should know. I personally think you should be there with him during this time."

Sterling frowned. "How can you think anything like that? He doesn't know me. And even if Angeline told him about me, Chenault and I are strangers."

"The two of you are brothers, Sterling. You can't hold against him what Angeline Chenault did to you all those years ago. And as far as I'm concerned, you can't hold it against her anymore either. She came to you and apologized and tried to make peace."

Sterling began pacing and muttering before coming back to stand before Colby. A dark scowl covered his face. "Do you know what you're asking of me?"

She met his gaze. "Yes. I'm asking that you do what you know in your heart is the right thing. I think you should go to the hospital and be with your brother during this time. I have a feeling he needs you."

"He may resent me being there."

"I honestly don't think he will. Otherwise, why would he have tried contacting you?" A confused expression then shone on Colby's face. "How did he know Kyle Garwood would know how to reach you?"

"It's well known in the business world that Kyle and I are business partners on a number of ventures as well as good friends."

Colby nodded. "Are you going to go?"

Sterling rubbed the back of his neck, still unsure of what he should do. Again, against his will, he felt compassion for the woman who had turned her back on him, and now, thanks to Colby, he was beginning to feel compassion for his brother and what he was probably going through right now.

"I can't go. We're just getting back from our honeymoon, and I need to get you settled in. Have you forgotten I'm to fly to Spain next week to begin filming, and—"

"Stop making excuses, Sterling. Mac can meet us at the airport and take me to your home in the mountains. By the time I'm on my way, John can have the plane refueled and ready to fly you where you need to go. I'll be fine until you return. And I'm sure you'll get to Spain on time."

Pulling her close, he wrapped his arms around her waist. "Are you sure?"

"Sure of what?" she asked with a mischievous twinkle in her eyes. "That I'll be fine until you return or that you'll make it to Spain on time?"

Sterling grinned as he placed a kiss on her lips. Leave it to Colby to calm and soothed any frazzled situation. "I don't want to leave you, you know."

She smiled at his words. That was the first time he had even hinted at the possibility that maybe . . . just maybe, he liked having her around.

"You have to go, Sterling. It's time you let go of the past. Your mother asked for your forgiveness, and I think it's time you gave it to her . . . before it's too late."

Chapter 19

Colby stared out the car window. "What a lovely town. I think I'm going to like living here."

Mac gave her a dubious look. "If you do, you'll be the first wife of a Hamilton who did. All the others hated this place."

She remembered Sterling telling her that. "I don't see why. Who wouldn't like living in a quaint and quiet place that's located within a stone's throw of the Rocky Mountains?"

"A bunch of bored women with nothing better to do than sit around complaining."

Colby smiled. She really liked Mac. "How much farther is it to Sterling's home?" she asked, shifting around in the seat to take a look at a new hospital they had just passed. It seemed they had been riding for quite a while.

"Not much farther. His property is at the very end of town. We're already in Hamilton, North Carolina."

Colby raised a brow. "Is it a coincidence or do the Hamiltons have a city named after them?"

"In a manner of speaking it's named after them. Sterling didn't tell you all about his family's history?"

She shook her head. "Other than to mention there haven't been any girls born into the Hamilton family in over a hundred years, and the fact most Hamiltons are divorced men, he didn't mention anything else."

She then smiled. "Is there some deep, dark family secret he conveniently left out?"

Mac laughed. "No, in fact it's all true history, even though certain people living in these parts don't want to admit it. But it's all there on record."

"What is?"

"Have you ever heard of Alexander Hamilton?"

Colby laughed. "Of course, I've heard of Alexander Hamilton. I'm a teacher remember. And besides, history was my favorite subject in school. Alexander Hamilton was a prominent lawyer and statesman in the seventeen hundreds who went on to become the first Secretary of the Treasury under George Washington. He probably would have eventually become president one day if his duel with Aaron Burr had not ended his life."

"Hey, Teach, you're good," Mac said smiling. There was something about the look he gave her that spoke of admiration.

"I love history. Now what about Alexander Hamilton?"

"Well, the way the story goes is that while visiting this area, a beautiful slave girl caught Alex's eye and he approached her master about purchasing her. Not only did he buy her, but he purchased her parents, brothers, and other sisters. He brought them here, gave them their freedom, bought over a hundred thousand acres of land and built her a beautiful home."

"Since she isn't mentioned in the history books, I can only assume their relationship was rather discreet, especially since Hamilton was a married man," Colby said, fascinated with Mac's story.

Mac chuckled. "Some people claimed his wife knew all about Hamilton's black mistress, but it didn't bother her any. She had a grand place of her own in New York City where he officially lived. But from what I can tell, his heart was here with Lacey, and he came here every chance he got."

"Lacey?"

"Yes, Lacey. And even though they weren't legally married, Hamilton gave her his last name, and their ten sons were all Hamiltons."

"Ten sons?"

"Yep. Ten sons."

Colby shifted in her seat and turned around to face Mac when the car came to a stop at a traffic light. "Are you trying to tell me that Sterling is a decendent of Alexander Hamilton?"

Mac nodded. "And I bet of all the things you've ever read about Sterling in the newspapers and magazines, none of them ever mentioned his roots can be traced back to this country's first Secretary of the Treasury."

"How do you know so much about it?"

"Chandler Hamilton told me the entire story, and how later, after Alexander Hamilton died unexpectedly in that duel, people tried to take the land away from Lacey, but Alexander Hamilton was pretty smart. He had the land deeded to each of his ten sons. And he made sure it was put on file at a federal courthouse in Washington. The documents were signed by none other than his good friend, George Washington, who happened to be president at the time. So in all reality, this entire town belongs to the Hamiltons, decendents of Alexander and Lacey."

"That's amazing."

"Yeah, I think so, too. Sterling loves it here and the people here love him. There're other families living in these parts now, but everyone looks up to him as one of the few true Hamiltons. They're all proud of him and are very protective of him. He's a local boy who's done well for himself, and he gives back to this community. He has a scholarship fund that will give any deserving child from Hamilton a free college education. He's also the one responsible for having that new hospital built we passed a while ago."

Colby shook her head. She thought about the good deeds he had done for her two students. Edward Stewart had once told her Sterling was the most decent man he knew, and at the time she thought he had been crazy to make such a claim. But that was before she had gotten to know the real Sterling Hamilton. That was before he had captured her heart.

"Well, here we are."

Colby glanced around her. What she saw was absolutely breathtaking. She felt like a miniature person when she looked at the vast mountains surrounding them. Then she took a good look at Sterling's home. The two-story structure sat huge and spacious, nestled among a glen of trees with the mountains in the background and the Roanoke River running behind it.

"So what you think?" Mac asked as he came around to open the car door for her.

She turned to him and smiled. "I think I've come home."

When Sterling's plane landed in Jacksonville, Florida, prior arrangements had been made for him to be picked up and taken immediately to the hospital. As he sat in the chauffeur-driven car, he couldn't help wondering what Nicholas Chenault's reaction would be when he arrived unannounced.

He took a deep breath, wondering if he really should have come. Even now the thought occurred to him that it might be too late.

When the car pulled up in front of the hospital, he got out. He had spoken with the hospital officials from his jet. So that the hospital wouldn't become a circus with his arrival, and to not tip off the media, arrangements had been made for hospital security personnel to meet his car. He was then taken up to the tenth floor by way of a special service elevator.

When Sterling stepped off the elevator he glanced around and immediately saw Nicholas Chenault talking to a man who appeared to be a doctor. Sterling recognized Nicholas because he favored Angeline. He had her light brown coloring and light-colored eyes.

Sterling knew that he himself, was the spittin' image of Chandler. It was strange how one woman could give birth to two sons and they looked nothing alike. If anything, the only similarity they shared was their towering height. No one would ever guess they were brothers unless they chose to reveal that fact.

As if he had felt someone studying him, Nicholas Chenault glanced his way. Their eyes met. A part of Sterling wanted to feel resentment for the fact that this man had shared a part of his mother's life where he had not. He remembered how protectively she'd held Nicholas in her arms as a baby that day he had approached her and asked her to come home to him and his dad. Beginning that day, a part of him had resented the child she had preferred over him.

But not anymore.

Thanks to Colby, he'd been given food for thought. And plenty of it. She had been right. Nicholas Chenault had never done anything to him. And as he continued to look deep into his brother's eyes, he no longer saw him as an adversary. Nor did he see him as the "other child" that had gotten his mother's love when he had not. Instead, he saw a man in pain who faced the possibility of losing a parent he undoutedly loved deeply.

Sterling sighed. Nicholas probably loved Angeline just as much as he loved Chandler. In that case, he was going through pure hell.

As if they both made an important decision at the same time, Sterling and Nicholas began walking toward one another. It was Nicholas who offered his hand first in a firm handshake.

"I'm glad you came, Sterling."

Sterling relaxed when he felt the sincerity in Nicholas' words. "Thanks for notifying me."

Nicholas gave him a pained smile that was filled with warmth nonetheless. "She's your mother, too."

Sterling nodded, finally, after all these years, accepting Nicholas' words. "How is she?"

"There hasn't been any change. She's holding her own, although she hasn't come around since the surgery. Her doctor is afraid she may have slipped into a coma. I was just talking to him. You may be interested in what he has to say."

Sterling followed Nicholas to where the doctor was standing. He wondered how Nicholas would make introductions.

He soon found out.

"Dr. Thorn, I'd like you to meet my brother, Sterling Hamilton, and we want to know everything that's being done for our mother."

Colby had fallen in love with Sterling's home. The two-story house was large and spacious on the inside. It was apparent the house had been specially designed so that each one of the four bedrooms upstairs had a balcony that overlooked one of the many huge mountains. The sights were breathtaking.

Very nice, she thought as she settled into bed that night. The only thing missing was Sterling.

He had called earlier from the hospital and had told her Angeline Chenault's condition was unchanged, and that she hadn't regained consciousness. Their conversation had been brief and the only thing he'd said about Nicholas Chenault was that the two of them had met.

Colby drew in a deep breath. Even late at night she could smell the sweet fragrance of the wildflowers she had seen growing alongside the house. Tomorrow she intended to take a walk around the property. She had wanted to do that earlier today, but by the time she had unpacked it had begun getting dark.

The sounds in the distance of crickets and frogs intertwined with an occasional whooing sound from an owl. The noises were soothing and relaxing. Again she couldn't help but wonder how anyone could not like this place. She wouldn't be like those other Hamilton women who became bored and restless as they waited for their lumberjack husbands to return home. She would keep herself busy while Sterling was away. She might even apply for a job at the elemetary school in town. The thought of teaching again made her smile.

Now if she could only convince Sterling to keep her. She was determined more than ever to talk to him when he returned. She had news for him. Whether he liked it or not, he had a permanent wife.

Her last thought before sleep overtook her was that she was here to stay.

Dr. Thorn studied the two men who were sprawled out in the chairs in the hospital waiting room asleep. They had been there all night waiting for word of Angeline's progress. He had known the Chenaults for over twenty-five years and no one had ever mentioned Angeline had another son. Especially a son named Sterling Hamilton, the well-known movie actor. No doubt the media would have a field day when they found that out.

He cleared his throat and the two men woke instantly and stood. Although they weren't similar in physical features, except for their height, they both gazed at him with that same deep, intense stare. He could tell by the way they were looking at him, that they were expecting bad news.

It was Sterling who spoke first. "How is she?"

Dr. Thorn looked from one brother to the other. "Remarkably well for a woman who's gone through what she has. She's awake now, and I think I can say the surgery was a success, although she's not completely out of the woods yet. She has a lot of recovering to do and will need all the support she can get."

"Can we see her?" Nicholas asked anxiously.

Dr. Thorn smiled. "Yes. In fact, she's been asking for the both of you."

For the first time since meeting the day before, the two brothers looked at each other and allowed themselves to smile.

A few moments later both Sterling and Nicholas stood at the foot of Angeline's hospital bed. By the time they had gotten to her room, she had drifted back off to sleep.

"Mr. Chenault?" A nurse whispered softly as she entered the room. "You have a phone call at the front desk."

Nicholas nodded to the woman. He then turned to Sterling. "That's probably my office. I'll be back in a minute."

Left alone, Sterling allowed his gaze to linger on Angeline. In the hospital bed, she looked so tiny and frail. Her entire head was bandaged up and all sorts of machines were connected to her by way of various tubes. Sterling compared the woman he was looking at now to the one who had come to visit him in California. In less than four weeks, she had seemed to age almost twenty years.

Taking a deep breath he moved and sat in a chair at the head of the bed. No matter how he had felt toward her in the past, he would not have wanted this for her or anyone, not this sort of pain and suffering. At least Chandler had been spared that, having passed away in his sleep.

Suddenly Angeline's eyes opened weakly, and she looked at him. At first it appeared she was somewhat in a daze as she continued to look at him. And then as if she recognized him, a semblance of a smile tried to form on her lips and tears came into her eyes.

Sterling saw her attempt to raise her hand to him and took it in his. She tried to move her lips to forms words to make a sound and couldn't. In frustration, tears trickled down her cheeks and her lips began to tremble.

A part of Sterling wanted to get up and walk out of the room. He wanted to walk out on her like she had walked out on him. But he couldn't. Colby was right. He had to forgive and he had to forget.

Rising to his feet, he leaned over her, still holding her hand in his. "It's okay, Mother," he whispered softly. "Everything's going to be all right. The most important thing now is for you to get better. Nicholas and I are counting on it."

Angeline Chenault rapidly blinked back tears and looked up at Sterling with stunned disbelief in her eyes. Then slowly nodding her head she closed her eyes and drifted back to sleep with her small hand still firmly encased in Sterling's larger one.

"Mr. Wingate, there's someone here to see you, sir. It's Homer Morton of Morton Industries," Shirley Timmons announced over the intercom.

The expression on James Wingate's face became one of

surprise. Why on earth would Homer Morton be visiting him? He pushed aside the report he'd been working on. "Please show him in, Shirley."

James stood as he straightened his tie. It had been years since he had seen his former employer. He couldn't help but wonder why Homer Morton would be paying him a visit.

It didn't take long for him to find out when an angered Homer Morton literally stormed into his office.

"You've gone too far, Wingate, and I won't let you get away with it."

James was taken back by the man's angry words. "I have no idea what you're talking about."

Homer Morton's mouth twisted even more with anger. "You're lying, Wingate. I know all about what you did, and I won't let you get way with it. I can't believe you'd stoop so low as to use your sister to save your company."

"Use my sister to save my company?" James walked around his desk to face the man. "What the heck are you talking about, Morton?"

"I'm talking about the fact that somehow you found out Morton Industries was buying up Wingate stock."

James lifted a brow, clearly surprised. "Why would you be interested in Wingate stock?"

The man snorted. "Like you don't know. I wanted this entire operation, Wingate, and I had all intentions of getting it until you found out I was on the verge of taking over your company."

James shook his head, frowning. "I knew nothing about that."

"Yes, you did. Somehow you found out and used your sister to stop me."

James shook his head. The man had evidently gone mad. He knew nothing about Morton's allegations, and he couldn't imagine Colby knowing anything about them either. Other than holding shares in Wingate Cosmetics, she'd never taken an interest in the family business. Teaching was her love.

"I have no idea what you're talking about, Morton."

"I'm talking about your sister's marriage to Sterling Hamilton."

"What about Colby's marriage to Hamilton?"

"I don't know what's in it for Hamilton, but I do know you benefited from their marriage. You were able to save your company from me. While I was busy buying up your stock, Hamilton's company was busy buying controlling shares in mine."

James looked at the man, shocked and with disbelief. "That's not true."

"Oh, it's true all right. Your sister now owns the controlling shares of stock in my company."

"I think your being here did a lot to improve Mom's condition. I want to thank you again for coming."

Sterling nodded, not knowing what to say but knowing he had to be completely honest with Nicholas Chenault about how he felt. "I started not to come. I didn't want to at first but now I'm glad I did. I had to close this chapter in my life."

They were still at the hospital and Dr. Thorn had given them the use of his private office to drink some much needed coffee and to talk.

Nicholas got up and walked over to the window and looked out. "I hope you'll reconsider that, Sterling."

Sterling lifted a dark brow. "Reconsider what?"

"Closing this chapter in your life. How do you think I feel just finding out I have a brother?"

Sterling sat back in his chair. "I don't know. How do you feel?"

Nicholas turned to face him. "Shocked, suprised, betrayed. I felt all those things at first but now I feel glad and overwhelmed. And to think all those years I thought I'd been an only child."

Sterling shrugged and took another sip of coffee before saying. "You were."

"You still haven't forgiven her, have you?" Nicholas asked after a few minutes had passed.

Sterling took his hand and rubbed it down his face. "Yes, I've forgiven her."

"Then why do you want to close this chapter in your life? Why not fully open it and get to know Angeline."

Sterling sighed deeply. He wondered how he could make Nicholas understand. Colby was right when she'd said forgiving wasn't so hard, but forgetting was. "It's for the best, Nicholas. I've forgiven her but a part of me won't let go and forget just yet. You don't know what it's been like for me. You don't know all the garbage I had to deal with all those years."

Nicholas came back to the chair across from Sterling and sat down. "I think I have a good idea. Mom told me everything before she got sick. She even told me what she did to you that day in North Carolina when you were only a little boy. And while she was telling me I couldn't believe it. It was like we were talking about two different people. The mother I know and love just could not and would not turn her back on her child. But she convinced me she wasn't the same person then. When she walked out on you and your father she was barely seventeen."

Sterling drew back wearily. "Barely seventeen or not, she was still Chandler's wife and my mother."

"I know that and again I think I understand how you may feel, but I'm asking you to accept her now as she is, a warm and loving person. And accept me as I am, a man who desperately wants to get to know his brother."

Nicholas took a deep breath before continuing. "Don't close this chapter in your life. Give yourself a chance to know the Angeline Chenault that I know, and in time, hopefully you'll be able to forget the pain. And I want you to give yourself a chance to know me. There's more than just you and Angeline involved in this now. There's me."

Nicholas stood. "Have a safe trip back to North Carolina and tell your wife that I send my congratulations. I hope to get the chance to meet her one day."

Sterling nodded. "I'm sure that one day you will." Then he glanced down at his watch. "I've a couple of hours before my plane's ready to take off. How about lunch? I think you need a break from here. Do you know of any place nearby where we can grab a couple of sandwiches and engage in a private conversation?"

"A private converstion about what?" Nicholas asked.

"About you."

Nicholas frowned. "What about me?"

"Some weeks ago Kyle Garwood approached me about a business proposition concerning you and Chenault Electronics. At the time, because of personal reasons, I wanted no part of it. Now I'd like to take another look at it."

Nicholas' mouth tightened. "That's not what this is about, Sterling. That's not what I want from you. I'd much rather have a brother than a business associate."

Sterling heard Nicholas's words and felt the truth in them. A tender smile touched his lips. "How would you like to have both?"

Silence settled around the two men as the meaning of Sterling's words became clear. Nicholas returned the smile. "I'd like that."

Colby enjoyed her walk, which covered the vast area of Sterling's property. The trees were a mixture of pine, hickory, and oak. She also noticed signs of birch, maple, and hemlock. She smiled. Her class at school would have loved taking a field trip here during Back to Nature Week.

She sniffed the air to smell the fragrance of the camellias, dogwoods, and orchids. When she made it to the edge of the property she turned back around and took in her surroundings. The land that belonged to Sterling was beautiful.

In the distance, from where she stood high on one of the smaller mountains, she could see Sterling's home. And not too far away was the older house where he was born, the one Chandler had preferred living in until the day he had died.

Brushing off an old tree stump, she sat down. She had missed Sterling's phone call that morning while she'd been in the shower, and the only message he had left with Mac was that he would be coming home sometime today.

She was pulled out of her thoughts when in the distance she heard someone call her name. She lifted a surprised brow when she recognized James's tall form. She stood and began walking down the mountain toward him. When she got closer she saw the angry and intense look on his face.

"James? What is it? What's the matter?"

"I want the truth, Colby. I want to know the real reason you married Sterling Hamilton."

Chapter 20

Colby turned away from James and let out a long, shaky breath while she nervously ran a hand through her thick hair. "I don't know what you're asking me, James."

He gently turned her around to face him. "Don't you? If not, then let me explain things. I received a visit from Homer Morton of Morton Industries, and he's made some serious accusations. He's claiming his company tried to take over Wingate Cosmetics and in retaliation, Hamilton purchased a number of controlling shares of stock in his company and has placed them in your name."

Colby shrugged. "So, what's wrong with that? Sterling didn't do anything illegal did he?"

James frowned. "No, but I'd like to know how Sterling knew about the Morton Industries takeover attempt when I didn't, and why he purchased those shares of stock for you. What's he getting out of all of this?"

When Colby didn't answer, James took her hand in his. "We've never kept secrets before, Colby. I need to know the truth. Morton is not a happy camper. There's no telling how far he may take this, and I need to be prepared. He thinks I worked some deal with Hamilton and married you off to him to save Wingate Cosmetics. You and I know that's not true, but others may see it that way. So you have to tell me why you and Hamilton got married."

Colby looked at James before giving him a nervous little smile. "I married Sterling because I love him."

James nodded gravely. "I believe that. Now why did he marry you?"

Colby's eyes slid from James and she released her hands from his. "You don't think he could love me?"

"I'm not saying that and you know it. To be quite honest with you. I was totally convinced Hamilton loved you. But now . . ."

"Yes?"

"But now I don't know what to believe. I keep playing my conversations with Hamilton over and over in my mind, and I suddenly realized that at no time has he actually admitted to me that he loved you. He just acted like he did, and very convincingly I might add. And that's what worries me. I'm not sure if his actions were sincere or if it was playacting on his part."

Total silence surrounded brother and sister. After a few minutes had passed, Colby spoke. "Okay, I'll tell you everything, but please try to keep an open mind about what I'm telling you."

When James didn't say anything Colby went over and sat back down on her tree stump. "You may as well make yourself comfortable on that one," she said to James, indicating the other stump across from her. "This may take a while."

After James had taken a seat she started with her story. "I didn't meet Sterling in Richmond two months ago like I told you I had. I first met him barely a month ago. And I wish I could still claim it was love at first sight, but I can't. We were both on a mission, although they were totally different missions."

"What sort of missions?"

Colby took a deep breath before continuing. "For the first time I wanted to do something for Wingate Cosmetics and saw my chance. I flew to California in hopes that I could convince Sterling to do an endorsement for your new cologne, Awesome. I'd written to him with my proposal, so when he sent word through his attorney that he wanted to meet with me, I assumed it was about that."

"But it wasn't?"

"No, there was some sort of mix-up."

James frowned. "What kind of mix-up?"

With a soft sigh, Colby reached out and brushed a piece of fallen leaf off her shorts. Then she looked up at her brother. "He thought I had come to answer an anonymous ad he'd placed in selective newspapers around the country."

"What sort of ad?"

Colby hesitated briefly before replying. "He was looking for a woman to be the mother of his child."

At James's confused look, Colby further clarified. "He was looking for a surrogate mother."

"What!" James was no longer able to sit down. And his loud voice penetrated the quiet stillness of the entire mountainside. "Is he crazy? What woman in her right mind would do such a thing?"

Colby forced herself to say the next words. Meeting James's gaze direct, she said. "Me. To save Wingate Cosmetics from a takeover by Morton Industries, I agreed to have Sterling's baby."

Sterling paced back and forth in the cabin of his jet. Takeoff had been delayed due to thunderstorms and he was anxious to get home.

"We've been given the okay to take off now, Mr. Hamilton," John's voice came over the intercom. "It's time to buckle up."

Sterling smiled as he responded. "Thanks, John."

Then he took his seat and strapped himself in. He glanced down at his watch. He had planned on being back in North Carolina hours ago.

A tiny tremble rippled down his spine when he realized just how much he missed Colby and how she had constantly been in his thoughts. And just to think in a few days he would be leaving her to began filming in Spain. He wondered if she would consider going with him. Then he squashed that idea. Because of everything that had been happening lately, he hadn't spent the time he should have preparing for his next movie, and with Colby there it would be a lost cause. She would definitely be a distraction, one he didn't need. Spielberg had approached him months ago and convinced him he was the ideal man for the part in his next flick; and after reading the script he had agreed. And as with all his movies, he wanted to give this one his very best.

He shifted in his seat and thought of his meeting with Nicholas. Everything had gone well and after the two of them had placed a conference call to Kyle and Jake, it was basically a done deal that Chenault would get the financial backing it needed to do further research.

Sterling's thoughts slipped back to Colby as he relaxed in his seat. He would be in North Carolina in an hour or so. He couldn't wait to hold her in his arms, and he couldn't wait to make love to her again.

He smiled. He liked everything about her. She was a person who wasn't afraid to tell him exactly what she thought. And he knew the more time he spent with her, he was trodding farther and farther onto dangerous ground. If the truth be known, he kind of liked the idea of someone being there for him to hold at night, someone he could wake up with in the mornings, and like now, someone who would be there at home waiting for him when he returned.

He had never wanted those things from a woman. And he had never really thought about those things. Before Colby came into his life, he had prided himself on being Hollywood's leading bad boy. Although he knew he had won universal respect because of his talent as an actor, he'd never complained about the media labeling him the man who razzled and bed-dazzled the women. And he certainly had never given any thought to ever falling in love.

Until now.

Now he could clearly see how he could easily fall in love with Colby. He could see just how he could want her in his life forever. Already she was constantly in his thoughts, his dreams, and he missed her like crazy when they were apart. He smiled when he thought about her ability to arouse a sexual hunger in him that was mind-boggling. And for a man who had never taken any of his past sexual encounters seriously, that realization was downright scary.

He tried to shift his thoughts from Colby and concentrate on the activity happening outside the plane's window. But he couldn't. All he could think about was the time he had spent with her in Barbados. During those seven days, something had happened to him. Somehow after years of feeling alone and empty, Colby had filled a deep need within him. It was a need he hadn't known existed.

For so long he honestly hadn't had a clue what love was, at least not the kind of love a man had for a woman. In fact, he never thought he was capable of that kind of love. He knew how much Kyle loved Kimara and it completely astounded him because he knew it was an all-consuming kind of love. He figured that must have been the kind of love Chandler had felt for Angeline. And knowing that, he had never wanted to experience that kind of love. He had decided to stick wih the kind of love he knew about, the kind of love he felt safe and comfortable with. And that was the kind of love between a parent and a child. Chandler had been the perfect teacher of that kind of love.

He took a deep, shaky breath upon suddenly realizing that with Colby he wanted that other kind of love; the kind he had avoided for so long.

"What have you done to me, Colby?" he whispered quietly. But soon after he'd asked the question of himself, he immediately knew the answer. He knew at that very moment, beyond a shadow of a doubt, whether he wanted to or not, he had fallen in love with her.

"Ah, hell, this wasn't supposed to happen," he muttered to himself, tightening his hands into fists. He was never supposed to fall in love. He was supposed to spend the rest of his life without any emotional attachment to a woman. But in her own way, Colby had broken down his resolve and had bombarded him with all kinds of emotions. They were emotions he had never felt before, and more importantly, they were emotions he couldn't deny any longer.

Colby had snuggled her way into his heart.

"James, please be reasonable. It's like you haven't listened to anything I've said. You're refusing to listen. I've told you I have no intention of honoring that contract."

"But Hamilton doesn't know that, Colby. He thinks you'll be out of his life within twelve months after his child is born. And no matter what you want, he'll get his way because he has your signature on a legal document to make sure he does."

"But things can change before then. I'm hoping he'll want to keep me here with him and our child."

James pulled his sister in his arms. "Oh, Colby, I hope that will happen, too, but that may not be the case. You know of Hamilton's reputation. And although he wants a baby, I doubt he's ready to change his lifestyle and permanently become a married man. Right now all you are to him is a means to an end.''

"No, that's not true. We had a wonderful time together in Barbados. He likes having me around, James. I just know it. One day he's going to realize that both he and the baby will need me.''

"Don't get your hopes up on that, honey. Just because a man enjoys sleeping with a woman doesn't mean he's ready for a permanent relationship with her. Sterling's name has always been connected with numerous women and that may not change although he's married to you now. You may need to prepare yourself for that.''

Colby stiffened. "How can you say such a thing?''

"Because from what you've just told me, you and Hamilton don't have a real marriage. At least not in the real sense of what the institution of marriage is supposed to represent. The only thing binding between the two of you is a contract; a contract he expects you to abide by. The only thing the two of you share is a business deal.''

All it took was a look at the expression on Colby's face to let James know his words had hurt her. He reached out and pulled her to him. "I've sheltered you from so much, Colby, and maybe that's where I made my mistake. It's time you see things as they really are. Let me help you get out of this before it's too late. Once you get pregnant from him, Hamilton will demand his child. We need to consult my attorneys right away. Hopefully they'll be able to come up with some—''

Colby pushed herself away from James. "No. I won't leave him. Please try and understand that I have to do this, and not just for Wingate Cosmetics. I have to do this for me and for Sterling. He needs me, James. I know you think that sounds crazy, but deep in my heart I believe that. There's never been a woman in Sterling's life to really love him, believe in him, appreciate him, and trust him completely. And I want to be that woman."

"Colby, baby, listen to me for just—"

"No, James. I don't need you to try and protect me anymore. I have to handle this on my own. I want my time with Sterling. I have to believe that in the end, I can and that I will make a difference."

"And what if you don't? What if he still wants to send you away after your child is born? Just how will you handle that?"

"I refuse to even consider that possibility."

"You love him that much, Colby?"

She met her brother's probing gaze. "Yes. I love him that much. It's hard to explain, but I believe Sterling and I met the way we did for a reason. And I'm asking that you stay out of it and let me handle things. Promise me you'll let me work out things between me and Sterling on my own."

"Sweetheart, you're taking a big gamble on him."

She smiled faintly up at her brother. "The biggest gamble I took was going to California in the first place."

It seemed James held her gaze for the longest time before finally nodding. Then he reached out and captured her hand in his. "I'll always be here for you, baby. I love you. You know that don't you?"

Colby wiped away the tears that misted her eyes. "Yes, and I appreciate that."

Then she reached out and hugged him. "And more than anything, James Cameron Wingate, I appreciate you. And I love you, too."

Colby stared out of the window and watched the car pull up in the yard and knew it was Sterling. Getting up from the table she hugged herself and rubbed her arms, feeling nervous and apprehensive. Her conversation with James had brought up uncertainties she didn't want to deal with. They were things she hadn't wanted to think about. But she knew sooner or later she would have to.

Taking a deep breath she walked out the door and stood on the porch. When Sterling got out of the car, he stood leaning against it and stared at her. She gazed into his dark eyes and saw him appraising her outfit, an old faded shirt and a pair of denim shorts. It wasn't an outfit a wife would greet her husband in, especially if that husband was Sterling Chandler Hamilton.

"Welcome home, Sterling."

A huge smile tilted the corners of his lips and he slowly walked over to her. "I'm glad to be home."

Sterling started to tell her that the main reason he was glad to be home was because he loved her, but something held him back from saying those words. Instead he reached out and pulled her to him and placed a kiss on her lips.

"I'm glad to be home because I knew you were here, Colby."

Those simple words he'd spoken in a deep, husky voice totally dissolved any apprehensions Colby had. Loving him the way she did wasn't wrong. And she had to continue to believe that given time, he would come to love her, too.

She placed her arms around him. "I missed you."

Sterling smiled and tightened his arms around her. "I missed you, too."

He picked her up and carried her into the house. Once inside he placed her on her feet and closed the door behind him with a soft click. "I should have been here to do that when you first got here."

"Do what?"

"Carry you over the threshold."

Colby smiled. She wondered if he realized he was behaving like a happily married man, and not a man with every intention of ending his marriage some time in the future.

"Better late than never," she said, smiling up at him. "How's your mother?"

"She's progressing rather nicely."

"And your brother?"

"Nicholas is fine, too. But I don't want to talk about them."

"Oh? Who do you want to talk about?"

He pulled her into his arms, and moments before capturing her lips with his, he whispered. "Nobody."

Colby couldn't sleep anymore. She slowly eased out of Sterling's embrace, taking care not to wake him. He needed his rest.

He had tried to be tender when he'd made love to her, but she had shown him she hadn't wanted his tenderness. What she had wanted, and what she had needed, was exactly what he'd eventually given her, his complete possession, and the sharing of his heated passion.

She wondered if it would always be this way, whenever he returned home after being away; that overwhelming need to be joined as one with him in the most intimate way, where the only thoughts that could cloud her mind were those of him.

Over and over he had made love to her. Then she had fallen asleep in his arms only to be awakened later by the feel of his warm breath on her neck, and the feel of his hand moving slowly over her body, causing her flesh to become hot once again.

Finally, after neither of them could handle any more pleasure and survive the experience, they had fallen asleep exhausted and their strength totally consumed.

But something had awakened Colby. Something had pulled her back into consciousness. It hadn't been a sound that had awakened her, but a sudden thought, an alarming realization. She felt the need to think about it, work it out in her mind and come to terms with it. That need increased her urgency to be alone for a while.

Slipping into her robe, she walked barefoot across the room, opened the french doors, and stepped out onto the dark balcony. She drew in a deep breath of the clean, crisp smell of the mountain air, wishing it could somehow cleanse her soul.

The great irony of it was that she had known from the very beginning what she was getting herself into. Sterling hadn't made any promises to her. He had made it clear up front that he wasn't looking for a permanent wife. But she had let herself believe she could make a difference in his life; a difference he would soon come to accept. Now she wasn't sure that would happen.

"Colby?"

Sterling's voice startled her. She'd thought he was still inside sleeping. She slowly turned around to him. "Yes?"

"Are you okay?"

She only hesitated a moment before answering him. "Yes, I'm fine. I'm just enjoying the night air."

"Would you like some company?"

"Sure, but I thought you were sleeping."

He came to stand before her. The musky scent of him combined with the potent smell of pine needles and mountain laurels, stirred her senses and made her even more aware of him.

"I was asleep, but I woke up and reached out for you and you weren't there." He put his arms around her, drawing her closer to him.

Colby leaned against him, absorbing his strength. She so desperately needed it now. He always managed to convey an aura of cool confidence. The only time she'd seen that confidence waver even just a little was when he had told her about Angeline Chenault's visit. It was during that time that she had seen straight through Sterling's pretense at being cool, confident, and nonchalant.

"Do you want to tell me what really drove you out here?" he asked softly, as he leaned down and caressed her face with butterfly kisses.

"Talk to me, baby. Tell me what's bothering you." Then he drew her deeper into his arms as his hand smoothed gently across her shoulders and back.

"James came to see me today," she finally said, knowing he'd been waiting patiently for her to answer.

He eyed her thoughtfully before saying. "This sounds serious."

Colby nodded. "He found out about that Morton Industries stock you gave me. Homer Morton visited him and accused James of marrying me off to you to save Wingate Cosmetics."

"So what did you tell James?"

"I told him the truth, all of it."

Sterling raised one eyebrow at her. "In that case, I'm surprised he didn't hang around to bump me off."

She shrugged. "I talked him out of it."

"I appreciate that."

He sat down on a bench and pulled her down next to him, taking her hand in his. "And just what did you say to him that saved my life?"

Colby glanced up at him and wondered how Sterling would handle what she was about to say to him. "I told him I had no intentions of honoring that contract between us."

"And he fell for that?"

"Yes, because it's the truth, Sterling. I can't give up my child," she said seriously, and honestly.

Sterling released Colby's hand and stood. He stared down at her. His expression was unreadable. "You're totally serious aren't you?"

Tilting her chin she stood and faced him. "Yes, so you might as well go ahead and sue me."

He reached out and wrapped his arms around her waist

and pulled her to him. "I'd rather continue to love you," he whispered before his head came down and his mouth covered hers.

Because Sterling's kiss had sent immediate shock waves coursing throughout Colby's body, it was an entire minute before the meaning of his words sank into her mind. She suddenly broke off their kiss. "What did you say?"

Sterling smiled at the look of disbelief on her face. "I said I love you. And don't worry about me suing you because there's no longer a contract. I contacted Edward before my plane landed today and ordered him to destroy it, as well as the prenuptial agreement. So now, Colby, you're stuck with me. Forever." Sterling pulled her into his arms.

"Oh, Sterling," she said as tears began clouding her eyes. She felt as though she had just awakened from a dream—a wonderful, glorious dream. The knowledge that he loved her sent her pulse in overdrive.

"Colby?"

She lifted her head and looked up at him. The moon's light silhouetted his features and she could see the intense look that lined his face. "Yes?"

"How do you feel about me?"

She was surprised he even had to ask. There was a glint of mischief in her eyes when she said, "You have moved up a notch above Denzel," she said teasingly. "And since I've gotten to know you better, I even like you much better as a man."

"Colby!"

"What?"

He lifted her face to meet his eyes. The look in his expression was serious. "I have to know how you feel about me."

She looked at him, reading the anxiety in his eyes. Then it suddenly occurred to her that this was all new to him, these emotions he was experiencing. And it was important that he know just how she felt. As far as he was concerned, no woman had ever really loved him before.

She lifted her hand to rub gently across his beard. "I love you, Sterling, and I have loved you for some time. I fell in love with you in California. I realized how I felt about you the day you took me to your home in Malibu. I love you with all my heart and soul."

He stared down at her for a long moment before saying, "Thank you for loving me."

Colby gazed into his eyes with all her love clearly shining in hers. Her voice was soft as a whisper when she said. "It is my pleasure."

The reddish-brown highlights of dawn seeped across the mountains and into Sterling's bedroom. His eyes were open. He had awakened during the predawn hours.

Colby sighed in her sleep and snuggled closer to his body. Instinctively, he wrapped his arms around her, holding her close. Her body felt heavenly curled up against his. And her perfume, that arousing feminine scent he'd come to accept as part of her, surrounded him.

He gazed down and regarded her thoughtfully. Their marriage wouldn't be normal by any means. Their home life would be chaotic and their private life would be non-existent. And they would have to work harder than most married couples at building and maintaining a solid relationship. But as he stared down at her, he knew she was worth everything.

Colby shifted in his arms, slowly opened her eyes and looked up at him. She smiled.

Sterling felt has if his entire world opened up with that one smile, and he silently pledged to love her for the rest of his life. He pulled her closer into his arms and whispered the words, "I love you," before leaning down and touching her lips in a soft, gentle kiss.

Chapter 21

Colby stood on the porch and watched Sterling load his luggage into the trunk of the car. He was getting ready to leave for Spain.

She sighed heavily and leaned her head back to rest against the huge wooden post. He would be gone for a month and she would miss him terribly.

She couldn't help but think about the last five days they had spent together. Their time together had been private, precious, and intimate. They had walked hand in hand over every inch of his land, sharing stolen kisses during the day among the thickets of plants and trees, and then again at night underneath the dark, moon-kissed sky.

They had engaged in long serious conversations with topics ranging from the challenges she felt were facing school teachers today, to his desire to one day direct and produce his own movie.

He had also explained the things that went into making a motion picture telling her how the special effects were done and why he enjoyed performing most of his own stunts.

They had also talked seriously about their marriage. He had told her she was now his first priority in life, and he intended to make their marriage work. It was important that they fill their marriage with constant support, understanding, and open communication. Their marriage, like most celebrity marriages, would be faced with many challenges from overzealous fans wanting to know everything about them to the media trying to oblige their readers at any cost.

She had agreed that when he was on location making a movie for extended periods of time, she would stay with him whenever possible.

They also talked about what she wanted to do with her time. She loved teaching and if the opportunity ever presented itself for her to return to the classroom, she would consider it. He had no problem with that and even liked the idea of her wanting to teach in Hamilton.

By the end of each of their discussions, she'd felt within her heart that together they would be able to handle whatever pressures came their way. Love, faith, and trust would be the key ingredients to them having a successful marriage.

When Sterling placed the last piece of luggage in the car he turned and looked at her. His gaze was serious, thoughtful. She had no idea what he was thinking to cause such an intense look in his eyes because her own mind was filled with her own thoughts. They were thoughts of him and how much she loved him.

He slowly walked over to her and extended his hand to her. "Come on, baby. Let's go for a walk."

She nodded and placed her hand in his.

For the first few minutes they walked in silence. Then she spoke.

"Did you remember to pack your copy of the script?"

"Yes."

"What about your daily planner?"

"Yes."

"What about—"

He stopped walking and turned to her. He squeezed her hand gently. "I've packed everything."

She gave him a shaky smile. "I don't know why I'm asking you all these questions. You're used to all of this, going away, leaving the country to make movies."

Sterling stepped closer and looked deeply into her eyes. "No, I'm not used to this at all," he whispered huskily, fiercely. A strong hand reached out to gently touch the nape of her neck. "This is the first time I've ever gone away and left behind the woman I love."

He leaned down and touched her mouth with his, placing his arms around her waist and bringing her closer to his body. The kiss deepened as he used his tongue to fill his senses with the taste of her, and to fill her senses with the taste of him. He slid his hands from around her waist to her rounded bottom, running his hand obsessively and possessively over her smooth curves, and at the same time absorbing her whimpered moans of pleasure in his mouth.

Sterling broke the kiss and pressed his lips against the hollow of her throat, breathing deeply, erratically. "I love you," he whispered as his lips, moist and warm, inched their way to her earlobe.

"And I love you, too, so very much," she said in a trembling, choked voice.

Sterling lifted his head. He leaned back and gazed into Colby's eyes. They were glistening with tears that began running down her cheeks. She quickly swiped at them.

"Now see what you've done, Sterling Hamilton. I had promised myself I wouldn't do this. But see what you made me do."

He pulled her into his arms understanding completely. He didn't want to leave her either. "It isn't too late, Colby. You can change your mind and come with me if you want."

She smiled through her tears. "And let you accuse me of being a distraction. Never."

He grinned. "But you'll be a distraction I'd like. You know how much I enjoy spending time with you, baby."

Colby grinned. "Yes, well, at least while you're gone I'll be off my back for a while."

Sterling's laughter could be heard through the mountains and trees. "I thought you liked being on your back beneath me."

"I do." She took a deep breath and placed her hands on her stomach. "If I didn't get pregnant before from our time in Barbados, I'm probably pretty pregnant by now."

Sterling's hand covered hers. "How soon will you know?"

Colby shrugged. She would have a pretty good idea within the next couple of weeks. "How soon do you want to know?" she asked him.

He smiled smugly. "I already know. It's you who's the doubtful one."

The smile Colby gave back to Sterling was tender, loving. He was convinced he had gotten her pregnant in Barbados. She reached up and wrapped her arms around his neck. "Time will tell, Mr. Hamilton. Time will tell," she whispered before pulling his mouth down to hers. And she realized as she curled into him, arching her hips closer toward him, just how much she wanted his prediction to be true.

Chapter 22

Colby sat on the blanket she had spread out on the ground and watched a squirrel dart from one tree to the other. She loved the beauty of this particular area on Sterling's land, a small clearing nested beneath a cluster of pecan trees. While he'd been home, Sterling had brought her here every day just to sit and talk. Sometimes, more often than not, they would also end up doing other things. She couldn't help but smile when she thought of those other things.

She placed aside the book she had brought with her to read. Her mind just wasn't on it right now. Sterling had been gone for ten days and she was missing him something fierce. At first he had called her every morning before he left for the movie set, and then again at night before he retired to bed. But for the past few days, he had only called in the mornings and then his conversations had been brief and rushed. And so far today, she hadn't heard from him at all. She wondered how things were going with the filming of his movie. Some critics had predicted it would be Spielberg's greatest achievement and with Sterling in the lead role, it would gross more than the amount being spent to make it. Sterling was one of the few actors who consistently delivered twenty-five million-plus movie openings.

Colby didn't know very much about the woman who would be his leading lady in this movie, Rachel Hill. He had told her he'd never worked with her before, and that she had starred in a British film a year ago that had been quite a success. However, this would be her first American film. Colby had seen a picture of the woman in a magazine and thought she was simply beautiful.

She managed a wry smile. Lucky for her this movie didn't call for any love scenes. At least she hadn't seen any when she had taken a peek at the script Sterling had left on the kitchen table one day.

Colby twisted around when she heard Mac call her name. She stood when she saw him and noticed the worried expression his face.

"Your brother just called, Colby. He's at the hospital. Cynthia may be losing the baby."

"Oh, no." Colby began racing toward the house. "I have to get to Richmond, Mac," she said, knowing James was probably going out of his mind about now.

"I can't believe James called and made the situation seem worse than it was," Cynthia said, smiling at Colby and frowning at James.

"That's okay. I just didn't know what to think when Mac said James had told him you'd been taken to the hospital and could be losing the baby."

Cynthia waited until after the nurse had left from taking her temperature before responding. "I complained about having a little stomach pain, and James literally freaked out."

"I was worried," James said in his defense, kissing his wife on the lips.

"Well, no harm's been done," Colby said. "Mac drove my Jaguar here in record time." She chuckled. "It's a wonder he didn't get a ticket."

"How long will you be staying," Cynthia asked.

"I'm staying in town tonight but I'm leaving to go back home first thing in the morning. If Sterling calls he'll be wondering where I've taken off to."

The doctor then entered the room and told James that Cynthia would be released in the morning. The pains had been from an overactive baby making Cynthia's abdomen slightly uncomfortable.

"Colby, do me a favor and take your brother home and put him to bed for a nap. I think this little excitement has worn him out," Cynthia said, laughing.

"Sure thing."

When Colby walked out of the hospital with James on one side of her and Mac on the other, she was unexpectedly surrounded by reporters. They were everywhere and were flashing their mikes and cameras in her face. Mac reacted quickly and placed himself between Colby and a number of the reporters.

"Have you seen this morning's paper, Mrs. Hamilton?"

"What comment would you like to make?"

"Did you have any idea about the affair going on between your husband and Diamond Swain?"

"Why did he order that she replace Rachel Hill in his latest movie?"

"Is it true he has left you for Swain and that he's filed for a divorce?"

Colby was taken a back by the bombardment of questions coming at her all at once. "What are you talking about?"

One reporter replied for the others. "We're talking about the picture and article appearing in this morning's paper."

Colby's face showed her confusion. "What picture? What article?"

No sooner had she asked the question, a newspaper was practically shoved in her face. She saw the front page picture of Sterling holding Diamond Swain in his arms. The headlines read THE HAMILTON-SWAIN FLING IS ON AGAIN!!

Colby frowned. Then she neatly folded the paper and handed it back to the reporter. "I can't believe someone would print such garbage."

"Then you don't believe it?"

"Of course, not."

"Did you know your husband asked that Diamond Swain replace Rachel Hill as his leading lady in the movie he's currently filming in Spain?"

"Did you know he's carrying on an affair with Diamond Swain while the movie is being filmed?"

Before Colby could respond the reporter continued. "That picure on the front page of today's paper shows them embracing right after he left her hotel room around three A.M. this morning."

"Come on, Colby, you don't have to listen to any of this," James said, taking his sister's hand and leading her away.

Another reporter seized that opportunity to yell out. "The truth is in that photograph, Mrs. Hamilton. You can't deny it. Take a good look at it and you'll see two people who care a lot for each other. It seems Sterling Hamilton is playing you for a fool."

An angry Mac pushed their way through the reporters. It was only after Colby was securely settled into the back seat of the car with James getting in with her and Mac at the wheel, that she gave into her tears and cried on James's shoulder.

James looked at his sister as she sat at the kitchen table eating the sandwich he had made for her. "I can't believe how calmly you're taking all of this," he said.

Colby stopped eating and glanced up at him. "Calmly? I don't call crying my eyes out on your shoulder taking anything calmly. I feel sorry for whoever wrote that article and took that picture. Sterling's going to be furious."

James came and sat down at the table across from her. "I take it you don't believe any of it?"

Colby thought long and hard about James's question. Sterling's relationship with Diamond Swain was something the two of them had never discussed since they had gotten married. But deep in her heart, she believed he would not be unfaithful to her. She refused to believe these past few weeks with him had been a lie and that he would think so little of her and sleep with another woman.

"No, I don't believe it," she answered softly.

"Then why were you crying?"

"Because I was mad. The media has gone too far. How can anyone stoop so low and print something like that. It's like those reporters want to think the worst of Sterling."

"Diamond Swain *has* replaced Rachel Hill on the set of that movie Hamilton is filming in Spain, Colby. The midday news confirmed that," James pointed out.

She nodded. "Yes, I know, but there has to be a good reason she was replaced by Diamond Swain."

"Okay, then explain the picture, Colby."

Colby shrugged, not wanting to think of the picture right now. "I can't explain it, but I'm sure Sterling will when he calls." She leaned back in her chair and held her brother's gaze.

"I trust him, James. And I believe he loves me just as much as he says he does because he has no reason to lie about it. I know you don't think he loves me but—"

"You're wrong. I do think he loves you."

Colby wasn't prepared for what her brother had just said. "What! Just a few week ago, when you found out about Morton Industries, you were almost certain he didn't."

James leaned back in his chair and smiled wryly. "Well, yes, but that was before Hamilton paid me a visit."

A surprised expression covered Colby's face. "Sterling came to see you? When?"

"When he was on his way to Spain. He thought we should settle the issue once and for all about your marriage and how he felt about you."

Colby was silent for a moment before asking. "What did he say?"

James chuckled. "Quite a lot. And what he said and how he said it left little doubt in my mind about his feelings for you."

He reached out for her hand. "But there are a lot of people who'll read that article and see that picture and believe the worst. That photo is pretty damaging."

Colby shook her head. "It's not damaging to me because I don't believe it, and I don't care who may read it and believe it. In my heart, I believe Sterling loves me and that's all that matters."

"I'm glad to hear you say that, Mrs. Hamilton," Mac said coming into the room. "I didn't mean to listen in but I just happened to be standing outside the door a few seconds ago."

He came farther into the room to stand in front of Colby. "I think we should leave this afternoon for North Carolina."

Colby frowned. "Why? What's wrong with waiting to leave in the morning as we planned?"

Mac sighed heavily. "I tried calling Spain and Sterling's not there. The person I talked to said he walked off the set to return to the States the moment he saw the headlines in the papers."

Colby blinked. "Sterling's on his way home?"

Mac nodded. "Yes." Then he looked at her thoughtfully. "And I have a feeling he thinks he'll find you packed and gone when he gets there."

Colby's face went completely blank at Mac's statement. However, James asked the question before she could. "Why would he think that?"

Mac's expression was solemn for a moment before he answered. "Because of the Hamilton curse. No Hamilton man has been able to keep a woman for long. All Hamilton women end up divorcing Hamilton men and leaving them."

Colby rolled her eyes to the ceiling. She remembered that bit of family history Sterling had once shared with her. She stood from her seat. "Well this Hamilton woman has no intentions of leaving. I married my Hamilton man for life. Get the car ready, Mac. We're going home tonight."

Chapter 23

"Where is she?"

Sterling frantically asked himself that question as he tried calling his home in North Carolina again. He was in his jet on his way back to the States.

The photograph of him and Diamond that appeared everywhere in the newspapers was damaging enough, but the article deliberately raised doubts of his faithfulness to Colby. It was just the type of thing they didn't need to deal with right now.

He released a deep sigh then tried calling James's house. There wasn't an answer there either. And he couldn't locate Mac. Where was everyone?

No sooner had he hung up the phone, than it rang.

He snatched it up immediately. "Colby?"

His face showed disappointment that the caller wasn't Colby. "Yes, Diamond, I'm fine. No, I haven't been able to reach Colby, and no, it's not your fault."

He nodded. "Everything will be fine once I talk to her and explain things."

He shook his head. "No. That won't be necessary. Just let me handle this. Colby has to trust me. Otherwise, our marriage will never stand a chance against this sort of garbage. Just sit tight and don't worry about me and Colby. We'll be fine."

He took a deep breath. "Okay, I'll keep in touch."

Sterling hung up the phone, hoping what he'd just told Diamond was true and that he and Colby would be fine. He looked down at his hands. They were trembling. He didn't want to think about the possibility that he could lose Colby over this.

He stood and began pacing the length of his cabin. He knew she'd probably seen the article by now and he had a lot of explaining to do. He just hoped that wherever she was, she believed he loved her more than anything. He couldn't imagine living his life without her.

He sat back down in his seat and gazed outside the window at the clouds, believing there had to be sunshine out there somewhere. The kind of sunshine to brighten the earth like Colby had brightened his life.

He refused to be another Hamilton who lost the woman he loved, and he simply refused to live his remaining years in heartache and pain.

He was determined to keep the woman he loved with him always.

It was late afternoon when Mac and Colby arrived back in North Carolina.

"I'm going to stay at my own place tonight," Mac said after opening the door to let Colby in. "You and Sterling will need plenty of privacy."

Colby nodded. Mac's place was on the other end of Sterling's property. He stayed there whenever Sterling was in town, and only stayed with her in Sterling's home whenever he was away for protection against possible trespassing reporters.

After checking out the place he came back to her and let her know everything was okay. Then he teasingly told her there weren't any reporters hiding out under the beds.

"And you really think Sterling's on his way home?"

"Yes, I'm almost certain of it," Mac replied. "I've been trying to reach him in the air but keep running into some sort of interference. There must be bad weather somewhere."

Colby nodded. "I'm going to get settled in. Good night, Mac, and thanks for everything."

"Don't mention it. I promised Chandler a long time ago that I'd look after that boy. And I'm meaning to keep my word. You're good for him, Colby. You're just what he needs."

No sooner had Sterling's plane landed at the airport in Raleigh, than a helicopter was standing by to fly him the rest of the way to Hamilton. Bad weather conditions in New York had forced his flight out of the city to be delayed. It hadn't helped matters that he was still unable to get in touch with Colby.

He gave a sigh of relief when the copter landed in the clearing on his property. It was night, and he could barely make his way though the darkness, but he didn't intend to stop until he held Colby in his arms.

A showered Colby had just slipped into her nightgown when she heard the sound of a door opening downstairs. She grabbed her robe, wondering if it was Mac returning. He usually knocked before entering.

"Colby!"

The sound of Sterling calling her name thundered

loudly throughout the house. Excitement pricked her every nerve. He was actually home!

Tossing her robe aside she raced out of the room. She stopped at the landing and stared down at Sterling who was standing at the bottom of the stairs looking up at her with dark, intense eyes. She loved him so much and no matter what, she believed he loved her.

"Hi," she said quietly, watching him watch her. She had seen the relief on his face when he had seen her. Mac had been right. Sterling had actually thought there was a possibility she wouldn't be there.

"Hi, yourself," he said, huskily. "We need to talk don't we?"

She nodded, knowing he was referring to the article that had appeared in the newspaper that morning. "Yes.

Sterling said nothing else for a moment but continued to look at her. He then said, "I know we need to talk, but I have some questions I need answered right now."

"What are they?"

"At anytime after seeing that picture and reading that article did you think it was true? At anytime did you doubt my love for you? And do you doubt my love for you now?"

Colby knew she had to be completely honest with both him and herself. A part of her, the part that knew and accepted she was not as beautiful and glamorous as the women he was used to dating, especially someone like Diamond Swain, had tried considering the possibility that it had been true. But she had crushed the idea before it had gotten a chance to fully take root in her mind.

"At first when I saw it, and saw you holding Diamond Swain in your arms, I really didn't know what to think, and I didn't want to believe those accusations. But then after I thought about it, I knew I couldn't believe it, and that I wouldn't believe it. I believe in my heart that you love me and there's a good reason for that picture."

Her smile was bittersweet when she continued. "At least there better be a good reason, Sterling Hamilton."

He smiled. "There is."

"Good. Now can I come down to get the hug I so badly need?" Colby asked softly.

Sterling didn't think he could possibly love her more than he did at that very moment. He needed her more than he needed his next breath. Kyle had been right when he had said Colby was a precious gem.

He held out his arms to her and she flew down the stairs toward him. He caught her, staggering a little at the force of their combined weight. No sooner was she in his arms than he captured her mouth with his, kissing her with a passion that conveyed his love and appreciation of her trust. A part of him had been so afraid she wouldn't trust him and that she wouldn't be here when he arrived.

When he lifted his head she asked him why he had stopped. "Because if I don't stop, I'm going to end up carrying you back up those stairs and making love to you. But first we need to talk."

He picked her up in his arms and instead of carrying her up the stairs like he really wanted to do, he carried her into his study.

Colby looked up at Sterling with widened eyes. "Let me make sure I have this straight. Diamond Swain is married to your friend Jake Madaris?"

Sterling nodded, smiling. "Yes, they've been married a little over a year now. But because of Diamond's need for privacy, she and Jake are keeping their marriage a secret. There are members of Jake's family that don't even know yet."

Colby shook her head. "But why?"

"It's a long story and to tell you all of it, I'll have to go back to the very beginning and explain how Jake and

Diamond met. I'm the one who introduced them, but it was never either of their intentions to fall in love."

He smiled ruefully. "It was similar to our situation. It just happened."

Sterling pulled Colby closer to him as she sat in his lap. "Diamond has always been a good friend to me, nothing more. We used our friendship to keep the media speculating about us. It served as good publicity. But there has never been anything sexual between us. And after she married Jake, he suggested we continue the charade so the media wouldn't find out about their marriage. That way Diamond could keep her personal life, the one she shares with Jake, private."

Sterling turned Colby around in his lap. "When it was discovered that Rachel Hill was snorting cocaine in her dressing room, she had to go. It was Spielberg's decision, not mine, to call Diamond. She had been his first choice anyway, but Diamond had turned down the part because of a prior commitment. It was sheer luck for him that she had just finished filming in New Mexico and agreed to fly to Spain."

"When was the last time you had seen her?"

"I saw her that week I spent in Texas with Jake. She was spending a couple of weeks at the ranch with him. She had arrived the week his nephew, Clayton Madaris, got married although she didn't attend the wedding with Jake since no one knows they're married."

Sterling held Colby tight in his lap. He inhaled sharply her very special scent. "I talked to both Jake and Diamond before coming home tonight, and they're willing to make a statement to the press announcing their marriage if the article that appeared in the papers this morning has caused problems between us. I told them it didn't. But I want you to tell me how you feel about it. Diamond, Jake, and I are willing to bring everything out in the open if—"

"No, that's not necessary. No matter what the papers

say, I trust you and I believe in you and that's all that matters."

He leaned down and kissed her lips. "I nearly went crazy when I couldn't reach you earlier today. My mind tried convincing me of the worse, but my heart refused to believe you would have so little trust in me. But then that picture did look pretty convincing, and all I could think about was the Hamilton curse."

Colby rolled her eyes. "There's no such thing as a Hamilton curse. But there is a such thing as bad choices. I hate to say this but all the Hamilton men before you simply made bad choices."

She smiled sweetly at him. "Now getting back to that picture, where was it taken? The article claims it was taken right outside Diamond's hotel room door at three in the morning."

Sterling nodded. "Unfortunately, that's probably true. Because Diamond was thrown into things at the last minute, she hadn't had time to prepare for her part in the movie before hand. So I volunteered to go over the script with her. Diamond is sort of a huggy person and when I was leaving, she hugged me to thank me for my help. That was all there was to it, but, of course, the papers wanted to make it out to be more than that."

He gently squeeze her hand. "I'm sorry. I just didn't think how bad something like that would look. Jake trusts me with Diamond completely, and I'm so used to not caring what others think. But now I do care what others think because I have you to think about. I don't want anyone thinking you're being made a fool of or that you're unloved."

"I've told you, Sterling, it doesn't matter what others think as long as—"

"It matters to me. You're my wife and I love you, and I want the whole world to know that. I plan to call a press conference in the morning and publicly deny I'm having an affair with Diamond."

Colby looked up at him. "That may not be necessary."

Sterling raised a brow. "Why not?"

"Because if I guess correctly, tomorrow the media's interest will be shifted from you and Diamond to Angeline Chenault."

Sterling was quiet for a moment before asking. "What do you mean by that?"

"What I mean is that I received a call from Nicholas Chenault tonight and it appears Angeline is concerned with all the bad publicity the papers are giving you and Diamond, so she has decided to do something about it."

Sterling looked at Colby thoughtfully, making sure he was following her. "She wants to shift the media's attention elsewhere?"

Colby nodded. "Yes. She has decided to place the heat on herself. She's holding her own press conference in the morning and she's going to announce that she's your mother."

"What! Does she know what she's doing? The media will have a field day with that. They've been trying to figure out who my mother is for years. They'll start digging into her past, hounding her for information, and smearing her good name."

"Yes, I know," Colby said smoothly. "And I think those are the things she's counting on happening."

Sterling looked astounded. "Why?"

"To shift the attention from you to her. By the time the papers finish broadcasting her annoucement, the news regarding you, Diamond, and Rachel will be old news. At least it'll take a backseat to your mother's revelation."

Sterling placed Colby out of his lap and onto the seat next to him. Then he stood and walked over to the window. Since leaving Florida he had been in contact with Nicholas daily regarding Angeline's condition. Then when Angeline had gotten better where she could talk on the phone, he had spoken to her countless times.

"I can't let her do that. She's a sick woman. Although she's no longer in the hospital, she's still not completely well. I won't let her do it."

"I told Nicholas you'd probably feel that way, but he told me to tell you that Angeline's mind is made up, and there's no stopping her. She's going to do it."

A few minutes passed before Sterling spoke. "And she's willing to do that for me?"

"Yes, she and Nicholas both are. He'll be subjected to just as much heat from the media as Angeline."

Colby sat for a while and stared at Sterling's profile as he stood across the room. She couldn't believe he was actually there with her, and that because of his love for her he had walked off the set of his movie and immediately flown back home to her. She could feel her throat swell with the emotions she felt. She ached to tell him how much she loved him, and she ached to show him how much she loved him.

She got up and walked over to where he stood looking out the window. She knew he was thinking hard about what she had just told him about Angeline. His mind was in turmoil and she intended to soothe it in a very special way.

She curled her arms around him. "Sterling?"

"Umm?"

"Are we through talking yet?"

He turned around and slowly smiled at her and took her into his arms, bringing her closer to him. "Yes, sweetheart, we are."

She returned his smile with a seductive one of her own. "Good, let's go to bed."

* * *

Sterling and Colby had just finished making love again when the sun rose to a brilliant hue over the top of the mountains, announcing it was a brand new day. They lay in each others arms, happy with the love they shared for each other and at the moment, completely drained of any strength to do anything but wait to revamp their energy.

"How much longer will it be before you know something?"

Colby smiled as she entwined herself deeper into Sterling's arms. She knew specifically what he was talking about. "I could find out today. I'm a day late already."

"You don't have to find out on my account," Sterling said, smiling happily at her. "My son will be born sometime next March."

Colby chuckled. "You think so?"

Sterling grinned. "Yes, nine months from June is March."

She shook her head. "I'm not talking about the timing. I'm talking about the baby's sex. You still think Hamiltons can't have girls?"

"Yes."

"All right then, are you willing to make a deal?"

Sterling raised a brow. "What kind of deal?"

"If I have a girl, I want a lifetime of special moments from you."

"Baby, you'll get those regardless of whether we have a son or a daughter." He pulled her closer into his arms. "I want to thank you for giving me the most precious gift I've ever had."

Colby looked up at him. "And what was that?"

He met the question in her eyes with a serious expresssion in his own. He reached out and took her hand and brought it to his lips. "That one special moment, the day you became my wife. God must have known I needed someone like you in my life and sent you to me. I will always believe that and cherish it."

Threading his fingers through her hair, he caught a loose part with his fist and gently lifted her head to give him easy access to her mouth. He loved this woman and he would make sure that for the rest of her life she got all the special moments she deserved.

Epilogue

"Chandler is crying, Sterling," Colby said sleepily. "It's feeding time."

Sterling came immediately awake. Unlike most people, he enjoyed these two o'clock feedings. It was a special time to bond with his child.

He padded in his barefeet across the hall to the nursery where Chandler Hamilton was crying. Reaching down he picked up his child.

Colby had refused to take a sonogram during her pregnancy to determine the sex of their child. "Some things should remain a surprise," she had said. And Chandler's entrance into the world had been totally that for him.

Up until the time the doctor had uncovered her in front of his eyes to prove that his wife had indeed given birth to a girl, he had been so sure she was having a boy.

It wasn't that he had preferred a son over a daughter, it was just that he'd actually thought he couldn't produce a female offspring. He and Colby had brought the era of all male Hamiltons to an end with the bundle of joy he held in his arms.

And she was indeed a bundle of joy to everyone, especially to her grandmother Angeline and her uncle Nicholas. Sterling smiled when he thought about the growing close relationship between him, his mother, and his brother. And now that Chandler was born, Angeline's and Nicholas's visits to North Carolina were rather frequent.

He gazed down at his daughter. She was simply beautiful. He would have to get his shotgun ready in sixteen years when she began dating. Unless, however, the young man was one of Kyle's sons, since he seemed to have a lot of them to go around these days. Kimara had given Kyle two more sons. Keenan and Kellum.

Sterling's smile widened. He and Colby would have to do a lot of overtime to catch up with the Garwood clan. "But we can do it if we try, can't we, Chandler?" he cooed to his daughter.

"Do what?" Colby asked coming into the room. Since she was still breast-feeding, the two o'clock feedings could not be done without her. Like Sterling, she also enjoyed this special time with their daughter.

She looked at her husband. He looked so good shirtless and wearing only his sexy, boxer style, silk underwear. He was one very sexy man, and now that Wingate Cosmetics' ads for Awesome were everywhere, everyone knew what she had always known . . . Sterling Hamilton was awesome.

The advertisment featuring him had taken the country by a storm and Wingate's sales for its newest cologne had skyrocketed beyond their wildest dream. It seemed that all women everywhere wanted their men to wear Awesome. But Colby knew she had the real awesome man.

"What can we do if we try?" Colby asked Sterling again.

He smiled at her. "Have just as many babies as the Garwoods."

Colby frowned. "Don't even think it, Sterling Hamilton. No one can have as many babies as Kyle and Kimara, and

I don't even plan on trying," she said, taking their child from his arms. Chandler was barely four months old and already her husband was thinking about having others. And so was her brother. He was trying hard to convince Cynthia that James Jr. needed a sister.

"What about a Garwood-Hamilton wedding sometime in the future?" he asked his wife. "And then if we have another daughter, she can marry Jake and Diamond's son. "I like the idea of a Madaris-Hamilton match one day."

Colby lifted a brow. Evidently Sterling thought he was pretty good at putting marriages together since he'd done a fairly good job of putting theirs together. "Jake and Diamond don't have a son, Sterling."

"Not yet they don't. But hopefully, they'll get their act together soon enough. Neither of them is getting any younger."

Sterling watched as Colby breast-fed their child and a deep feeling of love and pride washed over him. He leaned down and kissed her lips. "Do you know what I think?" he asked smiling.

"No, what do you think, Sterling?"

"I think you're more valuable than the most precious gem, and that you satisfy all my needs."

A smile formed on Colby's lips with Sterling's compliment. "And you, my darling husband, have surpassed Denzel in my book, and as a man I think you're totally awesome." Her eyes darkened from the heat she saw radiating in his gaze.

"I also think if we're not careful and behave ourselves, we just might catch up with the Garwoods," she whispered seductively

He laughed. "At least we have plenty of room up here on our mountain."

She grinned. Although they visited their home in California often, this place, here in the mountains of North Carolina, was what they truly considered home. "Yes, we do have plenty of room up here, don't we?"

Colby reached out and let her fingers lightly trace the masculine lines of Sterling's face. "I love you."

He inhaled her fragrance. Her scent was unmistakably . . . Colby. "And I love you, sweetheart. Always."

ABOUT THE AUTHOR

Brenda Jackson lives in the city where she was born, Jacksonville, Florida. She has a Bachelor of Science degree in Business Administration from Jacksonville University. She is married to her high school sweetheart and they have two sons attending college. Presently, she works for a major insurance company. She is also a member of the First Coast chapter of Romance Writers of America, and is a founding member of the national chapter of Women Writers of Color.

Dear Readers,

I hope you enjoyed *One Special Moment*. I had fun writing Sterling and Colby's story, as well as revisiting with Kyle and Kimara Garwood.

I am presently working on my next book, which is tentatively titled, *Fire and Desire*. This is Trevor Grant and Corinthians Avery's story. The sparks . . . and the passion (the fire and the desire) are leaping off the pages as I pen this story. So get ready. You asked for it and you are definitely going to get it. Prepare yourself for some enjoyable and exciting reading. It is scheduled to be released in May 1999.

To those of you who can't get enough of those Madarises, sit tight. Jake Madaris has a story in the works and so does baby sister, Christy Madaris. And look out for those Maxwell brothers. You will definitely see Alex and Trask again, as well as Sterling's brother, Nicholas Chenault.

I just love writing connecting books. Individually, every book I write will be a totally satisfying love story. And together, the entire collection of my books will create a compelling saga of one's family love and deep devotion, which will encompass their friends as well. I hope they will be stories you will enjoy and cherish forever.

You can write me at the following.

> Brenda Jackson
> P.O. Box 28267
> Jacksonville, FL 32226

I would love hearing from you, and promise to write back if you include a business-size, self-addressed, stamped envelope. Also, please check out my Web Site at: http://www.tlt.com/authors/bjackson.htm

> Take Care,
> Brenda Jackson

THE MADARIS BROTHERS TRILOGY

Praise for TONIGHT AND FOREVER

"This is a terrific book, filled with love in all its guises. Ms. Jackson brings passion and tenderness, faith and trust, together with friendship and does it so well."
—The Paperback Forum

"TONIGHT AND FOREVER . . . is so well written and entertaining that readers of all genres will enjoy the experience."
—Affaire de Coeur

"Mrs. Jackson's impressive debut novel is a silk and satin fantasy grounded in sensual reality."
—Romantic Times

"TONIGHT AND FOREVER is a genuine love story . . . an outstanding experience readers won't forget for a long time."
—Rendezvous

Praise for WHISPERED PROMISES

"Brenda Jackson has written another sensational novel . . . stormy, sensual and sexy—all the things a romance reader could want in a love story."
—Romantic Times

Praise for ETERNALLY YOURS

"Ms. Jackson has done it again! . . . another Madaris brother sweeps us off to fantasyland. **ETERNALLY YOURS** is a 42-carat diamond!"
—Romantic Times

"ETERNALLY YOURS . . . A truly touching and heart-felt story that is guaranteed to melt the hardest of hearts."
—Rendezvous

"Filled with family love, brotherly antics, sensuality, and just enough intrigue and surprises ... **ETERNALLY YOURS** is a story rich with fascinating characters. Too bad there are no more Madaris brothers."
—Affaire de Coeur

COMING IN SEPTEMBER . . .

COMMITMENTS (0-7860-0558-0, $4.99/$6.50)
by Carmen Green
Economist Fox Giovanni is a workaholic. She is finally persuaded to retreat to a friend's home in a small town in North Carolina. She doesn't expect to be swept off her feet by Van Compton, the drop-dead gorgeous carpenter who is working on the house.

INTO THE NIGHT (0-7860-0559-9, $4.99/$6.50)
by Robyn Amos
Young actress Coco Vanderbilt is sure that her brother is innocent of the murder he is accused of, and that her photographer has the evidence to clear his name. She will use every trick up her sleeve to uncover the truth. But she doesn't expect to go against her photographer's bodyguard, Jax Jaxon . . . or to lose her heart in the confrontation.

FOLLOW YOUR HEART (0-7860-0560-2, $4.99/$6.50)
by Raynetta Manees
Famous singer, Meekok Moore, will not be pressured into appearing more provocative for the public. She flees to her Georgia hometown, where she is simply Tameka Morgan. When she meets Ty Barnett, a man of God, she must choose between her two worlds. Ty is determined to show Tameka that he is the only man for her and that nothing else is as important.

THE BEST FOR LAST (0-7860-0561-0, $4.99/$6.50)
by Gail McFarland
Noelle Parker opted to take a frightened little girl home rather than turn her over to Child Protective Services. Now she faces charges of kidnapping. Devastated, she turns to Jamal Harris for legal support. He willingly provides her with that and much more . . . he fulfills the dreams Noelle only dared to experience through romance novels.

Available wherever paperbacks are sold, or order direct from the Publisher. Send cover price plus 50¢ per copy for mailing and handling to Kensington Publishing Corp., Consumer Orders, or call (toll free) 888-345-BOOK, to place your order using Mastercard or Visa. Residents of New York and Tennessee must include sales tax. DO NOT SEND CASH.